Oric And The Alchemist's Key

Lesley Wilson

Cataloguing-in-Publication entry is available from the National Library of Australia.

ISBN: 9780995422001 (paperback)
         9780995422018 (ebook)

Thanks go to my friends Anne Wheeler and Patricia Bryant for their assistance and encouragement in the writing of this book.

Thanks, also, to my husband, Mike, who has made it possible for me to spend so much time glued to my computer keyboard.

Chapter One

Oric Runs for his Life

Esica Figg crept from his hiding place behind a dusty wall-tapestry. Blinking in a shaft of early-morning sunlight, he surveyed the bodies that lay strewn across the floor.

Marauders had struck at dawn. After a night of carousing, the inhabitants of Dunburton Manor were too befuddled to offer resistance. The invaders cut them down without mercy, stole everything of value, and left a pyre of furniture burning in the centre of the Great Hall.

Anger replaced Esica Figg's fear. He cared not one jot for the murdered people of Dunburton, but he did care about the silver he had loaned the incumbent Lord. Now it was gone – stolen along with everything else of value in the manor. Figg's business was moneylending and he stood little chance of recovering his loss. Frustrated, he beat his fist against the wall. His desire to become the wealthiest man in the realm had taken a huge step backward.

Smoke from the blazing furniture seared Figg's throat. Poised to make his escape, the sudden slam of a door arrested his movements. Hastening back to his hiding place behind the tapestry, Figg peeped through a hole in the fabric.

A tall, thin boy raced into the Great Hall and came to an abrupt halt beside the still form of an old man.

"Master Deveril! Master Deveril!" The boy dropped to his knees and rubbed the man's blue-veined hands. "Are you hurt?"

The Dunburton alchemist's eyes flickered open.

"Praise the Lord!" the boy gasped. "I thought you were dead."

Deveril fluttered his hands. "Pay attention, Oric, for I have little time left." His voice was surprisingly strong for one so near death. Figg, hiding only feet away, could hear every word.

From around his neck Deveril took a chain with a key hanging upon it and pressed it into Oric's hand. "This key unlocks the secret to great wealth. You must promise to keep it safe. If it falls into evil hands, untold disasters could occur."

Oric curled his fingers over the key. "I promise, Master Deveril. But I am confused. What kind of disaster? And where is the wealth you speak of?"

But the old man had drawn his final breath.

Slowly, as if in a dream, Oric stood up. The pyre of furniture had become a blazing inferno sending billows of acrid smoke around the Great Hall. Coming to his senses, Oric sped toward the door, pulling the chain with the key over his head as he ran.

A spark landed in the tinder-dry tapestry, setting it ablaze. Figg, driven from his hiding place, struck viciously at the small tongues of flame that licked the front of his tunic. His personal conflagration extinguished, he hastened after the boy. Come what may, Figg meant to gain possession of the alchemist's key.

-oOo-

Oric ran through the woods, not caring that bramble thorns tore at his limbs. He had no idea where to go, nor did he care. Master Deveril was dead. Could there be anyone who would ever show him kindness again?

Oric recalled his brush with death, and shuddered. He would have met the same grisly fate as the other Dunburton inhabitants had he not been out on an errand for the alchemist. Hunger rattled his belly, for he had put nothing in it since the previous night's supper. He picked a few blackberries, but they did little to satisfy his appetite. Pulling out Deveril's key, Oric stared at the ornate double-knot engraved upon its shank. The symbol meant nothing to him, but he determined to honour his promise to Master Deveril and guard the key with his life.

Coming upon a stream, Oric followed the narrow watercourse. He prayed that it would lead to a settlement. Dusk produced intimidating shadows; fatigue and emotion took their toll and Oric fought the desire to weep. Kneeling at the water's edge, he drank deeply. His thirst slaked, he clambered back up the bank. In the distance a tiny light glimmered. Oric did not know it, but he had reached the lands of Sir Edred of Bayersby.

-oOo-

Ichtheus paced his kitchen domain, wishing he were not apothecary to Sir Edred of Bayersby. Wolves had savaged the Bayersby herds, and Sir Edred had led his men into the forest to slay the offending beasts. Exasperated, Ichtheus slapped the air with his bony hands; the huntsmen rode recklessly and there would be injuries aplenty. Regardless of the late hour, Ichtheus would be expected to cobble the battered men back together again. He sighed, feeling his age. An assistant would help to lighten his load, but he had yet to find someone suitable.

Heavy tapestries hanging from the manor walls failed to stop the cold draughts that whistled through every crack and cranny. Ichtheus rubbed his aching joints, eyeing his truckle bed beside the fire. How he longed to crawl into it and sleep. Instead, he picked up his mortar. He was about to grind a mixture of herbs when a tapping sound stilled the pestle in his hand. Replacing his equipment on the table, he inched open the iron-studded door that gave access to the outside compound. Ichtheus squinted into the darkness, and almost died of fright when a golden-haired youth toppled head over heels through the doorway and came to rest on the stone flags.

Ichtheus poked the intruder with his toe.

The boy clamped thin, dirty arms over his head. "Do not hit me, sir! Please do not hit me. I mean no harm. I just want a safe place to sleep and a little food for my empty belly."

"Hit you? No one is going to hit you," Ichtheus replied kindly. "Get to your feet, young fellow. You have no need to be afraid of me. What is your name?"

The grubby bundle of rags uncoiled reluctantly. "Oric, sir," whispered the boy.

Ichtheus provided a substantial meal, and then chased the boy into the yard to wash his grimy hands and face. After a good scrub, Oric crept back into the kitchen.

Eyeing him speculatively, Ichtheus guessed the youngster to be around fourteen or fifteen years of age. His eyes, blue as a fair summer sky, shone with intelligence, and a mop of unkempt straw-coloured hair surrounded his freckled face.

Oric sneaked a look at the elderly gentleman, with flowing white hair and beard.

Could this stranger be trusted, he wondered? Since he had little to lose, Oric told Ichtheus his sad story.

"I have only vague memories of my parents," Oric began. "My father worked as a scribe for the Lord of Dunburton. Mother was a companion to the lady of the manor. Both my parents were struck down by a fever when I was a small boy. Had Master Deveril, the Dunburton alchemist, not become my mentor and protector, I dare not think what might have become of me." A look of pride crossed Oric's face. "Master Deveril taught me to read and write."

"Is that so?" said Ichtheus, an idea beginning to filter into his mind. "Carry on, lad."

Oric struggled with his emotions. "Three days ago a band of raiders sacked Dunburton Manor and the surrounding village. Almost everyone was killed. I was out on an errand for Master Deveril; otherwise I would also have died. I returned to the manor as Master Deveril breathed his last." Oric recalled his mentor's final action, but chose not to mention the key that the alchemist had entrusted into his care.

"I am in need of an apprentice," said Ichtheus in the spur of the moment. "With some training, you might fit the bill. What do you think, Oric?"

A grossly overweight woman sashayed into the apothecary's section of the kitchen, stilling the reply upon Oric's lips. She raked the scene with gimlet eyes. "So who do we have here?"

Mother Morghan, housekeeper, nurse and would-be herbalist, was a necessary evil. Without her to take over duties on his behalf, Ichtheus would remain tied to Bayersby Manor. The Lady Myferny, Sir Edred's wife, set great store by the woman, but Ichtheus suspected Mother Morghan to be more witch than herbalist. He groaned. Right now, she was the last person he wanted to see. Barely disguising his irritation, he snarled, "Clear off, woman, and mind your own business."

Oblivious to the apothecary's displeasure, Mother Morghan meandered across to Oric and dug him none too gently in the ribs. "Huh! He ain't up to much, is he?" She sucked her gappy teeth noisily. "Where is he from? I ain't seen him hereabouts before."

Ichtheus took a chance. "Oric is my new apprentice. He is here to stay, so you had best get used to him."

Mother Morghan sniggered. "He looks that skinny; I reckon he ain't up to the job." Filling her pot with ale from a wooden barrel, she flopped into a battered chair beside the fire. "Best get rid of him before Sir Edred sees him."

Offended, Oric decided he did not much like the look of her, either. "Aye, missus," he countered, "What yon apothecary says is right. I am the new apprentice, and I plan to stay."

Ichtheus nodded at Oric's off-hand acceptance and returned to the mixture in his mortar. He glowered at Mother Morghan with distaste. The woman was continually sticking her fat nose into his business, and right now he wished it were chopped off and under his pestle for grinding.

Mother Morghan slurped her ale, spiteful thoughts whirling around her mind. For years she had coveted the apothecary's position. Drawing up her fleshy lips like the top of a drawstring pouch, she imagined her role in the future with Esica Figg, the moneylender. He had promised her a prominent position once he deposed Sir Edred. Master Ichtheus' days at Bayersby Manor were surely numbered.

The clop of hooves outside announced Sir Edred's return, and Ichtheus went into the compound to greet him.

Sir Edred leaped down from his horse and thrust his sword into the hands of a waiting squire. Lady Myferny ran into her husband's arms and planted a kiss on his bearded cheek. "I am glad to see you home unscathed, my lord."

"And I am pleased to be back," replied Sir Edred, returning his wife's kiss. "We have slain three wolves, but many more still roam the forest."

The dead animals, tied by their feet to poles, were carried between six men. Sir Edred ran his fingers through the wolves' thick fur. "These hides will boost our winter bedding, but they are poor compensation for the damage done to our livestock."

"Never mind the livestock," cried Lady Myferny. "Some of your men are injured."

Sight of Lady Myferny always gladdened Ichtheus' heart, but he never ceased to be amazed by the effect her presence had on Mother Morghan. The housekeeper, normally bone idle, tackled several chores at one and the same time. Little wonder Lady Myferny thought the wretched woman such an asset.

The huntsmen's injuries ranged from minor scratches to serious wounds. One had broken his wrist. Another fellow had gouged an eye on a tree branch. The worst casualty had suffered a severe mauling from one of the wolves.

Under Master Ichtheus' tutelage, Oric learned that bishop's-weed, chervil and Solomon's-seal diminished bruises; salve of primrose, adder's tongue and shepherd's purse aided with the healing of wounds. Fascinated, Oric watched his mentor sew together deep gashes with a thread of horse hair. When it was time to straighten the bones of the broken wrist, Oric lent his strength to hold the patient steady.

Well pleased with his new apprentice, Ichtheus looked for a suitable reward. Oric had arrived at Bayersby Manor barefoot, so Ichtheus handed over a pair of his own boots.

With cold weather fast approaching, Oric gladly accepted the gift – even though the boots were worn and rather large.

Hours later Oric crawled inside the huge inglenook fireplace. Feeling chilly, he stirred life into the fire with a stick. His action dislodged a pile of smouldering logs, sending a cascade of orange sparks onto Sir Edred's sleeping wolfhound. The dog yelped, jerked awake by the pinpricks of searing heat. Oric hastily brushed the hot cinders from the animal's coat. The dog, named Parzifal, licked Oric's face, and then slumbered on. Oric drifted off to sleep with his cheek pressed against the comforting warmth of the dog's rough hair.

-oOo-

Inside his dingy shop in the village of Kilterton, Esica Figg pored over a pile of grubby documents. His spidery handwriting, describing strategies for deposing the current Lord of Bayersby, covered many pages. To achieve his aim Figg needed an army, but mercenary soldiers cost money. His coffers were filling with the aid of a gang of bully boys and some street urchins, but the progress was slower than Figg liked. If the Dunburton alchemist had told the truth, possession of the mysterious key might provide the extra funds he so desired. Figg rolled up his parchments, and slammed down his quill. Despite considerable effort, he had not yet found the boy with the key.

Chapter Two

Market Day Adventure

Several days spent caring for Sir Edred's wolf-hunt casualties disrupted Ichtheus' routine and he was relieved when his domain returned to normal. "The Lord be praised," he muttered as he bid his last patient farewell.

Oric rattled about, trying to restore order in the medicine chest. Ichtheus smiled with satisfaction; the new apprentice was shaping up well.

Filling a drinking pot with ale, Ichtheus stretched out on his truckle bed. "Methinks you deserve a break, lad. Tomorrow is market day in the village of Kilterton. Would you care to accompany me and help with my medicament stall?"

"Aye, Master Ichtheus, I would!" Oric fingered the key hidden under his tunic. He had tried several locks in Bayersby Manor, all to no avail. A chance to seek new keyholes was an opportunity too good to miss.

To get to the market in good time, Ichtheus arose before dawn. He donned a bonnet with long earflaps and a dark-green cloak. His leggings, made from tough canvas, were cross-laced with leather garters and a pair of ankle-high boots encased his narrow feet. Climbing onto the donkey, Ichtheus settled himself into the saddle and tucked his legs in front of two panniers full of medicaments. "Giddy-up Braccus," he said, gently kicking the donkey into motion. Oric, wearing his second-hand boots, followed after his master on foot.

Ichtheus set a brisk pace along an old Roman road; Bayersby Manor was soon lost in the pre-dawn gloom. Soon the sun crept over the horizon, burnishing the windswept moors with golden light. Feeling euphoric, Oric filled his lungs with fresh, country air.

"You must never treat these moors lightly," Ichtheus warned. "I maintain a great respect for this part of Yorkshire, especially in winter when the earth is blanketed by snow. Men have lost their way and died in the frozen wilderness." He stretched his arms wide, "But on glorious summer days like this, the place soothes my soul."

Oric understood exactly what his master meant.

Purple heather faded to palest mauve and disappeared into hazy infinity. Sweet, flowery perfume filled the air. High above, a skylark warbled, adding its tuneful melody to the sound of bleating sheep and droning bees. Oric watched the little bird spiral upwards until it became a tiny, black dot in the pale-blue morning sky.

Glancing back to make sure Oric had not fallen behind, Ichtheus caught sight of Sir Edred's wolfhound skulking along amongst some tall ferns. "Ye gods, what is yon mutt playing at? Send him home at once, Oric. The last thing we need is to look out for him all day."

Oric flapped his arms. "Shoo! Go back home, Parzifal!"

The dog collapsed in a heap on the muddy track, wagging his tail half-heartedly. He had clearly taken to Oric, and he intended to follow his new friend come what may.

"Clear off, you scrofulous mutt," Ichtheus yelled.

Parzifal took no notice.

"You certainly have him well-trained, Master Ichtheus," Oric tittered. "One word from you and he does exactly as he pleases."

Ichtheus wriggled in his saddle and glowered. "Mind your manners, boy, or I shall send you home… along with the dog!"

Belly to the ground, Parzifal inched forward. Crescents of white beneath the brown of his eyes gave him a comically doleful expression.

"Look at him," Oric chortled, "crafty dog moves only when he thinks we are not watching."

"Aye, well, we *are* watching, and he cannot come." Ichtheus remained adamant.

"What if I throw a few rocks at him? I could do with a bit of target practice," teased Oric.

"You will do no such thing!" Ichtheus snapped. "If anything untoward happens to that wolfhound, Sir Edred will likely chop us up for dog meat."

Oric paled at the idea. "Perhaps we should let Parzifal come with us. That way I can keep an eye on him."

Dreading the thought of turning back, Ichtheus agreed. "Very well, but for goodness sake call the dog to heal."

Oric whistled, and Parzifal bounded forward. He shook his leonine head, and splattered Ichtheus with globules of drool.

"Wipe that silly grin off your face, boy," growled Ichtheus, mopping saliva from his leggings, "else I shall fetch you a clout."

Oric's smile widened, for he knew his master's words to be an empty threat.

Anxious to continue with their journey, Ichtheus prodded Oric with his switch. "Get a move on. At this rate the market will be finished before we arrive." He dug his heels into Braccus and, in a foul mood, rode on.

Prior to their departure, Mother Morghan had complained non-stop. "Who do you think you are, swanning off again?" She had rubbed her sweaty face on her grubby apron, and kicked lady Myferny's cat Caedmon out of her way. "I have only one pair of hands and more than enough to do with them, without having to cope with your workload on top of everything else!"

Ichtheus shuddered at the memory. No wonder he was in a bad mood. The woman was a harridan, and bone-idle to boot. But what choice did he have? If he wanted to attend the market someone had to stay behind to keep an eye on things. In exchange for the apothecary's services Sir Edred provided food, a bed, and a small wage. The money Ichtheus made from his medicament stall gave him a feeling of independence and provided him with a few luxuries.

Rugged moorland gave way to gentle fields and neat copses as Oric and Ichtheus began the steep descent into the sheltered vale of Roxdale.

Ichtheus leaned back to maintain his balance and his saddle slipped. "Od's blood, Oric! Did I not instruct you on how to properly fasten the girth around Braccus' belly?" The saddle slid sideways and downwards until, with a bone-jarring thud, Ichtheus landed on top of the spilled baskets of merchandise.

Braccus lowered his head, peeled back his top lip and snickered. Parzifal went about his own business, leaving Oric to pacify the apothecary, re-saddle the donkey, and gather up the jumble of medicaments.

Ready to resume their journey, Ichtheus looked around for Parzifal. "Where is that stupid dog?" he snapped, twitching with irritation.

Behind a nearby stone wall a crop of golden wheat swirled with irregular waves. Every now and again, Parzifal catapulted into sight. With his ears flapping, he turned his head swiftly from side to side before disappearing amongst the tall stalks again.

"Look at that crazy mutt!" Oric guffawed. "He must have wandered in amongst the wheat and lost his way."

"Aye," replied Ichtheus, laughing almost as hard. "I reckon he is leaping up to see where he is going." Wheezing and gasping, Ichtheus mopped his streaming eyes. The day was definitely improving.

Arriving at Roxdale Beck, Braccus approached the ford and waded into the icy waters. Ichtheus eyed the brackish, swirling mass, thinking it far too close for comfort. He dragged his cloak above his knees, crossed his bony shanks atop the saddle, and put his trust in the sure-footed donkey. Oric followed, carrying his precious boots.

They had almost reached the other side when Parzifal missed his footing. For a heart-stopping moment, he disappeared into a churning pool of murky water. To Oric's great relief, the dog swam to the far side and scrabbled up the muddy bank. He shook himself with spectacular vigour, sending a deluge of cold water over the donkey's rear end. Startled Braccus lurched along the road at a smart canter. Ichtheus fell back across the donkey's rump and was thoroughly shaken about.

Oric gave chase.

"Grab the bridle before I lose my seat," cried Ichtheus, clinging on for dear life.

Oric caught and calmed Braccus, and helped Ichtheus to sit upright.

The old man glared at Oric's humour-filled face. "Do not dare to utter one word, boy! Not one single word!"

Overwhelmed with mirth, Oric had no words left to utter. Parzifal trotted along blissfully unaware of the upset he had caused.

On the crest of a low rise, Ichtheus reined Braccus to a halt and pointed to a settlement spread out below. "There lies the village of Kilterton. It may look harmless from here, but mark my words, Oric, when we arrive among the market-day masses you must remain vigilant. Not everyone you meet is as innocent as they appear. Amongst the ordinary folk of Kilterton, there lurks a form of low life that will steal, cheat and maim."

Acutely aware of the key that nestled against his breastbone, Oric placed a protective hand on his chest. To lose the key before he had unravelled Master Deveril's mystery was too awful to contemplate.

People intent upon enjoying the market thronged Kilterton's wide thoroughfare. Voices were raised in competition with hawkers and a cacophony of squawking, bellowing, and heehawing livestock brought to the market for sale or exchange. Countrywomen gossiped in the village square whilst their men-folk swilled liquor in the alehouse.

"There will be brawls at the close of day," Ichtheus remarked, eyeing the packed inn. "We must get away from Kilterton before dark."

The vibrant atmosphere thrilled Oric until he caught sight of a pitiful, moth-eaten bear. A dwarf jabbed the poor creature with a stick to make it dance. Oric hated to see animals ill-treated and, seething with anger, he strode over to the dwarf. "Hey, what say I poke you with the stick? I would rather see you dance instead of yon poor bear." The dwarf shrugged, made a rude gesture, and moved off down the street with his bear in tow.

Thirteen-year-old Dian Cole watched the altercation

from the doorway of her parents' cottage. Disgusted by the dwarf's market-day routine, she applauded the youth who had attempted to defend the bear. The boy made eye contact with her, and Dian smiled. The boy blushed and dropped his gaze.

"Who is that young fellow?" Dian asked her older brother.

"Ain't never seen him before," replied Josh Cole. "He is a newcomer to the market."

Word soon spread that the apothecary had arrived. A long queue formed in front of Ichtheus' well-stocked table as country folk patiently awaited treatments and advice. A surge of delight coursed through Oric; it was going to be a rewarding day.

The apothecary's assistant had no idea how wrong he was.

Chapter Three

Friends and enemies

Ichtheus' customers thinned and Oric begged leave to look around the village. Well pleased with the morning's takings, the old man flapped his hands in generous dismissal. "Aye, be off with you, lad, enjoy yourself, but see that you stay out of trouble."

Not knowing where to begin his search for likely keyholes, Oric chose the sunny side of the street first. Finding no locks to try he paused outside Kilterton's inn, deliberating whether or not to enter. Snatches of conversation coming from within were all about violent robberies that had recently occurred in the district. Oric moved on, not wanting to spoil his day with bad news.

Across the street, a gang of urchins squabbled under a horse-chestnut tree. Oric stopped to watch the game they were playing with some fallen nuts. The noisiest member of the group swaggered over and confronted Oric.

"What you looking at?" the boy demanded.

Oric smiled hopefully. "I was watching your game. Can I have a turn?"

The boy thrust his face forward, his hot breath fanning Oric's cheek. "Why should we let you join in with our fun? Clear off, else I will give you a thrashing." To back up his threat the boy raised both fists and jabbed the air around Oric's head.

"Give over, Ned," shouted one of the smaller urchins. "Let the lad be." Young Joe was no fool. The newcomer worked for the apothecary. Most likely he would have money and plenty of it. "What say I take you on for a copper coin," he added, handing Oric a shiny chestnut with a length of plaited horsehair threaded through a hole in the nut's centre. A similar brown nut dangled from Joe's outstretched hand. "On the count of three, make your strike."

Oric wound the horsehair around his finger. Holding the nut in his other hand, he lined up his aim.

"One, two, three!"

Oric swung the nut down hard, smashing Joe's target to pieces.

"Beginner's luck," snarled Joe, threading horsehair through a new nut.

Oric proved a deft hand at the game, with a strong and true aim. He trounced both urchins within a few heartbeats. Poor losers, Ned and Joe turned ugly.

"We will fix you… clever beggar." Ned's face was a mask of jealous menace.

Joe bared his small, greenish teeth. "Aye, you had best watch your back from now on, Master Clever Dick!"

Refusing to stump up the money Oric had won, the boys sloped off.

Oric had no idea that Ned and Joe were employed by Esica Figg as thieves, or that the unpleasant encounter would be the first of many.

"Pay no heed to those two," said one remaining youth

scuffing his bare feet in the dust. "I reckon they are nowt but wind and water." A wide smile transformed his ruddy face. "I am Josh Cole." He jerked his thumb at the girl by his side. "And this is my sister, Dian."

Oric's heart skipped a beat. It was the same girl he had encountered earlier in the day.

Dian smiled, dimples indenting her rosy cheeks. "What is your name? You are a newcomer to the district are you not?" Golden freckles dusted the girl's small nose, and her hazel eyes twinkled with mischief. She looked to be around thirteen years of age.

"My name is Oric, and I am recently apprenticed to the Bayersby apothecary." He flushed crimson for the second time that day. Dian was the prettiest girl he had ever seen.

"Shall you attend the next market, Oric?" Josh interrupted. "If you could spare the time, I could do with a lesson on how to smash chestnuts the way you just did. I would like to beat those two vagabonds for a change, they are…"

A thin, grubby woman cut Josh's words short. "Josh! Dian!" she screeched. "Have you nothing better to do than skulk about in the street? Get yourselves home at once. Work aplenty awaits you."

"Ye gods," exclaimed Josh, his ruddy face crumpling with consternation. "That's our Ma! She reckons Ned and Joe are a bad lot. If she saw Dian and me near them, she will beat us for sure."

Oric watched his two new friends scamper along the street, hoping they would not get into too much trouble. He also hoped he would meet them again; especially the girl.

Returning to his mentor's stall, Oric noticed a tall, gaunt man standing in a shop doorway across the road. "Who is yon fellow?" he asked, nodding in the stranger's direction. "I do not like the look of him."

"Your instinct serves you well, Oric," growled Ichtheus. "He is Esica Figg, the moneylender. Yon villain causes more upset amongst local families than a fox in a chicken run. Apart from driving folk to ruin with outrageous repayment demands, I believe he is also involved in other kinds of wrongdoing." Ichtheus shrugged his bony shoulders. "Despite surreptitious investigation, I have been unable to prove anything untoward."

Figg locked up his shop, and took a stroll along the high street. Many of the stall-holders owed him money. Each one of them would pay back twice as much as he had borrowed. Figg nodded and smiled, unperturbed by the black looks he received from his debtors. Soon he would have sufficient funds to employ the first of his mercenary soldiers and a master at arms to drill them.

The sour whiff of tallow from the candle maker's stall transported Figg back to his apprenticeship in his father's candle-making business. White scar tissue on his hands and arms reminded him of the hot wax burns he had suffered; none of them worth the indifferent financial reward he had received. Meanwhile, in the shop next door, a moneylender had amassed funds with apparent ease. When Figg senior died young Esica sold the business, pocketed the money, and travelled north. Reaching the village of Kilterton he had set up a moneylending establishment of his own. Several lucrative years had swiftly passed, but still he was not satisfied. Now Figg had his sights set upon Sir Edred's manor and all the rights and privileges the position afforded.

Keen to inveigle Ichtheus into borrowing money, Figg approached the apothecary's stall. Gathering repayments from the apothecary would provide a legitimate reason to visit Bayersby Manor on a regular basis. The more information

Figg could glean about Sir Edred and the workings of his manor the better.

Not wishing to meet the moneylender, Oric crawled under his mentor's table. Safely out of sight, he filled spare vials with liquorice juice from a large flagon.

"Good day to you, Master Figg," said Ichtheus, nodding curtly. "May I help you?"

" Oh, ho, 'tis not *your* help I seek," smirked Figg. "But *I* might be able to help *you*."

"Help me?" Ichtheus spluttered. "How in the world can *you* help *me*?"

"By offering you a loan," Figg replied, twisting a greasy rat tail of hair slowly around his forefinger. "I am willing to arrange very reasonable repayment terms."

"I am not interested in a loan," Ichtheus snapped indignantly.

Sitting under the table, Oric detected his mentor's icy tone.

"However," Ichtheus continued, "I am interested in your dealings with other folk around the district."

"That, sir, is none of your business." Having no desire to undergo a barrage of difficult questions, Figg turned on his heels and stalked back to his shop. He stood in the doorway and watched two of his young employees rob shoppers with nimble efficiency. He despised the boys, but he needed Ned and Joe's help to swell his coffers. Across the road, another, vaguely familiar youth popped up beside the Bayersby apothecary. Figg's heart skipped a beat. It was the boy from Dunburton – the boy that held the alchemist's key. Hardly able to believe his stroke of good fortune, Figg immediately began scheming how best to kidnap the youngster.

Next to Figg's table, an old crone shoved a lumpish man onto a wooden block. The fellow mouthed a few obscenities at the woman, and clanged a handbell. "Come all you sick serfs and villeins. Try our pink potion for pale people," he shouted.

The old crone fetched her son a vicious clout to the back of his legs with a stick. "You great oaf," she shrieked. "I could do better than that wi' me tongue cut out. Shout a bit louder for gawd's sake; else we'll be here all day."

"Charlatans," Ichtheus muttered. "I dread to think what their ghastly mixture contains." He pulled harder on a rotten molar anchored in the lower jaw of his friend Uther Tidwall, the bootmaker. Uther, upon whose chest Ichtheus was kneeling, let out a yell as the offending tooth plopped free. Oric ducked to avoid a spurt of crimson blood and dabbed at the patient with a rag. Ichtheus apologised to Uther, angry that he had allowed himself to be distracted.

A malodorous stench, similar to a fish stall at the end of a hot day, insinuated itself into Ichtheus' nostrils. He raised his head and glowered at Oric. "What is that fearful stink? Check your feet, boy, to see that you have not stepped in something obnoxious."

The source of the smell sidled into Ichtheus' peripheral vision. It was the old hag from the opposing stall across the road. Unhurriedly she picked up, examined, sniffed and prodded every item that Ichtheus had for sale. Oric was about to tell her to be off, but the pressure of Ichtheus' hand upon his boot reminded him to mind his manners.

"Hey, Uther! Who is that unsavoury woman?" Ichtheus whispered. "Have you seen her before?"

Uther struggled into a sitting position. "Oh, her! She is a newcomer hereabouts." Drizzles of frothy blood oozed from the corner of the cobbler's mouth. "Her name is Hersica Horzefell. The ugly bruiser advertising their potions is her son, Zebediah. Rumour has it that he is a nasty piece of work."

Ichtheus, upon his knees beside his patient, peered at the Horzefells from beneath his table. "As far as I can see, they are not doing much trade."

The ugly couple gave Oric the creeps. "Poor trade or no, Master Ichtheus, I would not trust that pair further than I could spit."

Finished with her inspection, the woman returned to her own stall. Figg immediately engaged her in animated conversation, all the while stealing furtive glances at the apothecary's table.

Convinced that Figg's uncommon interest boded no good, Ichtheus wished it was time to pack up and head for home.

Chapter Four

Egglebart's Big Fight

Trade around Ichtheus' stall remained brisk for the rest of the day and folk awaiting the apothecary's attention chin-wagged nineteen to the dozen. "By Gaw!" Oric overheard one old codger exclaim, "I hardly dare go out these days for fear of being set upon. 'Tis sheer luck no one has been killed."

A burly villager nodded his agreement. "Aye, but how do the thieves know who to attack? Only people with valuables seem to get picked on." He looked down his nose and tapped it with a forefinger. "I reckon someone is in the know."

Neighbour eyed neighbour and suspicion ran riot.

The press of people at Ichtheus' table parted to admit a tall, thickset man. Head and shoulders above the crowd, he stood out like a beacon. Awestruck, Oric goggled as the late afternoon sun turned the giant's shock of red hair into a halo of burnished copper. His one good eye shone from a deeply weather-beaten face; an empty socket was all that remained of the other eye. Without so much as a by your leave, the fellow wrapped Ichtheus in a vast hug.

Oric raised his fists and moved closer, "Hey! What are

you doing? Take your hands off Master Ichtheus!"

"Brave lad," the man exclaimed, trying to hide a smile. "'Tis not often I am issued with such a forceful challenge."

"This great oaf," Ichtheus flailed his arms in an effort to free himself, "was once a prizefighter of great renown." Seeing Oric's worried expression, Ichtheus hurried on, "But he is retired now and is naught but a gentle giant."

"Huh!" Oric was not impressed. "He looks more like a maniac to me."

The giant guffawed with laughter. "Nay, lad, you have naught to fear. I am as gentle as a lamb with folk I like. This fine apothecary was attending a battle with Sir Edred when I received my injury." He indicated his empty eye socket. "But for Master Ichtheus' timely intervention I would not only have lost my eye, but also my life." He squeezed the old man tighter, lifting him off the ground. "And our friendship has endured over the years, has it not, Ichtheus?"

"Aye, so it has, you great lummox." Ichtheus broke free and cuffed the culprit affectionately. "Oric, allow me to introduce you to Egglebart."

A hand like a side of beef encompassed Oric's small paw, and squeezed. "I am honoured to meet you, young sir. Any friend of Ichtheus' is a friend of mine."

Oric winced and, slightly pacified, returned the pressure.

Introductions over, Egglebart turned his attention back to Ichtheus. "I was hoping to find you here. Before this day is done, I may have need of your ministrations one more time."

"How so?" Ichtheus eyed his friend suspiciously. "Do not tell me you have entered into another prizefight." He wagged his finger. "Have I not warned you? You are getting too old to take risks."

Egglebart had the grace to look shame-faced. "I know, I know! But someone has put up an irresistible prize. Added to my savings, the money is all I need to buy a smallholding. One more bout, then I promise to have done with the sport."

"Can I watch the fight?" Oric hopped from foot to foot, his eyes pleading.

"Aye! Get along with you. I will pack up the stall." Ichtheus had hoped to leave the market early, but what difference would a few extra minutes make? If Egglebart's past performances were anything to go by, the contest would not last long.

Excited at the prospect of some spectacular entertainment, Dian Cole joined the crowd. Pushing through to the front row, she was delighted to find herself next to Oric. "Hello, again," she murmured.

Oric wanted to do cartwheels. Instead, he stuttered like a fool. "Oh, er, fancy bumping into you again!" He cursed himself silently. *What an idiot!* Here he was standing next to the prettiest girl he had ever seen and his stupid tongue would not work properly. When Josh pushed in, Oric was both relieved and irritated.

Brothers! Dian thought. *They were nothing but a nuisance.* She wanted to learn more about the apprentice, but every time their paths crossed something always stopped them from talking.

Oric's face fell when Egglebart's enormous opponent, aptly named Cruncher, swaggered out of the inn. Surely Egglebart could be no match for this bruiser.

Of a similar opinion, Esica Figg viewed the proceedings with satisfaction. He had chosen Cruncher with care. The pugilist's record was unblemished, and he was not renowned for fair play. Any local warrior who took up the challenge would surely fail to win.

As Figg hoped, word of his secretly donated prize spread and a large crowd assembled to witness the fight. The locals backed Egglebart, the man they knew. Figg chafed his hands together as he anticipated the financial killing he was about to make. Not only that, if things went according to plan, he would soon have his hands on the alchemist's key. *Ay, ay,* he thought, *what a splendid day.*

Stripped to the waist, Egglebart flexed his muscles at the cheering spectators. Cruncher entered the ring and the people booed.

The two fighters squared up.

"I have seen yon bruiser before," a traveller beside Oric sniffed. "Cruncher makes his living from competition. Huh! If you could call it competition! He launches his bulk onto his opponents and squashes them till they submit." The traveller winked at Oric. "And it never takes long." He cocked his head at Figg collecting coins hand over fist. "The only winner this day will be that money-grubbing snake taking wagers."

Oric soon understood that speed and intelligence gave Egglebart the initial advantage. The big man jabbed playful thrusts at Cruncher and nimbly danced around. Goaded like a maddened bull, Egglebart's hirsute opponent bellowed in fury as he delivered his first, hefty swipe. Rubbing his mouth ruefully, Egglebart dodged more thrusts and planted several of his own. Blood from Cruncher's battered face spattered the crowd.

Dian squealed and covered her eyes with her hands. Oric would like to have put his arm around her, but Josh stood his ground between them.

Loving the excitement, the spectators howled their local man toward victory.

"EGGLE-BA-ART! EGGLE-BA-ART! EGGLE-BA-ART!"

Distracted by the crowd's noisy adoration, Egglebart's attention wandered. Cruncher seized the opportunity and locked his hands around Egglebart's neck. Egglebart thrust his arms up inside the man's hold and attempted to grip him in the same way, but Cruncher's neck was wider than two hand spans. For several heartbeats the two heavyweights swayed together in a macabre embrace. With his windpipe squashed almost flat, Egglebart fought for breath. In desperation he dropped his right arm and slammed his fist into Cruncher's belly.

Winded, Cruncher eased his grip upon Egglebart's throat.

Crumpling to his knees, Egglebart sucked in great draughts of air.

Without giving his opponent a chance to rise, Cruncher set about Egglebart until he toppled face down in the dirt. Standing proud, he pounded his chest in undisguised glee.

The crowd booed.

Egglebart remained in a semi-conscious heap.

Cruncher prepared to launch himself upon Egglebart's prostrate form.

"Watch out Egglebart," Oric yelled. "Yon bully is coming at you again."

Egglebart was not nearly as feeble as he pretended. In the blink of an eye he rolled out of Cruncher's way.

Cruncher hit the ground with a bone-jarring thud. Egglebart straddled his back, forcing the man's arms up between his shoulder blades.

Cruncher screamed in pain.

The crowd howled with delight.

Dian peeped between her fingers.

"Are you prepared to give me a fair fight?" Egglebart yelled.

"Aye, anything you say," Cruncher squealed. "If you break my arms I will be in no fit state to fight anyone."

Egglebart allowed Cruncher to stagger to his feet and then encouraged him to lumber forward. Each time

Cruncher came close, Egglebart ducked away. Cruncher panted with effort and, blinded by his own sweat, he failed to dodge Egglebart's onslaught of vicious jabs.

Oric saw that Egglebart's opposition was mostly brawn and little brain and he yelled his encouragement along with the hysterical crowd.

Egglebart delivered a final poleaxe blow that felled Cruncher to the ground. The huge man lay spread-eagled on his back, gasping like a freshly landed trout. Blood from his wounds trickled into the earth.

Figg spewed venom, his hopes of a financial killing dashed in a few short moments. His agreement to pay Cruncher only one quarter of the prize money was now null and void, for the entire amount would go to the victor. Not only had Figg lost his stake money, but to avoid a lynching, he was faced with paying out the people who had backed Egglebart to win. Try as he might, Figg could think of no escape from his costly predicament.

Inside the inn, Egglebart claimed his reward.

"I know not who put up the prize," the ruddy-faced innkeeper explained. "A scruffy urchin was waiting for me when I opened up this morning. He thrust this pouch into my hand and told me to give it to the winner." With an eye to boosting his trade, the innkeeper continued hopefully, "As the victor, I trust you will buy pots of ale all round."

Enjoying his moment of fame, Egglebart jangled the leather pouch over his head. "Aye, drinks for all, for I have funds aplenty."

"Be quiet!" Ichtheus hissed, tugging on Egglebart's sleeve. "Lord knows what rogues might be listening. We do not want to find you down some dark alley with your throat slit."

"You worry too much." Egglebart thrust a pot of ale into Ichtheus' hand. "Have I not just proved myself invincible?

No-one would be game enough to bandy blows with me."

Ichtheus eyed his friend doubtfully. Blood mixed with dirt caked Egglebart's chest, and the flesh around his one good eye was beginning to swell. "I would not wager on your success if anyone were to challenge you now."

Egglebart guffawed and wiggled his two front teeth. "Look, they are hanging on by a thread. Pull them out; they have been well paid for. I shall not miss them."

Ichtheus fished the tooth extractor from his pouch and handed it to Oric. "Since Egglebart's teeth are all but out, you may as well finish the job."

Following his mentor's instructions, Oric removed the offending teeth. He then stared at the inn's rafters, agonising over which medicament would aid his patient's recovery.

Egglebart guffawed again. "Look at the expression on yon apprentice's face. Anyone would think he held my very life in his hands."

"Aye, that could easily be the case if disease infects your gums." Ichtheus replied tightly.

A flicker of uncertainty crossed Egglebart's face.

Ichtheus waggled a finger under the big man's nose, "You would do well to pay attention to us, my friend. To save your gums from rotting, you must swill your mouth with sage water every morning. For extra protection, rub the tooth sockets with a sage leaf." He turned to Oric. "Can you remember that?"

Oric nodded enthusiastically. The more he learned, the more fascinated he became in the art of healing.

Eadbald Cole observed the procedure and, in his drink-fuddled state, he wondered what all the fuss was about. Who needed an apothecary to draw teeth? The money-grubbing old coot probably charged far too much for doing the deed. If only the prizefighter had asked, Eadbald would have fixed him up for the price of a pot of ale.

Keeping out of her father's sight, Dian Cole also watched Oric. The young apprentice was clever, of that she had no doubt. However, she was irritated to see that he attracted the attention of several village girls. Dian longed to speak to him, but rather than risk a drunken tongue-lashing from her father, she quietly left the inn and waited outside. At the very least, she intended to bid Oric goodnight.

After the day's lucrative trading Ichtheus' pouch bulged with silver, but he was less than pleased with the bartered livestock they had acquired. He recalled the gruesome hour he had spent with a rich merchant and cringed. The fellow had everything from head lice to haemorrhoids and had traded a donkey in exchange for treatments.

Oric fondled the sturdy animal's soft, cream muzzle. "Just as well we gained this second beast. I swear we have twice the goods we started with."

"Aye, pack up quickly, lad, before we are given any more," Ichtheus glanced nervously from left to right. "I will fetch the dog."

Parzifal, tied to a tree, munched on a juicy bone. Several more bloody delicacies awaited his attention. "Where did they come from?" Ichtheus asked suspiciously.

"I gave them to him." Oric grinned wickedly. "The butcher asked for some potions, and we did a trade."

Ichtheus slammed his eyelids shut. "Please tell me, boy, that you have not given Tewdric Bascoomb laxatives and diuretics for his wife." He prised one eye open and skewered Oric with a terrible look. "Do you have any idea of the trouble you may have caused?"

Oric shook his head, his enthusiasm fading rapidly.

Unpleasant visions of the butcher's wife, Helled Bascoomb, filtered into Ichtheus' mind. "For weeks the butcher has badgered me for purging medicaments, believing they would, if administered in large enough doses, flush away his wife's evil temper. Knowing the potions would not achieve the desired result I have steadfastly refused Tewdric's requests." Ichtheus smacked his forehead with the flat of his hand. "If Mistress Bascoomb discovers whence those potions came, my life will not be worth living."

Anxious to change the subject, Oric gathered up the donkey's reins. "Do you need a hand to mount, Master Ichtheus?"

Ichtheus made several attempts to clamber on and, with Oric's aid, he finally settled amongst the packages strapped upon Braccus' back. Oric swung his own leg effortlessly over a pile of merchandise on the second donkey. Ichtheus watched his apprentice enviously. *Oh, to be so young and supple.*

From across the road, Esica Figg watched and waited. At his surreptitious nod, the Horzefells followed after the apothecary and his apprentice.

Chapter Five

Attempted Murder

The apothecary's departure from Kilterton was undignified. A goose, led by Ichtheus on a long cord around her neck, hissed and flapped. She spooked Braccus, causing him to buck. Ichtheus clung on. Oric was soon in trouble, too. He sneezed repeatedly as feathers from two chickens in a wicker cage flew up his nose.

Folks sniggered and nudged each other, some barely able to contain their mirth as they watched the spectacle.

Parzifal, thinking it all a wonderful game, ran in and out of the donkeys' legs, yapping and snapping.

"Get out of the way, bonehead," Oric yelled. The new donkey, unsettled by the noise, skittered sideways. Oric lost his grip on the coop and the chickens crashed to the ground. The donkey continued to prance and Oric joined his feathered friends.

"You need to get a firmer grip on yon animal," wheezed an old farmhand. The man's weather-beaten face creased with humour as he grabbed the donkey's bridle.

Seated on a bench outside the inn, Dian observed Oric's

struggles. Oric scrambled to his feet and came almost nose to nose with her. Two dimples indented Dian's rosy cheeks as she tried not to giggle. The blood rushed to Oric's face, and again he felt foolishly inadequate. Ye gods! Whatever must the girl think of him?

"What ails you now, boy?" Ichtheus reviewed their scattered possessions. "Pick up the coop and carry the chickens. I will lead the donkey. You can follow along at your own pace, on foot, and for goodness sake keep Parzifal out of my way."

Sighing, Oric obeyed. "So much for me riding home," he said, giving Dian a sickly grin.

Dian reluctantly trailed back to her parents' cottage. Her father, Eadbald Cole, earned his living doing odd jobs around the village; he would soon return from the inn to demand his dinner. Well aware that her father's earnings were paltry, Dian wished that he did not spend so much of his income on ale. Her mother, Frida, was little better, for she also liked a tipple. With few funds left over to buy food, the Cole family often went hungry. Depression settled upon Dian like a dark cloak. She longed to escape, but where could she go?

-oOo-

Anticipation stirred Figg's innards as he watched the Horzefells leave the village in pursuit of the apothecary and his apprentice. If everything went according to plan he would soon have his hands on the apothecary's takings, the boy, the alchemist's key and, for all he knew, a vast fortune. Finished with the market, he stowed his table away and locked up his shop. Mounting his mare, he set off for St Griswald's Church.

Figg had discovered St Griswald's whilst out collecting loan repayments from farm-tenants and cottagers. The regular priest had abandoned the church, and its nearby manse, in favour of greatly superior lodgings beside Kilterton's new priory. Deserted, the old buildings had soon fallen into overgrown disrepair. A gloomy crypt beneath the church provided an ideal place for what Figg had in mind. As part of Sir Edred's estate, the buildings, hidden by a thick copse of trees, were only a short distance from Bayersby Manor.

A few days after finding the church, Figg had hidden most of his money there. He imprinted upon his brain each and every headstone above the graves in which he had buried his silver. Relieved that he had found a safe place to store his wealth, Figg relaxed for the first time in many moons. He instructed the Horzefell family to move from their hovel on High Moor into St Griswald's crypt, and informed the remainder of his band of villains that they had a new meeting place.

-oOo-

Lavender twilight descended upon Oric and Ichtheus as they made their way home from the market. Damp mist rose from the earth and seeped into moorland hollows, transforming them into milky-looking pools. Bracken grew head-high on either side of the road and, hampered by the chicken-coop, Oric soon lost sight of his master. Whoever would have thought that two chickens could weigh so much? For two sticks he would release the wretched creatures and dump the cage.

Parzifal gazed at the birds and drooled.

Oric stopped to rest awhile and rubbed his sore arms. The day had been interesting, medically speaking, but the opportunity to try Deveril's key in any of Kilterton's locks had not presented itself. At his current rate of progress, the mystery might never be solved.

The memory of Dian's laughing face temporarily wiped all thoughts of the key from Oric's mind as he blushed scarlet for the third time that day. How he wished she had not witnessed his embarrassing mishap with the chickens and the donkey. He would like to know the girl better, but would *she* wish to befriend such a buffoon?

Hersica and Zebediah decided upon Digby Ford across Roxdale Beck as the ideal ambush site. Outside the village, they left the main road and took a shortcut. Unhampered by baggage, they soon came to the shallow crossing. Tall bracken gave them adequate cover as they settled down to await the apothecary and his apprentice.

Ichtheus and his animal entourage arrived at the ford. In the middle of the crossing, the new donkey's leading rein pulled taut.

Exasperated, Ichtheus looked back. "Pish! What is the matter now?"

The new donkey, it seemed, had an aversion to water. Ichtheus tugged on her rein, but she steadfastly refused to enter the swiftly flowing beck.

"Where the devil is Oric?" Ichtheus muttered. "The lad is always missing when I need him most."

With insufficient room to turn in the narrow ford, and the leading rein too short to reach the other side, Ichtheus had no alternative. Sighing hugely, he removed his boots, rammed them into a pannier, and slid into the water. Sharp stones cut into his bare feet, and he cursed. Paddling through the shallows, he arrived back on the road a good deal wetter than he would have liked, and faced the unyielding donkey.

Ichtheus yelled for Braccus to move forward. Braccus

responded, but the other donkey remained rooted to the spot. The leading rein snapped under the strain. Braccus whooshed forward to the other side of the ford and began to crop grass in a leisurely fashion. The goose, looking happier than she had all day, gleefully filtered water through her beak.

Ichtheus pushed back his bonnet to scratch his itchy scalp. Hang it all, he had probably picked up head lice from the merchant who paid for his treatment with the donkey, and she was already causing him trouble.

As if she read his mind, the little animal glared at Ichtheus and dug her hooves more firmly into dry ground.

Ichtheus slapped her backside. Nothing! He tried yanking her halter. Nothing! It was as if the donkey had turned to stone. And still no sign of Oric.

Carefully approaching the donkey's rear, Ichtheus prayed she would not kick. She did not, for she had a sweet nature. She simply hated water.

Ichtheus tried pushing the donkey.

She sat down.

Ichtheus resisted the urge to kick the animal's backside. If the awkward apology for a piece of horseflesh had carried less of value, he would have left her behind. Facing the donkey, Ichtheus pressed his body against her rump and shoved.

Hersica peeped through the fronds of bracken. "Just look at yon silly beggar!" she mouthed, digging Zebediah in the ribs.

Immune to his mother's stink, Zebediah huddled closer and whispered in her ear. "Will I do it now, ma?"

"Aye, we will deal with the old man first and then wait for the apprentice to arrive." What the moneylender wanted with the boy was beyond Hersica's comprehension; he looked as thick as clarts.

Observing the apothecary, Hersica shook with silent laughter. "The apothecary has got himself into a right pickle with the donkey. Finish him off, Zeb, and put him out of his misery."

Veins knotted in Ichtheus' neck as he strained to shift the donkey. A vaguely familiar odour drifted into his nostrils. Feeling uneasy, he tried to recall where he had last smelled the rancid stink.

Too slow to defend himself against Zebediah Horzefell's blow, Ichtheus crashed to the ground. Stunned, and pinned down in the dirt, he slewed his eyes to see Hersica Horzefell goad her son.

"Go on, Zeb," Hersica screeched. "Strangle the life out of him."

Zebediah encircled Ichtheus' neck with claw-like hands.

Ichtheus struggled in the big man's grasp.

"You silly old fool, you stand no chance against my big son." Ghastly cackles erupted from Hersica's skinny frame.

In a daze, Ichtheus observed Hersica's filthy toes. They poked out through gaping holes in her boots only inches from his nose. At close quarters she appeared more repulsive than ever. Strings of seaweed hair hung in murky loops across her face and her black clothes were little more than rags.

Zebediah tightened his grip.

Starved of oxygen, waves of blackness engulfed Ichtheus.

Still lugging the chickens, Oric emerged from the bracken. Seeing the melee at the water's edge, he carefully placed the coop on the ground. Drawing a small dagger from its sheath, he ran silently forward. The Horzefells, engrossed in despatching Ichtheus, failed to hear him coming.

Nor did they see the streak that was Parzifal.

Oric plunged his dagger into Zebadiah's upper arm, missing a major artery by a whisker. With a piercing scream of agony, Zebediah exhaled a gust of sour breath and loosened his grip on Ichtheus' neck.

The black void receded, and Ichtheus scrambled to his feet.

Not to be outdone, Parzifal sank his teeth into Zebediah's backside.

Zebediah squealed like a stuck pig. "For the sake of all that's holy, have mercy!"

"Huh!" Ichtheus rasped. "How different things are, now the boot is on the other foot."

Hersica took one look at the furious dog, dragged up her ragged skirt, and scuttled back along the path in the direction of Kilterton.

Parzifal shook his captive's backside like a terrier with a rat.

Zebediah's screams reached a crescendo. "Call your dog away afore he tears my arse off."

"Order the dog to leave go, Oric." Ichtheus held his throbbing head. "I cannot stand the racket."

Freed from Parzifal's sharp teeth, Zebediah lurched upright. Clutching his ravaged buttock with one hand and his wounded bicep with the other, he hastened down the same track as his mother.

Parzifal followed to make sure the rogues kept going.

Deciding the water was less of a threat than the noisy altercation on her side of the beck, the frightened donkey plunged across the ford.

Parzifal returned to the scene of his victory with bits of cloth hanging from his jaws. He put his front paws up on to Ichtheus' shoulders and licked the old man's face.

"Ooh, my sainted aunt! What a day!" Quite out of character, Ichtheus hugged the dog, and then Oric.

Thus the bond between the three was irrevocably forged.

Chapter Six

St Griswald's Crypt

Exhausted after their unsuccessful assault on the apothecary and his apprentice, Hersica and Zebediah Horzefell stumbled down the worn steps into St Griswald's musty crypt.

"Where the devil have you been?" Figg hissed, his lips drawn into a tight, angry line. "You left the market hours ago. Did you rob the apothecary? Did you finish him off?" He craned his neck to see over the heads of his hapless employees. "And where is the apprentice? Did I not instruct you to bring him here?"

An ill-matched group of people, gathered around a sulky fire, watched the proceedings expectantly. Rastus, the elder Horzefell brother, sat apart from the rest. He glared contemptuously at his mother, thinking her more unsavoury than ever. As for his brother, Zebediah, the fool was naught but a lumbering clod.

"Ain't our fault the apothecary got away," Hersica whined. "We never bargained for the savage dog, nor did we expect the apprentice to creep up from nowhere and stab my Zeb." Her voice rose in shrill ululation. "Just look at him,

Master Figg! The poor sod is half dead."

Figg's icy retort sliced through her protestations. "Be silent, you useless, feeble-minded trollop! Not only have you and your numbskull son failed to rob and kill the Bayersby apothecary, you have also omitted to bring me the boy." The apprentice's welfare was of no concern to Figg, but he desperately wanted Deveril's key. Once he had the key in his possession he intended to dispose of the youth. What was a simple plan had suddenly become complicated. "Now the apothecary knows who his assailants are, he will have the entire populace on the lookout for you." Figg gazed at Hersica and Zebediah like a hawk upon its prey. "Because of your bungling inefficiency, neither of you can afford to be seen in Kilterton again. You, Hersica Horzefell, will remain here in St Griswald's crypt." He stabbed the air with his forefinger, "As for you, Zebediah, you are a naught but a brainless fool. You will go to Scutterskiff Keep. Perhaps, under adequate supervision, what little brawn you have can be put to good use."

Situated on the shores of Lake Brinwath, Scutterskiff Keep was two days' ride from St Griswald's. The isolated Norman tower provided an ideal place for Figg to amass his mercenary army.

Relieved not to be in Figg's bad books for once, Ned and Joe giggled and spluttered into their bowls of rabbit stew, but their mirth was short-lived.

"So you find the situation amusing, do you?" Figg's voice dripped malice. "I warn you, I will brook no mirth over inefficiency."

The two youngsters jumped up, spilling their supper. Puddles of greasy liquid congealed around their feet.

Figg sidestepped the lumpy mess. "And where, might I ask, are *your* day's thievings?" He delivered hefty swipes to the boys' ears. "If I find that you have kept any money for yourselves, I shall flay your hides."

Hersica's face twisted with anger, though she lacked the courage to speak out. Who did Figg think he was, speaking to folk like that? Not that she gave a tinker's cuss for the two snivelling brats, but how dare that worthless piece of scum revile the Horzefell family? Hersica slopped rabbit stew into two wooden bowls and thrust one under Zebediah's nose. One day the moneylender would get his just desserts, and Hersica intended to be nearby when he did.

Figg shifted his attention to two warriors, lounging against a stone coffin. He raised his eyebrows in query, he asked, "How goes your training program at Scutterskiff Keep. Are the numbers of recruits increasing?"

Cadoc, the senior of the two, shrugged. "Aye, master, the numbers are growing right enough. I only wish I could say the quality was there." He nudged his battle-scarred companion. "What say you, Rafe?"

"You will not get the fighting men you want, Figg. Not with the paltry money you pay for foot soldiers and archers." Rafe made a throaty sound of disgust and spat yellow phlegm into the embers of the fire. "Real warriors, prepared to fight to the death, want to be well rewarded for the sake of their families."

Figg had no desire to spend a penny more than was necessary for he had a great deal of money out on loan. "Real warriors," he raged. "The devil take 'em! Any able-bodied man who can wield a sword, battle-axe or pitchfork will do."

Early next morning, Figg left with Rafe, Cadoc and Zebediah, to review the situation at Scutterskiff Keep for himself.

-oOo-

An uneasy peace settled upon the occupants of St Griswald's crypt, and Rastus managed to rub along with his mother. The hovel they had once inhabited on High Moor became a temporary hiding place for plunder when the gang worked the territory north of Kilterton. Figg paid regular visits with his donkey and cart to collect the stolen goods. Nevertheless, his wealth failed to accumulate as swiftly as he desired.

The whereabouts of Deveril's mysterious key continued to dominate Figg's thoughts. If he could get his hands upon it, all his financial worries would surely be over. Killing the apothecary's apprentice would be an added bonus.

Chapter Seven

A Spooky Night Out

After the terrifying encounter with Hersica and Zebediah Horzefell, Oric worried about the safety of his key. He felt vulnerable, but could not yet bring himself to share Master Deveril's secret with Ichtheus. Much to his relief, the Horzefells failed to appear at the next market or on any subsequent market day.

"I am not surprised," Ichtheus stated. "After attacking me at the ford, that pair will never dare to show their faces in Kilterton again. They are probably causing mayhem in some other place far away." Nevertheless, Ichtheus failed to shake off his nervousness, especially when he ventured abroad late in the day.

Summer faded into autumn, and a sudden cold snap exacerbated a fever epidemic that spread through Bayersby Manor. Oric worked harder than he had ever done before, and he learned many new herbal recipes from his mentor. One mixture which eased coughs and colds was made from the residue of bruised liquorice-root boiled in spring water, pressed, and heated over a fire until it became thick. Another potion made from horehound and honey proved excellent for expectorating tough phlegm from the chest, and Oric ladled it into the afflicted with gusto. As day followed day, he became more fascinated by nature's remedies.

Life at Bayersby Manor differed in so many ways from the time Oric had spent at Dunburton. There, the lord of the manor had hunted or jousted most days, then indulged in night-long carousing sessions. As a common serf, Oric's time was spent performing back-breaking, menial tasks. Master Deveril's company at the end of each long day had been the only bright spot in his life. Oric thanked his lucky stars that he had found Bayersby Manor and Master Ichtheus. If he could strike up a friendship with Dian Cole, his happiness would be complete.

-oOo-

During one of her regular welfare rounds on Sir Edred's Kilterton tenants, Lady Myferny discovered that several families were unwell. Believing the rich owed a duty of care to the poor, she hastened home to ask Ichtheus' advice. "Their symptoms are similar to the malady that struck down many of our Bayersby servants," she explained. "Is there anything we can do to help?"

"We still have a goodly stock of liquorice-root potion," Oric interjected, hoping that Dian was not amongst the infected. "The medicament worked well, here. It will surely help the village folk, too."

"Aye, and I have some butterbur," Ichtheus added. "A concentrate of the root mixed with wine will stop folk from wheezing and aid their breathing." He disappeared into his storeroom and reappeared with a large flagon. "If we are dealing with the needy, we must assume that they will have no liquor of their own."

In her parents' one-room cottage, Dian ran herself ragged. Her brother, Josh, huddled miserably in a corner, his face flushed with fever. The rest of the Cole siblings sprawled on the floor around him. Dian, the last member of the family still upright, mopped fiery brows and administered sips of water. Her mother slept in the only chair. Eadbald Cole returned home briefly, but, seeing the sickly state of his family, he refused to set foot indoors and scuttled back to the inn. Frida Cole slumbered on, leaving her eldest daughter to cope as best she could.

Exhausted after a busy night, Dian worried over what she should do next. Josh looked a little better, but some of the younger children had taken a turn for the worse. She stared at them in desperation. Who would look after them when she left home?

Dian's fourteenth birthday was looming close. It was only a matter of time before her parents moved her out, and her father had already suggested that Master Figg might pay a good price for a strong servant-girl. Dian shuddered, trying to shut out the disturbing thought.

Oric and Ichtheus made the journey to Kilterton, and began calling at each cottage in turn. They doled out medicaments wherever necessary, and reassured worried parents. At last they arrived at the Coles' cottage and, praying that Dian had escaped the epidemic, Oric rapped upon the door.

"What are *you* doing here?" Dian gasped at the sight of Oric. Ashamed of her parents' unsavoury living conditions, it was her turn to blush. Her embarrassment lasted only a heartbeat, for she was keen to obtain help for her family.

Coughs and wheezes reverberated around the single

room. Ichtheus sized up the situation and produced butterbur root from his sack. "Fetch in the flagon of wine, Oric."

"Please, keep the liquor out of Mother's sight," Dian whispered. "Given half a chance she will sup the lot."

"We will concoct the potion at once, and remove any leftover liquor," Oric replied. "Butterbur has a bitter taste, your mother will not want to drink too much of it even though it is mixed with liquor."

Impressed by Oric's abilities, Dian wished he were not so shy.

Ichtheus chuckled quietly. The young lady had an interesting effect on Oric. Not normally tongue-tied, the lad seemed to have trouble with the simplest of sentences in her presence.

At the end of a long day, Oric and Ichtheus returned home to find Mother Morghan in another of her foul moods. Oric took one look at the woman's sour expression and headed for the stables. To avoid an evening of unpleasant confrontation, Ichtheus decided to visit a friend who lived on the moor. He piled on extra clothes to ward off the frosty autumn weather and prepared to leave.

Parzifal, thinking he was being deserted, wore a hangdog expression, rolled on his back, and stuck all four legs in the air.

Captivated by the dog's antics, Ichtheus gave in. "Oh, come on, you scruffy heap, I have not the heart to leave you behind."

Candlelight spilled out from the open kitchen door and illuminated Oric as he crossed the yard. He had bedded down the donkeys for the night, and stalks of straw protruded from his fair hair. He grinned, exposing two rows of even, white teeth.

"You going out are you, Master Ichtheus?" He stamped his feet and blew hot breath on to his frozen knuckles.

"No, no, Oric, I am dressed like this to go to bed!" Ichtheus' voice oozed sarcasm. "Of course I am going out, boy!"

"Can I go with you?" Oric's eyes sparkled. "All my chores are done."

Ichtheus had looked forward to a quiet gossip with his shepherd friend, Nathaniel. But in his current nervous state, he reasoned that a little company along the way might not be such a bad idea.

"If you wish to accompany me, boy, you had best hurry and get ready. We have a long walk ahead of us." Ichtheus picked up two bottles of his best nettle wine, wrapped a pot of stewed pigeons in a woollen sack, and stepped outside.

Pale moonlight turned ordinary things into strange shapes, and Oric stuck close by his master. Barely twenty paces past the door, he slipped on an icy puddle and almost dragged Ichtheus down.

"Lovely moon tonight, Master," Oric remarked by way of diversion.

"'Od's blood, lad, you attract disaster wherever you go!" Ichtheus smothered a smile as he hauled the boy to his feet.

Icy draughts clawed at Ichtheus' lungs with every breath he took, and his exhalations vaporised in the sharp air. "For goodness sake get a move on, Oric! We need to walk fast just to keep the blood from freezing in our veins." Only part way through autumn and the weather had already taken a turn for the worse and Ichtheus shivered, dreading the fast approaching winter.

Parzifal, unaffected by the cold, bounded back and forth like a puppy.

The path from Bayersby Manor to Nathaniel's home at Rigg Farm took Oric and Ichtheus past St Griswald's Church. Since services had ceased, local folk no longer used the narrow walkway. Vegetation once regularly cut back had grown in abundance. Holding their lanterns high, Ichtheus and Oric battled through the tangle of branches until they broke though into St Griswald's moonlit churchyard. An owl hooted eerily and its wings beat a soft tattoo as it rose into the night.

Oric eyed the gravestones, made sinister by shadows. "This place is creepy." He sidled closer to his master, inadvertently stepping on the hem of Ichtheus' cloak.

Half-choked, Ichtheus yanked at the material and spoke with a confidence he did not feel. "Nobody has worshipped at this place for many a long day. There is naught here but cobwebs and bats." He marched across the graveyard, but secretly he longed for the refuge of Nathaniel's warm farmhouse.

Hersica Horzefell squinted at the intruders through a gap in the church door. "Hey, Rastus take a look at this. Who do you suppose yon folk are?"

Shoving his mother roughly to one side, Rastus pressed his eye to the crack, "Ye gods, 'tis the Bayersby apothecary and his apprentice!" Dim as a lamp needing oil, Rastus gave no thought to capturing the intruders. "We cannot allow them to wander around here at will," he exclaimed. "Master Figg would have a fit if he knew."

"Aye," Hersica wholeheartedly agreed with her son. "If they return we had best get rid of them."

-oOo-

The rest of Oric and Ichtheus' walk to Rigg Farm continued without event. They were cold and hungry by the time they came upon Nathaniel's cottage. A few sheep, retained for breeding purposes, were penned against a wall of the house to protect them from severe weather and wolves. The remainder of the flock had been slaughtered; salted down to provide food during the winter months.

"How nice to see you, Ichtheus," Nathaniel beamed happily, drawing his friend inside the warm cottage. "Fancy you turning out on a bitter night like this. You must be frozen."

Hanging their outer garments on wall pegs, Ichtheus and Oric hunkered down beside the fire.

"You could not have chosen a better time to visit, for I have a blockage in my nose." Nathaniel snorted vigorously to prove his point.

The snub-nosed, woolly-haired shepherd reminded Oric of the sheep he had seen outside.

Nathaniel blew his nose noisily. "'Tis not so bad during the day you understand, but, come bedtime, I am hard-pressed to breathe."

"What would you recommend, Oric?" Ichtheus asked, pushing his apprentice forward.

Oric tilted Nathaniel's head back and peered up his nostrils. "I can see no obvious blockage. Since we have brought no suitable medicaments, the treatment will need to be simple." He gave Nathaniel's nose a gentle squeeze, "Do you have any beetroot?"

"Aye," Nathaniel replied. "I put some down in straw to last me through the winter."

"Good" Oric nodded his approval. "Boil up some beets and snort a little of the cooled juice. It will cleanse your nose and clear your head. In the unlikely event of your condition worsening, I shall send you some water of adder's-tongue."

Immensely proud of his apprentice, Ichtheus sang Oric's praises. "Under the circumstances," he concluded, "I would have advised exactly the same treatment!"

"By gum!" Nathaniel looked Oric up and down, surprised that a person of such tender years could be so knowledgeable. "How old are you, boy, and where are you from?"

"I am not sure of my exact age. Fourteen, maybe fifteen years, I think." Oric retained no memory of his arrival at Dunburton, and images of his parents were hazy. "According to Master Deveril, the lord of the manor took us in and set my father and mother to work. My parents died of a fever when I was but an infant. That is all I can tell you."

Ichtheus and Nathaniel soon engaged in lively conversation, and Oric's attention wandered. Every new place provided a challenge to find the lock that might respond to Deveril's key. But Nathaniel's simple cottage had no locks at all.

The shepherd dropped more logs onto the fire.

Parzifal yawned, stretched, and fell asleep. His cheeks puttered gently with each snore, and his feet twitched in a doggy dream.

Ichtheus heated the pigeon stew and spooned generous portions onto three wooden platters. Each fat bird, surrounded by turnips and onions, dripped with delicious gravy. Conversation stilled until the bones were sucked clean. Belching gently, Ichtheus reached for the first bottle of nettle wine. A short time later they opened a second bottle. The imbibers stretched out before the fire, feeling lazy and mellow.

Nathaniel produced a flagon of mead, and mellowness swiftly degenerated into intoxication. "I say Ichtheus!" Nathaniel slurred his words, "Did you hear about that old crone?"

Ichtheus raised his eyebrows drowsily. "What old crone?"

"The one they branded a witch." Nathaniel paused for effect. "I heard that some half-wit locals dragged the poor old hag from her hovel and carried her to St Griswald's Church. 'Tis said they never gave her a chance to defend herself. 'Tis said the fools built a pyre in the middle of the graveyard and burned her alive." He shook his head blearily. "What a terrible way to die."

Ichtheus looked stunned. Perhaps the Horzefell woman had not escaped after all. "How long ago did this happen?"

"A while back, but some folk believe the old crone has returned to haunt them," Nathaniel rolled his eyes in delicious horror. "And serve the ignorant peasants right, I say!"

Oric's Adam's apple worked overtime as he swallowed nervously. "We came by way of St Griswald's. Is there not another way home?"

"I have heard no such rumour," Ichtheus growled scathingly. "'Tis naught but village tittle-tattle. Nothing troubled us on the journey here, and I am not expecting any untoward occurrences on the way back. Besides," he cackled, "one whiff of our breath will knock any unsuspecting ghost flat on its back." Rising unsteadily to his feet, he piled on his outer garments. "Come, 'tis time we were on our way, boy, haunting or no."

Chapter Eight

Churchyard Witch

Outside Nathaniel's cottage, the cold air struck Oric and Ichtheus like a body blow. An icy moon sailed in an ocean of night sky, towing silver clouds in its wake. In a hurry to get back to Bayersby Manor and his warm bed, Ichtheus set a brisk pace.

Oric followed with the dog.

The only member of the trio not staggering was Parzifal.

"What ails you, boy?" Ichtheus slurred. "You will have me fall upon my backside if you continue to run into me like that. Pish! Can you not hold your liquor?"

Oric gave a hiccupping titter. "'Tis not my fault, Master Ichtheus, 'tis you that has over imbibed, not I!"

They soldiered on, tripping over each other until St Griswald's Church loomed into sight. Nathaniel's talk of witches and ghosts overrode Oric's good sense, and he hung back. He had guts aplenty for everyday things, but ghosts were another matter altogether.

"What a great booby you are," chafed Ichtheus, cuffing Oric's ears affectionately. "Come, we shall sing a song to cheer ourselves." Without further ado, he launched into his favourite hymn.

Oric joined in half-heartedly. Neither of them had an ear for music, and the noise they made set Parzifal to howling.

Moonlight cast long shadows, creating a black and silver scene. Trees took on sinister shapes, and a sudden breeze made an old yew tree creak. The owl hooted from his perch in the bell-tower, causing Oric's neck hairs to stand on end.

An urge to relieve himself overtook Ichtheus. While he fumbled with all his extra clothing, Oric and Parzifal sloped off around a bend in the pathway. Ichtheus was in full-stream when the pair reappeared, running as if chased by demons. Oric crashed into his master, and bowled him over. Unable to turn off his flow in time, Ichtheus pissed copiously into one of his boots.

"Damn your eyes, boy!" Ichtheus staggered to his feet, "What in heaven's name are you about?" He shook his foot. "You blithering fool… look what you have caused me to do." He set his wet boot on the ground, and was disgusted to hear it squelch.

Oric's voice rose from hoarse whispers to high squeaks of sheer terror. He grabbed Ichtheus by the arms. "Master! Master! I saw it. Her! *The thing!*"

"What thing, boy? What *THING*?" Ichtheus shouted and shook Oric as if he were a rag doll.

"The witch! You remember! The one we talked about with Nathaniel. That old hag that was burned! I saw her around the corner," Oric pointed a shaking finger. "She is there, I tell you. All of a quiver and a dither, she smiled and beckoned to me."

"What rubbish, boy!" Filled with nettle wine, mead, and bravado, Ichtheus strode down the path to investigate.

Parzifal loped alongside, rumbling with growls. Feeling less brave by the minute, Ichtheus rounded the bole of a giant oak-tree.

"Oh, my sainted aunt!" he gasped, his bravado deflated like a pig's bladder pricked by a dagger. He seized Parzifal's collar and huddled into the oak's dark shadow. Summoning every ounce of his courage, he took another peek around the tree trunk.

Not more than twenty strides away an old woman sat upon a rickety cart. She dithered and beckoned, just as Oric had described. Something was in the trees, too. Pallid, disembodied faces floated about as if imbued with a life of their own.

Prickled from head to foot with gooseflesh, Ichtheus lost his nerve. He turned and fled on liquid legs towards the churchyard gate. Parzifal chased after his master. Now horribly sober, Ichtheus stopped at the gate to make sure the apparitions did not follow. He tried to catch his breath and slow his racing heart. It would never do to let Oric see him in this state. Oh, dear, no! The lad would never allow him to live it down.

Oric was hiding in a ditch.

"Get out of there, boy! There is nothing to be afraid of," Ichtheus bluffed in his boldest voice. "The ghost you saw is naught but a trick of the moonlight. However, to spare you further distress, we shall traverse the churchyard's outer wall instead of cutting across the middle."

The sight of his master's rigid face stilled Oric's tongue, but he did not believe a word Ichtheus said.

They hurried around the churchyard's perimeter. Only when they had gained the cover of the overgrown footpath did they slow their pace. Not a word passed between them until they arrived back at Bayersby Manor.

Still shaken, Oric bid his master a subdued goodnight and crawled, fully clothed, into his inglenook corner.

Ichtheus removed his boots and dropped thankfully onto his truckle bed, but he took a long time to fall asleep.

-oOo-

Mirth was not something the Horzefell family indulged in very often, but at this moment Rastus and Hersica were shaking with unrestrained glee.

"Did you see the silly old fool?" Hersica screeched. "And did you ever hear such a racket? Trying to sing… hah! They sounded like tomcats from hell." Tears ran down her lined cheeks and made tracks in the dirt. "I scared the apothecary witless, beckoning to him from yon barrow, like as not he lost control of his bowels with fright!"

Rastus clutched his aching sides. "I doubt we shall see that pair here again. You did a grand job," he praised Ned and Joe, who were equally doubled up with laughter. "Am I not a crafty beggar, coming up with such a clever idea? Holding those oil lamps under your chins when you were up the trees was a stroke of genius." Rastus erupted with more horrible squeaks and wheezes as he visualised the urchins' distorted faces. From a distance they had looked like disembodied ghouls as they climbed from branch to branch. Just for the fun of it, Rastus had grabbed a lamp and joined in.

The church door banged, making everyone jump. Figg had returned.

"What is the cause of your hilarity?" In a foul temper, Figg's icy voice sliced through the crypt.

Flushed with success, Rastus related how he had rid the churchyard of the apothecary and his apprentice.

"You imbecile," Figg shrieked. "You had those pests within your grasp and you let them go free?" Almost beside himself with rage, he held up his thumb and forefinger a hairsbreadth apart. "And you think it funny that we came this close to discovery?"

The inhabitants of the crypt cowered under the intensity of the moneylender's abuse.

Figg's eyes glittered like shards of ice. "If you miss another chance to kill Master Ichtheus, I shall not be responsible for my actions. And, next time the opportunity arises, seize the apothecary's apprentice and bring him to me… alive."

-oOo-

The following morning Oric tried to assemble his thoughts, but he could make no sense of the things he had witnessed at St Griswald's the night before. Surely he had imagined the ghostly old crone in the graveyard. Nevertheless, he was in no hurry to return to the old church, and he hoped his master would forget the whole sorry incident.

Ichtheus crawled from his bed. Sober, and in the cold light of day, his intellect told him there was more to the strange goings on at the old church than met the eye.

Chapter Nine

Oric Confronts a Wild Boar

The Horzefells' disastrous encounters with the Bayersby apothecary caused Figg to distrust the abilities of his henchmen. The motley crew sprawled around St Griswald's crypt did little to boost his confidence, and he wished he could replace them. If mercenary soldiers were as easy to come by as female servants his problems would be solved. Eadbald Cole, the village drunk, had offered to sell his daughter, but the price he asked was too high. Figg decided to bide his time. When Cole ran out of liquor money, his asking price for Dian would tumble. Figg smirked; the young girl was worth waiting for. Not only was she a hard worker, she was also a very pretty piece.

Figg forced his attention back to the situation in hand, and clapped his hands to gain everyone's attention. "Mother Morghan informs me that the Bayersby heir has completed his education at Roxbrough Abbey, and is travelling home today. Since Lady Myferny's wealthy sister lives in Roxbrough town, young Master Guwain will be carrying valuable Yuletide gifts for the family at Bayersby Manor."

Fig looked directly at Rastus. "Lie in wait for the boy and his manservant. Kill them both. Seize everything of value, including their horses. Take Ned and Joe to assist you." A humourless smile played upon Figg's lips, "And, to safeguard the Horzefells' continued good health, I recommend that you execute your task efficiently."

Each successful robbery brought Figg closer to fulfilling his ambition. Money to pay his mercenary army was accumulating and, if things went according to plan, he would soon be Master of Bayersby.

-oOo-

Autumn turned into winter, and freezing fogs rolled down from the moors. Puddles in the yard froze treacherously solid, and spiky icicles stabbed down from Bayersby Manor's eaves. The festive season, with its many jollifications, was fast approaching, and an influx of visitors arrived daily.

Ichtheus filled his cheeks and let the air escape in an elongated fart-sound of disgust. The section of kitchen he usually called his own had turned into a devil's cauldron of milling, argumentative servants. Tension was palpable, but Oric enjoyed the underlying feeling of excitement.

Responsibility for Yuletide decorations usually fell upon Ichtheus. With a cartload of other work ahead of him, he attempted to bow out of the task.

Lady Myferny was determined to change his mind. "Dearest Ichtheus, please work your magic once again." She grasped his hand, her violet eyes pleading. "You always make everything look so beautiful."

Ichtheus thought of Lady Myferny's regular trips into Kilterton where, in times of trouble, she was always the first to offer Sir Edred's tenants a helping hand. Gazing at the beautiful, generous woman, Ichtheus felt it would be churlish to refuse her simple request. Besides, a foraging trip would provide him with the perfect excuse to escape the noise and the nasty cooking smells that currently permeated his domain. He went in search of Oric and found him experimenting with a new potion. "Cease what you are doing for the time being, lad, we have a busy day ahead of us."

Delighted to be included in his master's excursion, Oric could hardly wait to set off. "Where are we going?"

"Across the valley to Scraggswood Forest," Ichtheus replied. "We shall find an abundance of holly and copper beech trees growing there." He packed dried fruits, oatcakes to eat with slices of goat's cheese, and a flagon of ale. Wrapped in warm cloaks, they set out, Ichtheus riding his donkey, Braccus, and Oric astride the new female donkey that he had named Otty.

-oOo-

Spittle flew from Rastus' mouth as he bawled at Ned and Joe. "You dare to challenge Master Figg's orders? Do as you are bid or I shall flay your hides."

Ned stood his ground. "Nay, Master Rastus! Robbing folk is all very well, but killing them is another matter altogether. Me and Joe want no part of it."

Joe's pinched face showed his uncertainty. He whimpered and hid behind Ned.

Rastus lashed out, his heavy staff coming down on Ned's shoulder. Ned jumped back, gasping with pain. "By heck, Master Rastus, you are a nasty piece of work and no mistake." He grabbed Joe's arm. "Come on, little 'un. We ain't having nothing to do with this effort. I would rather face Master Figg's fury than Master Hangman's noose."

His authority routed, Rastus turned on his heel and marched off. He did not need the lily-livered pair. He could do the deed by himself.

-oOo-

Scraggswood Forest exuded an exhilarating aroma of pine and damp earth. Pale sunshine slanted through the trees, infusing wisps of mist with ethereal light. Oric and Ichtheus moved slowly, enjoying the heady smell and talking in hushed tones.

"Why are we whispering?" Ichtheus guffawed, sending a flock of wood pigeons flapping upwards in fright. "There is no one to hear us."

Midday came, and they stopped in a clearing for a bite to eat.

Loops of drool hung from Parzifal's jaws as he fixed his gaze upon the food.

Ichtheus eyed the dog with distaste. "For goodness sake feed the brute, Oric. He is putting me off my meal."

An enormous holly tree at the far end of the clearing sported a fine crop of scarlet berries. "I knew we would find what we want in Scraggswood Forest," said Ichtheus, brushing crumbs from his tunic. "Cut off a few branches, Oric, but mind you select the ones with plenty of berries."

The best berries were at the top of the tree. Oric shinned up amongst the prickly leaves with a dagger clenched between his teeth. Sharp spines dug into his tender flesh and he howled with anguish. But overcoming the pain, he chopped off some suitable branches and dropped them to the ground.

The pile of holly grew, and a satisfied smile quirked the corners of Ichtheus' mouth. "That should suffice, Oric, you may come down now." Ichtheus rolled the holly in a leather hide and strapped it to Braccus' back. So far so good!

"Foof! Am I glad that job is over!" Oric jumped the last few feet to the ground, then sucked his pierced fingers. "If you ask me, 'tis a good thing the festive season comes but once a year."

After the holly, lopping a few low branches from a copper-beech tree proved easy.

Lady Myferny had also requested some mistletoe, believing it gave protection against witchcraft, disease, bad luck and fire. Oric spotted a few clumps of the white-berried parasite growing amongst the top branches of an ancient oak-tree. His stomach lurched. "Not sure I have the head for that sort of height, Master Ichtheus. It must be fifty feet to the top of that tree."

"Do not be faint-hearted," Ichtheus snorted. "When I was your age, I climbed far higher than that." He gave Oric a shove toward the base of the tree. "Just think of the view you will enjoy from the top."

Not the least bit comforted, Oric placed his foot on the tree's lowest branch and began slowly to ascend. He had almost reached his goal when the distant baying of hounds intruded upon his concentration.

Sir Edred had left the manor at first light to hunt boar for the Yuletide feast, but Oric had not thought the party was headed for Scraggswood Forest. Still, he reasoned, they did sound a long way off.

"Can you hear those hounds?" Ichtheus stretched his neck and shouted up the tree at a pair of legs, which was all he could see of Oric, "Sounds as if they are hunting to the north of here."

A few substantial chunks of mistletoe whistled past Ichtheus' ear, narrowly missing his upturned face. He gathered up the fallen branches and added them to the parcel of holly on Braccus' back.

"I can *hear* the hunters, but I cannot see them." Oric threw down more mistletoe. "Hey! Wait a moment…" The branches of the oak-tree shook as Oric strained to obtain a better view. "Two horsemen have crested a hill over yonder. They are leading a pair of loaded packhorses."

"I suspect the travellers might be Sir Edred's son and his manservant," Ichtheus replied. "They are expected home from Roxbrough today. The spare horses will be carrying Yuletide gifts from Lady Myferny's family."

"Ye gods! I do not like what I see." Oric shouted.

A note of panic entered Ichtheus' voice. "What do you see, boy?"

"I can see a man with a bow and arrow lying in wait!"

Ichtheus flapped his hands with fright. "Quick, climb down, Oric! We must warn the travellers before they are ambushed."

Rastus had picked a good spot. Young Guwain and his manservant were clearly visible as they rode their mounts over a nearby hilltop. Rastus primed his bow, pulled back the string to crease his lips and let fly. The arrow thudded into the young man's chest. A second arrow swiftly followed the first, knocking the manservant from his saddle. When neither victim moved, Rastus approached with caution.

Back in the oak tree, Oric's voice went up several tones. "Master Ichtheus, I believe I have just witnessed a double murder."

"Oh, my sainted aunt!" Ichtheus ran first one way then another. "How far off are they?"

"Too far away for us to catch the culprit." Half-way down

the tree, Oric's attention was grabbed from another direction. "Now I see the hunt. Mounted men and a pack of hounds are coming this way, but I cannot see what they are chasing."

Presuming his two victims were dead, Rastus stripped them to their undergarments. He rolled the bodies into a ditch and kicked a layer of fallen leaves over his victims. He mounted the best-looking horse and grasped the bridles of the others. Eyeing the bulging panniers, he smirked with delight. Even after he had hived off a few items for himself, Master Figg should have no cause for complaint.

A cave in the hillside provided Rastus with a hideout. Off the beaten track and well disguised by thick vegetation, he had never seen another living soul in the vicinity. Nevertheless, he spent many sleepless nights thinking about his fate should Figg ever discover his double dealing.

Sir Edred galloped across the fields, unaware of the attack upon his son. Horns blared and hot-blooded shouts accompanied a cacophony of baying hounds.

The tumult reached a crescendo. Ichtheus jumped up and down, trying to attract Sir Edred's attention. Horses, men and dogs, all going full tilt, thundered past on the other side of a dome-shaped bramble thicket.

A boar with a huntsman's spear embedded in its neck, galloped into the clearing. Its powerful shoulders narrowed to a small rump, and its black, bristly hide was gashed with scars from many past battles. Ichtheus froze to the spot, mesmerised by the animal's sharp, yellow tusks.

The boar had murder in its wild eyes – it clearly intended to gore Ichtheus.

"Run, Master Ichtheus, run!" Horrified to see the old man in danger, Oric half-climbed, half-fell down the oak-tree.

Parzifal beat Oric to the rescue. He leapt onto the oversized porker's back and sank his teeth into the tough skin just behind its ears. Distracted, the boar bucked and tossed, but Parzifal hung on. Ignoring its canine passenger, the porker once again fixed evil eyes upon Ichtheus.

Back on the ground, Oric ran at the beast shouting, trying to distract it away from his master.

Ichtheus, heart racing, looked for an escape route. Outrunning the creature was not an option. God's teeth! What was he to do? Left with only one option, he hurled himself on top of the bramble thicket. Suspended several feet above the ground, he clung on for dear life.

With its original target no longer in sight, the boar turned its attention to Oric. Seeing that his master was out of danger, Oric sprinted back to the oak tree. He managed to climb out of reach, but not before the boar's tusk had raked his calf. Denied its human quarry, the boar concentrated on ridding itself of the creature upon its back. Parzifal lost his grip, fell off and plunged to safety in the thicket. The frustrated boar waddled away, squealing and bleeding, with the spear still embedded in its neck.

"Are you all right, Master?" Oric called as he stepped down from the tree.

"No, Oric! I am not all right!" Ichtheus expostulated. "Get over here at once, and help me out of these blasted brambles."

Spread-eagled on top of the thicket, Ichtheus looked like a fly caught in a sticky cobweb. He wriggled, but his body weight caused him to sink further into the bushes until only his backside remained visible.

"Extricate me from here, boy," Ichtheus bellowed. "We have no time to lose!"

Ichtheus was well ensnared by thorns, and Oric was obliged to hack away chunks of his master's silver hair and beard to free him. Safely returned to the ground, Oric brushed stray whiskers from his master's clothes.

"Never mind about me," Ichtheus snapped. "We must hasten to Master Guwain's aid." Without stopping to adjust his attire, he climbed on to Braccus' back and urged the donkey into a swift trot.

Somewhere ahead, Parzifal barked.

They came upon the dog, standing in the bottom of a deep, dry ditch. He wagged his plumy tail and nuzzled into a pile of dead leaves.

A flaccid hand flopped out.

Oric slithered into the ditch and scooped away a layer of dead leaves to reveal two bodies.

The servant was dead, an arrow through his heart. Guwain had the pallor of a corpse, but Ichtheus detected a faint pulse. "Snap off the shaft, Oric. If we try to extract the arrowhead here, the young master might bleed to death before we can get him home." Ichtheus hastily tore strips of fabric from his tunic and bound Guwain's wound. Satisfied that the bleeding had slowed, he enlisted Oric's help to drag Guwain from the ditch and on to Braccus' back. "Leave the other poor fellow. We will send someone to fetch him later."

Blood trickled down Oric's calf, and Ichtheus tore another strip from his tunic. "How did you sustain this injury?" he asked.

Oric pulled a rueful face. "The boar ran faster than me. He gored me with his tusk before I managed to escape back up the tree."

At the end of his days' hunting, Sir Edred returned to Bayersby Manor. Striding up and down the great hall, he expounded to all and sundry how he had narrowly missed killing a monstrous boar. "One of my huntsmen managed to spear it, nevertheless the wretched beast escaped. Dammed hounds lost its scent." Sir Edred tugged at his russet beard,

"God knows where the creature went after that." He beamed hugely. "The first boar may have escaped but we captured another, much bigger beast." Sir Edred's blue eyes flashed as he imparted every gory detail of his final kill. "No one shall go hungry this Yuletide."

Frenzied shouts from the yard interrupted Sir Edred's tale, and he ran downstairs to investigate the noise.

Framed in the open kitchen door were Oric and Ichtheus, supporting Guwain's inert form between them.

Chapter Ten

A Life Saved

Ichtheus swept everything from the kitchen table and, with Oric's help, lay Guwain upon it. "Mother Morghan," he bellowed, "Fetch a bowl of warm water and some cloths."

In the ensuing panic, Mother Morghan's agitation went unnoticed. Master Guwain had been robbed, that was clear, for he was near naked. But why had Rastus Horzefell failed to kill him? *Esica Figg need not lay the blame at my door,* Mother Morghan thought indignantly. She had kept her side of the bargain by informing him exactly when the Bayersby heir was due to arrive home. It was not her fault Figg's numbskull henchman had bungled the job.

Mother Morghan took a deep breath to calm her nerves. As far as she could see, there was nothing to link her to the attack. Nevertheless, next time she saw Figg she planned give him a piece of her mind!

"We must remove this arrowhead before the wound festers." Ichtheus snatched a cloth from Mother Morgan's hand. "Here, put that bowl of water down on the end of the table where I can reach it." Turning to Oric, he said, "What medicament would you suggest we use?"

May I refer to your *Apothecary's Almanac*? Oric asked, reaching for his mentor's well-thumbed book.

Ichtheus nodded his approval. If unsure of the correct remedy, the lad was never too proud to look up the solution.

"A decoction of burnet leaves will defend against infection," Oric read aloud, "and, when Master Guwain regains consciousness, we are advised to administer the seeds in powdered form mixed with a little wine. The astringent quality of the herb is effective for staunching internal and external bleeding."

"Well done, Oric." Ichtheus experienced an inner glow of satisfaction. "Bring what we need from the medicine chest."

Impressed, Sir Edred patted Oric on the back. "This young fellow displays the makings of a very fine apothecary."

Thrilled by Sir Edred's compliment, Oric beamed.

Mother Morghan glowered. In her opinion, the apprentice was getting altogether too big for his boots.

Exercising great care, Ichtheus eased the arrowhead from Guwain's chest. Out cold, the patient never flinched. The boy had already lost a lot of blood, and Oric was appalled at how much more oozed out.

For several days Guwain remained under Ichtheus' watchful eye, drifting in and out of semi-conscious delirium.

Oric feared for the boy's life. As Sir Edred's only son and heir, it would be a disaster if the boy failed to recover. "Can we do nothing more to help him, Master Ichtheus? He is burning up!"

"See if you can unearth some tincture of mugwort." Ichtheus placed his hand on Guwain's dry and fiery brow. "We need to provoke sweating."

Oric mixed some of the medicament with equal parts of wine and water. He dribbled a small quantity of liquid down the glassy-eyed patient's throat and applied a neat tincture directly on to the wound. Glancing at Ichtheus for approval, he asked, "If the treatment works, Master Guwain should soon be sweating like a hard-ridden horse, should he not?"

"Aye," Ichtheus replied. "If we are successful, he will swiftly mend."

Despite Guwain's weakened state, Oric saw that the fifteen-year-old boy was handsome. Burgeoning muscles rippled under his fair skin; thick, russet-coloured hair surrounded his neat skull. His chin was square and firm, but Oric thought the set of Guwain's mouth was petulant.

Sir Edred checked on his heir regularly and, seeing little improvement, he raged up and down the kitchen, swearing vengeance. "I shall not rest until the perpetrators of this heinous crime are incarcerated. When I get my hands upon the culprits, they will wish their mothers had never given them birth."

"Pray, calm yourself, my lord," Ichtheus soothed – worried that Sir Edred might suffer an apoplectic fit. "At this rate, you will become my next patient."

Apart from visits to the women's solar for brief naps and to pray, Lady Myferny remained by her son's side. She stroked his brow, willing him to get well. Guwain responded to his mother's words – and to Ichtheus' ministrations. Soon he was able to sit up and take a little nourishment.

With the lady of the manor spending so much time in the kitchen, Mother Morghan jumped about like a cat on a hot trivet. She rubbed and scrubbed, bobbed and grovelled, until Ichtheus became heartily sick of the woman's deception. To his utter disgust, Lady Myferny suggested that an extra kitchen-maid should be employed to help ease the housekeeper's workload.

Mother Morghan departed for Kilterton in search of a new maid and, in her absence, some semblance of order returned to the apothecary's section of the kitchen... but not for long.

-oOo-

Mother Morghan's first port-of-call was the local inn. Over a pot of ale she explained her mission to the innkeeper's wife.

Seated next to the Bayersby housekeeper, Eadbald Cole immediately suggested his eldest daughter for the position of servant-girl. "Esica Figg offered a good sum for the wench," he whined, squinting at the housekeeper. "If you can better his offer, the girl is yours." The housekeeper haggled; nevertheless, the final agreement was far more lucrative than anything Figg had proposed. The deal done, Eadbald drained his pot and wiped drips of ale from his chin. The moneylender had bungled his chance of purchasing a fine wench and, as far as Eadbald Cole was concerned, it served the penny-pinching, skinflint right. Eadbald immediately passed half the money over to the innkeeper. "Keep me topped up with ale, landlord."

Well pleased with her deal, Mother Morghan secretly pocketed the change from Lady Myferny's funds.

Surrounded by her curious brothers and sisters, Dian answered the door to Mother Morghan's knock.

"I have purchased you from your father," the Bayersby housekeeper snapped, pushing past the round-eyed gaggle of skinny children. "Pack your belongings and be quick about it. I want to get back to Bayersby Manor before dark."

Relief washed over Dian. Now she no longer had to fear an uncertain future with Esica Figg. She was going to Bayersby Manor. Her heart sang. She had no possession to pack but she threw a shawl over her shoulders. Keen though she was to leave her parents, her joy dimmed as she farewelled her little siblings.

"Try not to worry," Josh soothed, seeing how upset his sister had become, "I will keep an eye on the children." He hugged her tightly. "Besides, you are not going far away. Whenever you have a day off, you can visit us."

Mother Morghan pushed Dian out through the cottage door. "You might need to polish up your housewifely skills, Mistress Cole, now your eldest girl is leaving." With a shiver of spiteful delight, she wondered what Master Figg would say when he discovered that the Cole wench had been snatched from under his nose.

-oOo-

At first sight of the new servant, blood rushed to Oric's face. He hung his head, hoping that Dian might have forgotten his ungainly performance with the chickens and the donkey on market day. Judging by her amused expression, she had not.

Recognising a familiar face, Dian hastened across the kitchen to say hello.

Oric's tongue stuck to the roof of his mouth. He garbled a greeting and, overcome with embarrassment, dashed off to pursue an unnecessary chore.

A few days later, an untimely outbreak of adolescent spots did nothing to improve Oric's confidence. Feeling wretched, he searched through the *Apothecary's Almanac* for a cure. The mixture currently adhering to the bottom of his mortar looked revolting. Perhaps he had misunderstood the recipe. He re-read the page. *Fresh root of wake robin, bruised.* Yes, he had done that. Now what? He followed the writing with his index finger. *Distil the crushed root with a small amount of milk.* He poured a few drops of goat's milk into the bowl and placed it by the fire to warm.

The bowl of medicament steamed, and Oric gave it a stir. Tipping the container on its side, he poured the hot mixture onto a cloth. *Nothing ventured, nothing gained,* he thought, applying the tincture to his spotty face. "Fuuuuss!" It was hot, and stung like fury. If the cure matched the degree of pain, his spots should disappear overnight.

Dian observed Oric's antics from behind a stout pillar. She would like to make friends with him, but whenever she smiled at him he blushed and mumbled excuses about having to work. Dian wished the Bayersby heir behaved in the same way. Despite his weak condition, Master Guwain pestered her. Afraid of losing her newly acquired position, she forced herself to remain civil in the face of his unwanted advances.

Whilst living at home with her parents, Dian had dreamed of marrying a nobleman. She longed to wear the beautiful clothes, the jewellery, and the shoes that wealthy ladies took for granted. But linking herself to a tyrant to obtain them was not part of her dream.

Frustrated by his lack of stamina, Guwain entertained himself by taunting the servants. Sprawled beside the inglenook hearth, he ordered a young serf to roast some chestnuts over the fire. The child did as he was bid, whimpering pitifully as his hands smarted from the heat. Guwain slashed at the boy's legs with the stick he used to poke the fire. "Never mind your stupid fingers! Just see that you do not overcook the nuts."

Dian's palm itched. If Master Guwain were her brother she would give him a good smack. But he was not her relation, and his behaviour was certainly not brotherly. Dian dreaded the Bayersby heir's return to full strength, believing he would make her life more difficult.

-oOo-

A fierce gale blew the remaining autumn leaves from the trees, and the daylight hours lessened as winter enveloped the countryside. The central fire in the great hall consumed logs as fast as the woodsman could supply them; the inglenook fire in the kitchen burned continually though the servants were ordered to bank the flames down at night to save fuel.

Guwain continued to improve, his health swiftly outstripping his temper. Heartily sick of the young man's attitude, Oric avoided contact with him. Sir Edred unwittingly exacerbated the antagonism between the two boys by continually praising Oric's bent for healing. Eaten up with jealousy, Guwain seized every opportunity to run Oric down… especially in the presence of Dian.

So much for hankering after a nobleman! Thought Dian. She would remain single and poor as a church mouse rather than marry someone with the nasty streak that Master Guwain displayed.

-oOo-

The sight of the wild boar that Sir Edred had killed and salted down prior to Yuletide disturbed Ichtheus. Skewered and suspended over a hot fire in the inglenook, the porker remained a constant reminder of the close shave he had experienced with its terrifying relative.

A portly female visitor, toasting her red chilblains not five feet from the hunk of meat, also gave Ichtheus cause for concern. Etheldrida, maid and companion to one of Sir Edred's guests, had arrived with her mistress the day before. When her services were not needed upstairs in the women's quarters, she spent her time in the kitchen. To make matters worse, she had formed a liking for Ichtheus.

Ichtheus noted that Etheldrida had the same physical characteristics as Mother Morghan, but there the similarity ended. Amiable, and with a heart as big as a boot, she made herself useful, however distasteful the task. Nevertheless, the large woman terrified him. "Every time I put my nose inside the kitchen," he whispered, ducking to avoid Etheldrida's roving eye, "the woman corners me." Ichtheus felt like a fugitive in his own domain. "I tell you, Oric, she will devour me as surely as that pig on the spit will be gobbled up at the Yuletide feast." He glowered at his apprentice. "And your perpetually grinning face helps me not at all."

"I reckon she fancies you for a husband, Master Ichtheus." Oric gave the spit a vigorous turn. "She would make a luscious armful. Go on, give her a nice cuddle!" He winked cheekily and continued to rotate the beast, salivating as the smell of roasting pork permeated the kitchen.

Ichtheus grimaced and jumped back to avoid droplets of hot fat that sprayed out from the pig.

"Master Ichthe-e-e-eus." Etheldrida's dulcet tones crooned across the room. "Where are you hi-i-i-iding?"

Seeing her bearing down upon him yet again, Ichtheus beat a hasty retreat to the stable. The company of his two donkeys was infinitely preferable to the mass of womanhood and the traitorous Oric.

Parzifal also preferred the cold stable to the battle for supremacy that waged between the visitor's dogs. Scrofulous mutts fought for every last titbit, and snarled over the warmest place by the hearth. Lonely and cold in the stables, Parzifal greeted Ichtheus like a lost friend.

Secure in their stalls, the two donkeys munched on

sweet-smelling hay and Ichtheus leaned against Braccus, enjoying his warmth and the quiet stable. Otty was in foal, and Ichtheus hoped the little one would bring a satisfactory sum of money when it was weaned, always supposing Oric could be persuaded to part with the animal.

"Oi! Ichtheus!" A battered face appeared around the stable door. "What on earth are you doing in here, man?" Egglebart's carrot-red hair and beard were liberally spiked with frost after his long ride from Kilterton. "Come into the manor, it is freezing outside."

In the general upheaval, Ichtheus had forgotten the Yuletide invitation he had extended to his burly friend. "Foof! Am I glad to see you! It will make a pleasant change to converse with someone intelligent." He endured an enthusiastic hug. "Pandemonium reigns inside the manor," he continued. "I escaped out here for a bit of peace. But never mind. Find a stall for your horse and we shall repair to the mayhem indoors to seek a bite of supper."

They crossed the yard and stepped into the steamy, crowded kitchen.

"Od's blood! No wonder you preferred the stable," said Egglebart. "'Tis busier in here than at a hanging in Kilterton."

Delighted to see the big man Oric regaled Egglebart with his part in the rescue of Master Guwain. Finished with his tale, he saw Dian watching from the back of the room and nervous perspiration beaded his top lip. Thank goodness he had not spotted the girl earlier; otherwise he would have been too tongue-tied to tell Egglebart his story.

Observing that Oric no longer held Egglebart's attention, Ichtheus followed the big man's gaze. His jaw dropped when he saw that his friend was staring at Etheldrida. Ichtheus was even more astonished to see the woman wearing a reciprocal, dewy-eyed look. "Goodness me," he whispered, drawing Oric's attention to the enraptured pair. "If I am not mistaken, that might be love at first sight."

"Aye, Master Ichtheus," Oric sniggered. "I think you might be off the hook."

Chapter Eleven

Guwain Causes Trouble

Despite Guwain's unpleasant behaviour and a heavy workload, Oric experienced the best Yuletide of his young life. On festival day Lady Myferny presented him with an outfit of serviceable clothes. Egglebart gave him a small dagger. And, because he had done so well with his studies, Master Ichtheus rewarded him with a handwritten copy of the *Apothecary's Almanac*. A knot of emotion choked Oric's throat when he read the message inscribed on the book's title-page:

To my most accomplished apprentice, Oric

From Ichtheus of Bayersby

Last but not least, Sir Edred produced a pair of new boots. "There you are, my boy. A reward for all the hard work you have done since your arrival at Bayersby manor."

Dian also fared well. Lady Myferny handed over one of her own cast-off kirtles, two brand new aprons, and a pair of lace-up slippers. Oric had carved a little bird for her and, quite overwhelmed, Dian kissed his cheek.

Giddy with delight, Oric missed the fleeting expression of jealousy that twisted Guwain's face.

Feasting continued for three days. Stew pots belched steam, and smoke from the fire added more soot to the already blackened rafters. Tantalising smells permeated the manor as cooks laboured from dawn until dark. Servants carried one heaped platter after another to the great hall, slipping and slithering on rushes made greasy with spilled food.

As well as Sir Edred's boar, a side of salt beef, mutton, and a haunch of venison were consumed with relish. Chickens and geese were necked, stripped of their feathers, and spit roasted or stewed. As Sir Edred had promised, no one went hungry. Minstrels played almost continuously and, after the ladies retired to their quarters in the evening, the men's songs and poems grew loud and bawdy.

Mother Morghan kept Dian on the run, leaving the maid little opportunity to engage Oric in conversation. Meanwhile, Oric helped with the preparation of food, attended to minor injuries, and administered to those miserable folk who overindulged on food and liquor.

Guwain asserted his superiority, adding to Oric's chores with a near-continuous string of unnecessary orders.

On the seventh day festivities ground to a halt. Exhausted from lack of sleep and sated with Yuletide excesses, guests prepared for the journey back to their own homes.

Ichtheus rounded-up stray children, and Oric made sure all the dogs left with their correct owners. Murky clouds promised snow, and Ichtheus prayed that everyone would make it safely home before the weather broke. Any idea of folk returning because of impassable roads was too awful to contemplate. Dian lent a hand with the removal of the holly, beech and mistletoe that Oric and Ichtheus had so painstakingly hung up. Determined to talk to each other, Oric and Dian both spoke at once.

"Go on, you first," Dian laughed.

"I hope the weather holds until people get back to their homes," Oric stuttered.

"So do I." Dian replied, her hazel eyes twinkling with mischief.

Oric concentrated on his new boots, trying hard not to blush. Here he was, face to face with the prettiest girl he had ever seen, and all he could talk about was the weather. To hide his confusion, he collected up an armful of wilted branches. Nodding and grinning like an idiot, he backed into a barrel. He lost his balance and fell, sending empty ale pots clattering across the kitchen floor. By the time he gathered himself together, Mother Morghan had sent Dian off on another chore.

With all the guests departed, Parzifal returned to the kitchen. He collapsed in a heap beside the fire, put his shaggy head on his paws, and heaved a contented sigh.

Ichtheus dropped into his chair and massaged his aching knees. Smothering a yawn, he said, "Fetch me a pot of mulled ale please, Oric. And whilst you are about it, draw one for yourself. You have certainly earned it."

The kitchen door creaked open and Egglebart sidled in. Drawing up a stool beside Ichtheus, he sat both hands dangling between his knees, staring into the fire. Eventually he announced, "I must return to Kilterton tomorrow. But before I leave, I um… er, have something to tell you."

Oric handed out pots of steaming ale and dropped a bundle of holly onto the blazing logs. The dried-up branches crackled and flared.

"'Tis Etheldrida," Egglebart blundered. "She is worried about you, Ichtheus."

Startled, Ichtheus raised his eyebrows. "Worried about me, whatever for?"

Loath to make eye contact, Egglebart struggled on.

"'Tis… well… what I mean is… Oh, hang it all, man, there is no easy way to tell you!" Throwing caution to the wind, he blurted, "I have asked Etheldrida to wed me, and she has said yes."

Ichtheus leapt to his feet and pumped Egglebart's hand. "But this is wonderful news. I am delighted for you both."

Egglebart was amazed. "You are not upset?"

"Why ever should I be upset?" Ichtheus asked kindly.

Egglebart shuffled as if he sat on spikes. "Well… er, Etheldrida warned me to go carefully for she suspects that you… um, may… er, have a special feeling for her." He drew his bushy eyebrows together in consternation. "She… er, I mean we, do not wish to hurt your feelings."

Ale coursed the wrong way down Ichtheus' throat, and he fought to regain his composure. "Yes, indeed, I certainly do… er, did have an amazing feeling for the lady," he spluttered, "but I could not offer her the life *you* are planning, Egglebart. Besides, I am so much older. Under the circumstances I am sure everything is for the best, and I give you both my blessing." Ichtheus' relief was palpable as he silently thanked his lucky stars for his own narrow escape. "I shall await an invitation to your wedding with eager anticipation."

To hide his mirth, Oric took off to the other end of the kitchen to refill their drinking horns.

Tears that coursed down Dian's face were not altogether the fault of the onions she was peeling. She beckoned to Oric. "Oh, dear," she whispered, her shoulders shaking with silent laughter, "Master Ichtheus and Egglebart are so funny." Glancing at Oric hopefully, she added, "Do you suppose I will be allowed to attend the wedding?"

"I hope so," Oric replied fervently, liking the idea of spending a work free day with Dian.

Egglebart bubbled on with enthusiasm. "I have enough prize money saved to purchase a smallholding on the south side of Kilterton. Our nuptials are to take place at Easter, which will give me time to put the place in order before Etheldrida moves in.

Ichtheus beamed. "A spring wedding, how delightful!" Ichtheus' smile faded. "However, I am afraid there is another, more serious matter I must discuss with you before you leave. Earlier in the year, I had a near brush with death at the hands of the Horzefells. This, coupled with other violent crimes that have recently taken place around the district, makes me suspect that some sort of plot is afoot."

"'Od's blood, Ichtheus!" Egglebart looked stunned. "Why did you not mention this before?"

Ichtheus shrugged his shoulders apologetically. "I was loath to spoil the Yuletide celebrations with such a grim topic. But now the holiday is over, something must be done. A pattern of sorts is emerging and we need to discover who is organising the robberies." Ichtheus drummed his fingers on the chair's arm. "The Horzefells lack the intelligence and, in my opinion, they are naught but hired villains. I am convinced some other, more sinister individual is at the root of all the trouble."

"Have you any idea who?" Egglebart asked, his face creased with concern.

"Aye," Ichtheus lowered his voice. "I suspect Esica Figg, but I have no proof!"

"Perhaps we should set up a meeting at the Kilterton Inn." Egglebart suggested. "We need to know if other folk have heard any rumours."

"I shall be interested to hear what our friends have to say." Ichtheus rubbed his red-rimmed eyes. "But we can do nothing more this night." Keeping on his clothes for warmth, he bid Egglebart a good night and lay down on his truckle bed.

Oric watched Egglebart walk across the compound to his makeshift quarters in the stables, closed the kitchen door softly and retired to his own sleeping place behind the fire inside the inglenook. The logs damped down for the night gave out gentle warmth and Oric's eyelids drooped. A sudden, muffled yowl catapulted him back into wakefulness.

From his place on the edge of the hearth, Oric watched a shadowy form creep across the darkened kitchen. He put out his hand to shake his master, but withdrew it when he realised the sinister shape was Master Guwain.

Parzifal raised a sleepy eye but, used to the son of the house, he did not stir.

Guwain struggled with a writhing sack. He tiptoed to a large wooden chest used for storing flour and lifted the lid. Propping it open with his head, he untied the sack and threw it inside. Shaking with silent laughter, he shut the lid and beat a hasty retreat upstairs.

"Blink me!" Oric whispered to the dog. "Methinks we have a jester in our midst." He left the hearth and stepped over to see what Guwain had dumped in the flour bin. Whatever it was emitted dismal howls.

Ichtheus slumbered on.

Mother Morghan snored and chomped in her chair.

Keen to discover what was going on, Dian crept from her bed to support Oric.

The yowling increased and muffled thuds issued from inside the chest. Just as Oric was about to lift the lid Mother Morghan woke up. She blinked rapidly and vacated her chair.

"Hey! What you doing, boy?" She thrust out her chin as she waddled towards the chest. "What are you hiding in there?"

"Do not lift the lid! I know not what lurks inside." Oric tried to stop her, but Mother Morghan knocked his hands away and wrenched open the chest.

Lady Myferny's cat, Caedmon, half-crazed with terror, made his bid for freedom. Engulfed by a cloud of flour, he landed four-square on top of Mother Morghan's bosom and dug in all his claws.

"Lawks alive," she screamed. "'Tis the Devil himself. Get 'im off me, boy! Get 'im off!"

Caedmon clung on for grim death.

Blinded by the flour, Mother Morghan screeched and twirled and smacked wildly at the creature hooked upon her front.

Parzifal joined in the fun. Barking hysterically, he jumped up and down, his teeth making hollow clicking sounds as he snapped at thin air.

By now all the servants were wide awake and enjoying the spectacle.

Caedmon let go and fled, spreading drifts of flour across the stone floor as he ran.

Doubled up with mirth, Oric failed to see the hand that delivered a stinging slap to his ear. Shocked, he came face to face with a furious Mother Morghan.

"Ouch!" Oric rubbed his battered ear. "What was that for? I warned you not to lift the lid."

Angered by the ruckus, Ichtheus jerked up his head from the pillow. "What in Heaven's name is going on?" Oric suffered his mentor's dressing down in silence.

Feeling sorry for him, Dian fetched a broom. "I will help you to clear up the mess." She eyed Oric with a puzzled expression. "I saw Master Guwain put that cat in the flour bin. Why did you take the blame?"

Oric shrugged, "I am only a servant, who would believe

me? Besides, I do not want to cause more trouble."

Sleep eluded Oric but it was almost a relief to stay awake, for visions of the Dunburton massacre had recently returned to haunt his dreams. Dreams! They were more like nightmares and, always ended with Master Deveril's warning.

"This key unlocks a door to great wealth. You must promise me, Oric, to guard it with your life. Never allow the key to fall into the grasp of an evil person. Were the secrets it guards to come into the wrong hands untold disasters might occur."

Before the alchemist could finish his tale, huge, fire-breathing serpents devoured everything. Oric's escape from the flames became increasingly more difficult, and he always awoke drenched with sweat.

The responsibility of guarding Master Deveril's key continually preyed on Oric's mind. He decided that the time had come to share his secret with Master Ichtheus.

Chapter Twelve

Encounter with Wolves

Ichtheus awoke with a sore throat and a throbbing head. Reluctant to leave the manor, Egglebart crushed Oric to his chest and then, holding him back, looked worriedly into his face. "Will the old man be all right, do you think?"

"Oh, aye," Oric nodded reassuringly. "'Tis naught but a chill made worse by tiredness. I shall dose him with horehound and honey; the mixture will ease his blocked tubes. I promise you, he will be as right as rain in a day or two."

Anxious to start work on the run-down smallholding he had purchased from Sir Edred, Egglebart glanced at the overcast sky. "If you are sure there is naught I can do, I had best be on my way. If it snows I could be trapped here for days." Egglebart's property lay several miles south of Kilterton and he would be relieved when the long journey was done.

Egglebart was right, the first snowflakes drifted down as he arrived at Kilterton. Dog tired and frozen to the bone, he decided to stay at the inn overnight. Two days of continuous blizzards followed, cutting off Kilterton and Bayersby from all other civilisation.

"Ichtheus, *ICH-THE-E-E-US!?*" Lady Myferny's voice echoed around the manor. "Where are you? Come quickly, a disaster has befallen us."

Thinking that a death had occurred, Ichtheus hastened into the great hall.

"Oh, Ichtheus," Lady Myferny wailed, "The problem lies with my cat, Caedmon."

Having fallen foul of the sleek tom on many occasions, Ichtheus had trouble hiding his delight. "The cat is dead, Mistress?"

"Dead? No, of course he is not *dead*. At least I hope he is not." Tears welled in Lady Myferny's eyes. "Caedmon failed to return home last night, and he is not yet back. Please, dearest Ichtheus, would you go out and seek him?" In her distress, she failed to see that her apothecary was unwell.

Ichtheus chose not to enlighten her. "There, there, do not take on so," he patted Lady Myferny's hand. "I will do my best." Shuffling back to the kitchen, he piled on extra clothes.

Horrified, Oric looked on. "Surely you are not going out in this dreadful weather, Master Ichtheus." He smiled despite his concern. "You seem to be donning more skins than an onion. Where on earth are you planning to go?"

"You had best wipe that smile from your face, boy," Ichtheus rasped between coughs, "and don a few layers of your own." He thrust a few useful bits and pieces into a sack and handed it to Oric. "Let us put our best foot forward, we have a cat to seek."

A blast of cold air swept through the kitchen as the door slammed behind the reluctant search party. Mother Morghan grunted and huddled further down into her chair. With a bit of luck the interfering old fool and his twittering apprentice might freeze to death.

A keen wind whirled powdery snow around the

compound and Oric blew into his cold hands. "Where do you suppose we should begin looking, Master Ichtheus?"

"Right here!" Ichtheus snapped, shivering in the biting cold. "Here, puss, puss," he called in a quavering voice. "Here, kitty-puss, puss."

"I am not surprised the cat has run off," Oric remarked darkly. "Guwain is always tormenting the poor creature."

They walked slowly out of the compound, all the while seeking feline footprints. Ichtheus shuffled along with Oric following close behind. So deep was the snow, neither could tell if they kept to the path.

Straying too close to an unseen ditch, Ichtheus plopped up to his neck in a deep drift.

Oric inched forward and, grasping his master under the arms, heaved him out of the snow. "You should take more care, Master Ichtheus, you seem to be accident-prone."

Ichtheus glowered, sneezed, and dragged his dripping nose along his sleeve. He tried to speak, but his words were cut short by a violent bout of coughing.

"You are risking your life if you remain outdoors in this weather," Oric scolded. "I shall take you home."

Ichtheus felt so ill, he put up little resistance. Settled on his truckle bed inside the inglenook fireplace, with a hot posset in his hands, his shivers finally ceased.

Oric spooned horehound and honey into his master. "Rest now, and let the medicine do its work." He retrieved Ichtheus' sack, and headed for the outside door.

"You are not proposing to go out alone, are you?" Dian called after Oric.

"I have to," Oric mumbled, dreading the bitter cold outside. "Lady Myferny's cat must be found."

"Wait! I will come with you." Ignoring Oric's protestations, Dian pulled on a pair of Mother Morghan's old boots and knotted a thick shawl over her kirtle. "We shall seek the cat together."

After a long and slippery climb, they reached High Moor. Ahead lay a vast, white wasteland. Oric stared at the undulating terrain, wondering where to turn next.

Bilious green clouds lowered overhead and more snow began to fall. The whirling flakes built in ferocity until Oric could barely see. "We stand little chance of finding the cat in this," he said, urging Dian to keep moving. She looked exhausted, and her hands and face were blue with cold. Concerned, Oric removed his cloak and wrapped it around her.

Visibility deteriorated, and they failed to spot a snow-encrusted building until they almost walked into it.

Oric felt his way around the walls, found the door and pushed Dian inside a dilapidated hovel. The place might not be up to much, but it would provide shelter until the storm passed.

A central hearth bore evidence of a recent blaze. Kindling lay nearby, and there was a plentiful supply of logs. Oric fished in Ichtheus' sack and brought out a tinderbox. He set fire to some twigs and watched as orange flames ate hungrily at the more substantial chunks of timber.

Huddled over the fire, Oric and Dian took stock of their surroundings. A rough table and two benches provided the only furniture, and a pile of ragged clothes filled one corner of the single room. Dian sifted through the filthy rags, looking for a hint as to the owner's identity. "Pwah! They stink," she said, squeezing her nose between a forefinger and thumb.

Oric left the fireside to lend a hand and behind the clothing discovered a bulging sack. "My word, what do you suppose we have here?" Bronze cruciform brooches, silver buckles and armlets spilled out on to the hovel's dirt floor. A leather pouch filled with coins and a pair of silver candle holders completed the haul.

Eyes sparkling with excitement, Dian stared at the pile of items. "Do you suppose this is a robbers' haul?"

"I think it is!" In his element, every trace of Oric's former shyness vanished. "When the snow clears, I will bring the cart and retrieve everything. Until then, we had best find somewhere else to hide this stuff in case the villains return."

The stack of logs provided the only suitable place to hide the booty. Oric swiftly demolished the pile and, retaining only a pouch of silver, he returned the remaining treasures to the sack and stacked the firewood on top. The stash would remain hidden beneath the logs, providing no one needed the fire to burn over a long period of time. Dian rearranged the ragged clothes in their corner, making sure they looked undisturbed. Shivering, she returned to the fire. Oric joined her, and they warmed their hands before the flames.

Time passed. The wind stopped howling and Oric peeked outside. "I think the blizzard is over. We should head for home before it gets dark."

Two steps from the hovel, blood-chilling howls sent Oric and Dian scurrying back inside. Less than twenty paces from the building stood a male wolf and its emaciated mate.

"What do we do now?" The tremble in Dian's voice was clearly audible. "I am sure those brutes have us earmarked for supper."

Oric spoke with a confidence he was far from feeling. "Hurry, I have an idea. Gather up some rags along with two stout branches from the hearth." Dian ran to do as she was bid. Oric tied strips of cloth around the end of each branch and thrust them into the flames. The rags caught light and he handed one of the flaming torches to Dian. "Wolves are afraid of fire. If they come too close, burn them."

Oric eased opened the hovel door.

One of the wolves raised its head, sniffed the air, and crept closer. Oric thrust his torch under the creature's nose. It inhaled a lungful of smoke, recoiled, and ran away.

"Thank God!" Dian's eyes were huge in her pale face. "Now we have only one beast to deal with."

The second wolf fixed Oric with an evil yellow stare. Undaunted, it continued to pad slowly forward.

Oric swished his torch back and forth. "The beast must be starving to risk an encounter with fire."

"What are we to do?" Dian hissed. "The flames are almost done."

The wolf sprang, its pointed fangs bared in a vicious snarl.

Oric lunged.

The wolf landed belly-down upon Oric's red-hot torch. For a shocked heartbeat it remained motionless. Then, with a howl of anguish, it turned tail and fled after its mate.

Oric chuckled, trying to make Dian feel less afraid. "Yon beast smells just like Parzifal when he sits too close to the fire."

Dian eyed Oric in wonder, thinking he had guts aplenty.

"Now," said Oric briskly, "let us hasten back to Bayersby Manor. The sooner we tell Master Ichtheus about the robbers' haul, the better."

The sky cleared. Myriad stars twinkled around the moon, and frost glistened in the pale light. Chilled to the bone, Oric and Dian plodded on through the snowbound countryside. They tumbled into drifts and hauled each other out. Their clothes and boots, encrusted with snow, dragged them down. When they finally staggered into the manor compound the only thoughts in their minds were dry clothes, hot possets, and a blazing fire to thaw their frozen bones.

With warmth only a few strides away, an awful thought struck Oric. "The cat!" he wailed. "We forgot all about the wretched cat."

"No need to worry," said Dian, pointing to several paw-prints that led into the stables. "I think we may have found our missing puss."

Inside a straw-filled stall, a shaft of moonlight illuminated Caedmon as he stood guard over a tabby female that was fondly licking five little kittens.

"That wise moggy must have sneaked in here after we left." Oric glowered at the tomcat. "And to think how we suffered out there, looking for him!"

"Aye, but think on," Dian consoled, "had we not gone to seek Caedmon, we would not have found the hovel or the robbers' haul."

-oOo-

Oric warmed himself inside the inglenook fireplace. At the sound of Sir Edred's voice, he dropped his pot of mulled ale and leaped into the kitchen.

"Ichtheus has informed us of Oric's bravery," Sir Edred bellowed, leading his wife into the kitchen. Where is the young hero? Lady Myferny and I wish to congratulate him."

Guwain stomped along behind his parents, his brows beetled in a furious frown. Hero? Hah! As far as he was concerned, the apothecary's apprentice had just hammered another nail into his own coffin.

"Well done, lad!" Sir Edred pressed a coin into Oric's hand. "Thanks to you, Ichtheus tells me that we may well recover some lost valuables." He winked knowingly at Ichtheus. "I took your reward from the pouch of silver that you so honestly relinquished into his care."

Overwhelmed, Oric stared at the coin. For the first time in his life, he had money to call his own.

Lady Myferny enfolded Oric in a perfumed embrace. "Thank you for finding Caedmon. I am impressed by your diligence and bravery." She hugged Dian too. "It was courageous of you to accompany Oric in Master Ichtheus' place." She reached for Ichtheus' hand. "And I would never have asked you to go out had I known how unwell you are."

Awoken from a deep slumber, Mother Morghan struggled to grasp what was going on. She failed to hear that Oric and Dian had unearthed a robber's haul, but she did understand that they had stumbled upon the Horzefell's hovel. As soon as the weather cleared, she must get over to St Griswald's to warn Master Figg. Lawks alive! He would be as mad as a rabid dog when she informed him that his moorland hiding-place had been discovered.

Chapter Thirteen

Sir Oswold Rescued

The countryside remained snowbound and Ichtheus discouraged Oric from returning to the hovel. "Only a madman would tackle the moor in this weather. Unless, of course, 'tis a matter of life or death."

"Huh!" Oric sounded thoroughly jaded. "Looking for the mistress's cat was a life-or-death situation?"

Ichtheus recovered from his ailment, but not before he had passed his germs on to other folk. Bayersby Manor reverberated with horrible coughs and sneezes, and Oric peered down throats to see tonsils the size and colour of damsons. "According to my *Apothecary's Almanac*, a decoction of cudweed mixed with milk for children, and wine for adults, will give relief to everyone."

Ichtheus nodded his encouragement. "Any potion that might bring an end to this debilitating outbreak is worth a try."

Dian also contracted the infection, but she refused to let it beat her. She supped Oric's medications and carried on, caring for the younger serfs as best she could. She missed her brothers and sisters and worried about their welfare.

The epidemic worsened, and Oric was devastated when one severely afflicted youngster failed to respond to the treatment.

"You did your best, lad." Ichtheus rubbed his forehead wearily. "We cannot play God. When He calls for the return of a soul, there is little we mortals can do. Besides, I suspect the lad had a weak heart." Plopping down on his truckle bed, Ichtheus eased off his boots. "Right now, all I desire is a full night's sleep."

His mind otherwise occupied, Oric failed to reply.

"Is something else troubling you?" Ichtheus asked.

Since the young serf's demise, Oric had become painfully aware of his own mortality. What if he died and some villain seized Master Deveril's key? The alchemist's words continued to haunt Oric and, for the sake of his sanity, he decided to put his trust in Master Ichtheus. "I do have a problem," he admitted, glancing around the kitchen to make sure they were alone. He pulled the key from around his neck and handed it to Ichtheus. "This little item is the cause of my concern." He explained how the key had come into his possession and Ichtheus listened without interruption. "So now you understand," Oric concluded, "why I must honour Master Deveril's dying wish and keep the key safe."

"Indeed I do, lad." Ichtheus lowered his voice. "I have just the place to hide your key." He leaned closer to Oric, "When I first came to Bayersby Manor, I dug a hole in the stable floor to accommodate a small iron box." Ichtheus grinned wickedly. "My few precious possessions have remained undiscovered ever since, for no-one ever properly mucks out the stalls."

Oric readily agreed to the idea, and handed over his key.

"Do you suppose this emblem offers a clue to Deveril's secret?" Ichtheus asked, staring at the double knot engraved upon the key's shank.

"I wish I knew, Master Ichtheus."

-oOo-

Overnight a thaw set in, and Oric awoke to bright sunshine. No longer weighed down by the responsibility of minding Deveril's key, he felt better than he had for many a day. He joined Ichtheus at the table and tackled the breakfast of bread and smoked eel that Dian set before him. "Are you rid of your sniffles this morning?" Oric asked, smiling at the wench.

"Indeed I am," Dian nodded. "Your medicine, followed by a good night's sleep, has worked wonders."

"We must make the most of this weather and replenish our depleted herbal rootstocks," said Ichtheus, munching down the last of his eel. He yelled for Mother Morghan, but received no reply. "Where can that wretched woman be? Go and seek her out, Oric."

Several moments later Oric returned to the kitchen. "Mother Morghan is nowhere to be seen, and no-one knows where she is."

"Pfft!" Ichtheus spat his disgust. "Then you will have to forage by yourself, Oric, for I dare not leave the manor unattended."

Thrilled at the prospect of getting away for a while, Oric went in search of Dian. He had, at last, mastered his shyness and now he enjoyed her company. He found her beside the well, washing clothes.

"Master Ichtheus wants me to forage for more medicinal supplies. Would you like to come with me? An outing will do you good."

"Thank you, Oric, I would like nothing better. But Mother Morghan will make my life miserable if I fail to finish my chores."

"But the housekeeper has disappeared," said Oric persuasively. "She will not be any the wiser if you sneak away for a little while."

"If you can wait a few moments, I have almost finished the washing." Dian wrung out the last of the clean garments and spread them over bushes to dry. "Now I am ready," she smiled, her eyes sparking with anticipation.

Fresh green shoots thrust through the earth and the season's first snowdrops nodded their dainty heads. Birds chorused as if to welcome the oncoming spring, and Oric whistled along with their lively cacophony. Equally delighted to be out, Parzifal wagged his tail as he gambolled along the muddy track. Dian breathed in the fresh country air and felt better with every step she took. Her winter-pale cheeks soon turned rosy in the brisk wind.

Skirting the moor north of Bayersby Manor, Oric kept an eye open for the items his master required. "Root of Nettle is at the top of Master Ichtheus' list, followed by Hemlock to make sedatives. If you spot any, Dian, please let me know."

At the edge of Scraggswood Forest, they came upon Nidderdale Brook. Oric looked for a suitable place to cross, and took a running jump at a smooth rock that protruded clear of the water. But the rock was nothing more than a mound of silt swirled up by the eddying torrent; he sank up to his knees in sticky mud and toppled face-down into the water. His arms trembled with effort as the fast current dragged him sideways. Using every bit of his strength, he crawled forward.

Never one to miss an opportunity, Parzifal used Oric as a bridge. Head to one side, tongue lolling, he awaited Oric on the opposite back.

Once Dian saw that Oric was in no danger, she began to laugh. "Oh dear," she cried. "Yon dog is no fool."

"Aye well, 'tis your turn now," Oric shouted as he

squeezed water from his saturated clothes. "Let us see if you can get across the brook without a soaking."

Dian tucked up her skirt and put one foot into the water. "Ooooh!" she gasped, "'Tis freezing."

"Do not venture any further." Oric held up his hand, not wanting her to get wet. "Walk a little way along the bank until we find a better place for you to cross."

A few strides brought Dian to a row of stepping stones and she hopped across them to join Oric and Parzifal.

A loud crash followed by angry shouts startled them. Parzifal scrabbled through the tightly woven branches of a dense hawthorn hedge and added his deep, rough barks to the noise. "Stay here, Dian, until I see what the ruckus is about." Without further ado, Oric, struggled through the hedge after the dog.

Dian peered through branches, but they were so thickly interwoven she could see nothing. *I am not waiting here,* she thought. Dropping to her knees, she crawled through the gap that Parzifal and Oric had made.

A horse with nostrils flared to the size of ale pots stood over the recumbent form of an armour-clad knight. At sight of Oric, the man clanged into a sitting position, "Sir Oswold at your service, young sir."

Oric smiled and proffered his hand. "I think it is I who can be of service to you. Please allow me to help you up. Whatever caused you to fall from your horse in the first place?"

"Fall?" Sir Oswold exclaimed. "I did not fall, I was ambushed."

The elderly knight struggled to his feet and Oric saw that he was missing an arm. "The rogues have maimed you." he gasped, staring at the stump. Seeing Dian, he beckoned to her. "Quick, come over here, I need your help."

Sir Oswold flapped his one hand. "Heavens, lad, that arm went long since. Lost the miserable thing in battle years ago! I have learned to manage quite well without it."

"Ah, that explains the lack of blood," said Oric, greatly relieved. Anxious to be on his way, he looked around for Parzifal. As usual, the dog had disappeared. Frustrated, Oric pursed his lips and whistled long and loud.

"That great monster belongs to you, does he?" Sir Oswold asked.

"In truth, he belongs to Sir Edred, Lord of Bayersby," Oric admitted, "but the dog may as well be mine, for I cannot step out without him following me."

"He saved my skin," Sir Oswold harrumphed. "I was attacked from the rear and knocked from my horse. Before I could draw my sword the robbers made off with my helmet, which toppled off when I fell. Had your dog not appeared when he did, I doubt I would have lived to tell the tale. The villains ran away at first sight of him, though one weasel-faced wastrel was not quite quick enough. The dog bit a chunk from the fellow's tunic as he escaped, and serve him right." Sir Oswold wrinkled his nose. "One of the miscreants stank like a dead cat."

The attack upon Sir Oswold reminded Oric of Ichtheus' encounter with the Horzefells, but he kept his own counsel. He needed to talk things over with his master before he voiced his suspicions.

Sir Oswold unstrapped his arm and leg guards. "Now, young man, if you would be kind enough to help me out of my breastplate, I shall be able to remount my horse. By the way did I hear you mention Sir Edred of Bayersby?"

Oric nodded, "You certainly did."

"What a fortunate coincidence!" Sir Oswold beamed his delight. "Sir Edred is a friend of mine, and I am on my way to Bayersby Manor. I have lost my sense of direction, how about you ride pillion and show me the way?"

Wet through, and blue with cold, Oric gladly agreed. His teeth rattled like a skeleton in a breeze, and he had not looked forward to the walk home. With Dian's help he dragged Sir Oswold's discarded armour behind a boulder and promised to retrieve it with Master Ichtheus' donkey and cart as soon as possible. Clasping his hands together, he gave the one-armed knight a leg up into the saddle.

Comfortably settled, Sir Oswold hauled Dian up in front. "Now, pass up my shield please." Sir Oswold was not inclined to leave his family heirloom behind. Made from pitch-coated leather stretched over a willow frame, the shield was painted with a fierce and fiery dragon. Nodding his thanks, Sir Oswold hoisted Oric on to the horse's broad rump. "Hold tight," he advised, jabbing the animal with his heels. With only one hand Sir Oswold had difficulty holding his shield and the reins at the same time. To overcome his problem, he had attached the reins to his stirrups and his kicking action pulled back on the bit in the horse's mouth.

Dian clung on to the pommel, but Oric almost lost his seat as the animal shied backwards. Parzifal, having returned from his wanderings, let out a yelp of pain when one of the charger's massive hooves grazed his front paws.

Glancing down to make sure the dog was not badly hurt; Sir Oswold encouraged the horse forward with a brisk command. Dian relaxed back against the comforting warmth of Sir Oswold's broad chest and dozed off.

Part way back to Bayersby a few wilted nettle stalks under the hedgerow reminded Oric of his original task. "Please would you stop for a moment, Sir Oswold? I am out on a mission and my mentor will skin me alive if I return to the manor empty-handed."

Oric slid from the horse and dug up a quantity of nettle roots. The hemlock would have to wait for another time. He thrust the muddy bundle into his sack, and clambered back onto his pillion position.

-oOo-

Puffing fit to burst, Hersica Horzefell scurried along the track ahead of her son. She held up the hem of her skirt in one hand, in the other she carried the knight's helmet. "That ambush was a complete disaster," she squawked. "And I reckon that knight will have made off with our cart by now."

"For pity's sake, slow down, mother. Yon wolfhound has given up the chase." Rastus halted, placed both hands on his knees, and heaved for breath.

"Praise the Lord," Hersica wheezed, "for it seems I cannot rely upon you for protection."

Rastus ignored his mother's barb. "I hid the cart well. We shall wait a while and then sneak back to see if the knight has gone."

Returned to the scene of their crime, Hersica and Rastus approached with caution. To their great relief the place seemed to be deserted. They discovered the knight's discarded armour behind a boulder and Rastus retrieved their cart from its hiding place.

"Master Figg knows nowt about this haul." Rastus squinted at his mother. "What say we keep this armour for ourselves? I could sell it on and split the money with you."

Never one to pass up a lucrative deal, Hersica nodded. "Aye, but where will you hide everything in the meantime?"

"None o' your business," Rastus hissed. "Rest assured I will keep it safe until I can find a suitable buyer."

Hersica helped Rastus lift the armour on to the cart. "Mind you cough up half what you get. I ain't no fool. I know what this stuff is worth." Having no desire to spend more time than necessary with her disagreeable son, she departed for the relative comfort of St Griswald's crypt.

Before setting off, Rastus waited to make sure that his mother did not sneak back. The last thing he wanted was for her to follow and learn the whereabouts of his secret bolt-hole.

Carved into a hillside below Bayersby Manor, the opening to Rastus' cave was made invisible by thick vines and creepers. There was no evidence of human visitation when he had first discovered the place, nor had there been any since he moved in. Rastus parted the greenery, pushed his cart inside, and stashed away the armour. He longed to rest a while, but he had arranged to meet Master Figg.

-oOo-

Whilst Oric was helping Sir Oswold, Esica Figg was journeying from St Griswald's to the hovel on the moor. The earlier foul weather had stopped him from collecting the plunder he knew to be hidden there; now he was keen to rescue the valuables as soon as possible. Arriving at his destination, he jumped down from the cart and tethered the donkey behind the building.

Hersica's rank stink lingered on inside the dwelling, and Figg gagged. Repulsed, he kicked through the few discarded clothes she had described, but bared the dirt floor without finding a single item of value.

Rastus chose that precise moment to enter the hovel.

Figg scooped up an armful of Hersica's tattered cast-offs and threw them in his henchman's face. "Where are the stolen goods you and your mother are supposed to have secreted here? If you have attempted to dupe me I will flay your hide." In a panic, Rastus picked through his mother's old clothes. Finding nothing, his innards quaked. "Do you suppose some other villain has been here and lifted it?"

The noisy arrival of somebody outside saved Rastus from further interrogation. "Hush," Figg said, shoving his employee behind the door. "Perhaps the culprit has returned."

Chapter Fourteen

Guwain In Trouble

Sir Edred had forbidden his son to visit the moors alone. Nevertheless, Guwain sneaked out of the manor at dawn, saddled his horse and made straight for High Moor to try and find the hovel Oric had discovered.

Heather-clad hills stretched as far as Guwain could see, and he soon lost all sense of direction. He shivered, wondering which way to go next. Urging his mount on, he prayed that he would not fall foul of the sucking bogs his father had described. His false courage spent, Guwain almost fainted with relief when he spied a broken down building ahead. He dismounted and cautiously inspected the outside area. A donkey with a cart was tethered behind the hovel. Euphoria overtook Guwain's fear. He would order the person within to guide him back to Bayersby. He returned to the front of the hovel and strode through the door.

In the gloom, Guwain failed to see two men that sneaked up from behind. A sack was thrust over his head and, blinded by dust, he writhed in an effort to free himself. "Do you have any idea who I am?" he yelled. "Let go of me at once, or you will answer to my father, Sir Edred, Lord of Bayersby."

Figg ignored Guwain's protestations and bound the boy tightly with a length of rope. He threw the boy to the ground, and pushed his henchman outside. "Something strange is afoot." Figg's voice dripped menace. "What is that boy doing here, and where are all my valuables?"

"I swear on my father's grave – I have no idea what is going on," Rastus babbled. "Mother told me that after the last robbery she hid everything under yon pile of old rags. It ain't my fault if the stuff has vanished."

"Swear on your father's grave!" Figg howled. "I doubt you know who your father is! Get back inside and find what we came for. If you fail, I will boil your miserable carcass in oil."

Back in the hovel, Rastus vented his spleen upon the sobbing Guwain. "Shut your mouth," he snarled, giving the boy in the sack a vicious kick. "I have enough problems without listening to your bleating din."

Rastus searched every nook and cranny in the hovel, but he found nothing of value. In desperation he sat down upon a pile of logs to think. The timber dislodged under his weight and many of the logs rolled to the ground. His knees went weak with relief when he saw that a sack lay at the bottom of the woodpile. Yanking it out, he wondered why his mother had changed the hiding place without saying a word. By Jove, he would give the old biddy the rough edge of his tongue when he returned to St Griswald's.

Slightly pacified by the recovery of his plunder, Figg left Rastus in charge of the hostage and departed for St Griswald's Church with the donkey and loaded cart. Guwain's howls of anguish diminished with distance and Figg thanked providence that the Bayersby heir had survived Rastus' pre-Yuletide ambush after all. A happy feeling stirred Figg's innards. If the situation was handled carefully, Sir Edred would pay a king's ransom for the release of his only son.

-oOo-

Mother Morghan hauled her bulk along the muddy track on her first outing since the winter blizzards had isolated Bayersby Manor. She had deserted her post, but she did not care. *The apothecary and his good-for-nothing apprentice will have to manage as best they can on their own,* she thought spitefully.

Keen to give Figg the news that his hovel hideout had been discovered, Mother Morghan hastened along the pathway toward St Griswald's Church. At the very least she expected a silver coin in exchange for the important information she was about to deliver.

Before stepping over the church's threshold, Mother Morghan scraped her mud encrusted boots back and forth on the doorstep. Hearing the noise, Figg hastily covered the plunder he had brought back from the hovel and silently ascended the crypt stairs. He glared at the mess Mother Morghan had made. "Ye gods, woman! You have less finesse than a rutting pig."

Mother Morghan clasped a hand to her heaving bosom. "Ye gods, man! Do you have to sneak about like a blasted ferret? You almost caused me to have a conniption fit."

Figg overrode his disgust. "Hold your tongue, woman, I have a job for you." He thrust a grubby piece of parchment into her hand. "Return to Bayersby Manor immediately and display this ransom note in a prominent place."

"Oh aye!" Mother Morghan shoved the note down the front of her linen vest. "And who, might I ask, have you kidnapped?"

"I have seized Sir Edred's heir," replied Figg. "He is currently at the hovel under the care of Rastus Horzefell."

An amused smirk flickered around Mother Morghan's fleshy lips. "When I tell you what I know, you might want to remove the boy elsewhere."

"What nonsense! The hovel provides a perfect hiding place." A facial tick belied Figg's cocksure tone. "Why should I want to move him?"

"Oh, no!" Mother Morgan waggled her head. "I have been had like that before. Not another word will I utter until you stump up my reward."

Figg dug in his pouch and hurled a copper coin at Mother Morghan. His surly expression clearly conveyed that she had tested her luck far enough.

Mother Morghan curled her fingers around the coin, silently cursing Figg's parsimony. "I am here to tell you," she said self-righteously, "that the apothecary's apprentice discovered your hideout a while back. You may be making a grave mistake by keeping Master Guwain at the hovel."

Figg struck Mother Morghan with the flat of his hand. "Why did you not mention this straight away?" He rubbed his brow with splayed fingers. "If Guwain's absence has been noted, a search party may already be under way, and the hovel could well be their first port of call." He pushed past Mother Morghan, causing her to sprawl face-down on the muddy doorstep. "However, no one may yet have discovered the boy's absence. Keep the ransom note until later in the day. I need time to transfer my hostage to a new location." Stepping over the housekeeper, he ran to fetch his horse.

Mother Morghan scrambled to her feet. Too afraid to disobey Figg's orders, she wallowed back to Bayersby Manor. At the appointed time she drew the ransom note from between her greasy breasts and, making sure the kitchen was deserted, tacked it to the top of the apothecary's medicine chest. In a filthy temper, she took herself off to the women's quarters.

-oOo-

Arriving back in the Bayersby compound, Oric slid down from Sir Oswold's horse and held up his arms to help Dian. Nodding her thanks, she prayed that Mother Morghan had not returned and noticed her absence. She scurried to the kitchen in Oric's wake.

"Am I glad to see you!" Ichtheus exclaimed, approaching Oric at a trot. A most ghastly crisis has befallen us."

"Lady Myferny's cat gone missing again, has he?" Oric remarked cynically. Whatever the 'cat'astrophe, he did not want to know. His only desire was to change into dry clothes, and huddle before a warming fire.

"*No*, Oric, 'tis *not* the cat," Ichtheus hopped about in agitation. "Master Guwain went out early this morning and he has not returned. This afternoon I discovered a ransom note affixed to the lid of my medicine chest." Racked with worry, Ichtheus gabbled on. "And the kidnapper demands that a considerable amount of gold be placed inside a hollow oak at the edge of Scraggswood Forest. The note states that Master Guwain will lose an ear if the ransom is not forthcoming by first thing tomorrow morning." Ichtheus' voice went up several octaves. "What is more, the villains threaten to continue chopping bits off the boy until payment is made in full."

An anguished groan from the kitchen doorway silenced Ichtheus. Oric raced across the room and caught Lady Myferny a heartbeat before she hit the flagstones in a dead faint. Dian ran to his aid and together they eased the lady onto a chair. Oric set light to a feather and held it under her nose. The acrid smoke brought life back to lady Myferny's inert form, and she began to weep.

"Oh, my lady," Dian exclaimed, frantically patting her mistress' hand. "Do not distress yourself, I am sure Master Guwain will be all right. Sir Edred will see to that."

Informed of his son's kidnap, Sir Edred's angry voice roared across the kitchen. "I have no intention of depositing any gold in any tree. Nor do I intend to sit on my backside to await further developments. I mean to have Guwain safely back home before dark. The cowardly mongrels that have seized my son will not see another sunrise." Sir Edred dropped to one knee beside his distraught wife. "You have my word upon it, my love."

Ichtheus offered to accompany the search party in case his medical skills were required. "Since Mother Morghan appears to be missing again, you had best remain here, Oric."

For the sake of speed, Ichtheus shunned his donkey and borrowed a horse from Sir Edred. Sir Oswold volunteered to join in the search, and the two elderly gentlemen clattered out of the compound gates side by side.

In their haste, nobody gave the hovel a thought.

-oOo-

With every able-bodied male out searching for Master Guwain, Bayersby Manor took on the silence of a tomb. Although she did not wish the boy any harm, Dian enjoyed a respite from Guwain's irritating attentions. She hoped it would take a while for Sir Edred to find him. Feeling guilty, she sat at one end of the long table chopping turnips and onions to boil for the evening meal. In no mood for concocting medicines, Oric fetched a knife and gave her a helping hand.

Hunger eventually drove Mother Morghan out of her hiding place in the sleeping alcove. Back in the kitchen, she tore a chunk of bread from a loaf and spread it liberally with goose grease.

For once Oric was glad to see the housekeeper. "Where have you been? Had you showed your face earlier, I could have gone out with the search party."

Mother Morghan rolled bread and dripping around her mouth, "I am sure Sir Edred can manage perfectly well without *your* assistance."

Repulsed, Oric glared at her. "Now that you are back, you can attend to any medical requirements that arise." Turning to Dian, he asked if she would care to go out.

"No, she would not!" snapped Mother Morghan. "The girl is here to work and there is plenty for her to do. Get about your business, boy, before I lose my temper."

"Ah, well," Dian whispered as Oric bid her farewell. "At least I got to see some of the countryside this morning. But please be careful. There are too many rogues abroad at present."

Determined to do something useful, Oric decided to collect Sir Oswold's armour from the site of the ambush. If he travelled on to the hovel, he could also retrieve the valuables he and Dian had discovered when they were out seeking Lady Myferny's cat. Filled with a sense of purpose, he harnessed Ichtheus' donkey to the cart.

Chapter Fifteen

Oric Captured

Esica Figg arrived back at the hovel, his face crimson with effort and his horse lathered in sweat. "Has anyone been sniffing around here?" he demanded of Rastus.

"Ain't nothing amiss as far as I can tell." Rastus eyed his dishevelled master pointedly. "Not here, that is." He hawked and spat. "Yon youngster gave up yelling shortly after you left. Never known anyone be so bleedin' quiet. I poked him with a stick a while back to make sure he ain't dead."

Figg dismounted. "Cease your blather, man! Our hideaway has been discovered. We need to shift the boy immediately."

-oOo-

Oric searched behind the boulder for Sir Oswold's discarded armour, but it was nowhere to be seen. He scratched his head and stared at the flattened grass as if, by so doing, the items of armour might magically reappear. Perhaps he was in the wrong place, but there was only the one big boulder.

What if the robbers were still lurking nearby? Thoroughly disturbed, Oric jumped back onto the cart. He slapped the reins and urged Braccus to trot away as fast as the rough terrain allowed.

Memories of the wolves he had encountered during his last visit to the hovel dissolved what little enthusiasm Oric had left. He missed Parzifal's company, and wished that Sir Edred had not claimed the dog for the day.

Minus its picturesque layer of snow, the hovel exuded a menacing evil. Fighting off waves of apprehension, Oric tethered Braccus to a stunted tree and crossed the sheep-cropped grass. He eased open the hovel's door and stepped inside. Before his eyes adjusted to the gloom, a sack was thrust over his head.

"Hey!" he yelped. "What funny business is this?" Oric tried to peer through the sack's densely woven fabric, but he could see nothing. Someone wrenched his wrists behind his back and roped them together. A sharp knee between his shoulder-blades forced him face down onto the dirt floor. "Let me go at once!" he cried, spitting out dust and threads of sacking.

"Hark at young Master High and Mighty," a wheezy voice exclaimed. "Who does he think he is?"

"Shut your mouth!" rasped another voice. "Get outside and see if the apothecary has accompanied the boy. If he has, finish him off!"

Oric was hauled upright and rough hands searched his person.

"Where is the key, boy?" Shocked by his assailant's question, Oric played for time. "Key! What key? I know nothing about any keys."

A vicious blow to his belly winded Oric.

"Do not play the innocent with me," snarled the

unknown man. "I refer to the key that once belonged to the Dunburton alchemist!"

As far as Oric could recall, he had told only Master Ichtheus. How did this stranger know of the key's existence?

Another blow caused Oric to retch. The sack was dragged down over his shoulders, his ankles were roped together, and his feet were kicked from beneath him. He hit the ground hard.

"If you move, I shall cut your throat!"

The man sounded vaguely familiar. Oric racked his brain. *Where had he heard the voice before?*

Outside the hovel thuds and scuffles abounded. Braccus brayed long and loud. Someone screamed, "God rot yon poxy donkey!"

Oric blessed Braccus' unreliable temperament, knowing that he would kick and bite chunks from any stranger that used him badly.

"You simpleton, now see what you have done!" Oric's captor screamed abuse. "The accursed donkey has run off. Catch the beast before it returns to its home stable."

Bound at ankle and knee, Oric was manhandled outside. He jumped along the ground like a demented hare until his thighs made contact with something solid. Losing his balance, he toppled down upon a hard surface. Someone lifted his legs and wrenched them around. A rolling, bucking motion soon indicated that he was on a moving cart.

Some time elapsed before the cart stopped. Battling waves of panic, Oric braced himself for the blow he imagined would end his life. Nothing happened. The clink of harness indicated that the animal between the shafts was being unhitched. Hoof-beats, loud at first, gradually faded away. Oric shuffled to ease his aching bones and his elbow made contact with something soft and yielding.

"Ouch!" Exclaimed a youthful voice.

Oric almost jumped out of his skin! "Who are you?" he demanded. "I thought I was alone."

"Well, you thought wrong," replied the voice. "Who are *you*?"

"This is ridiculous," Oric replied tartly. "Who gives a jot as to who is who? But since you ask, I am Oric of Bayersby."

"Oric! 'Tis I, Guwain. What in the name of Christendom are you doing here?"

"Being kidnapped, it seems," replied Oric dryly.

"Well?" Guwain challenged. "What do you propose to do about it?"

"My hands are tied, for the moment." Oric's sarcasm was lost on Guwain.

"Release me from these villain's clutches at once, boy, or you will have my father to answer to."

Oric rolled on to his side, curled his legs as far back as they would go and pushed his bound hands down inside the sack toward his ankles. The man, who had searched his person for Deveril's key, had missed the small dagger secreted inside the cuff of his right boot.

Guwain lashed out with his feet. "Stop bumping into me, you fool! I shall be black and blue at this rate."

"You will be minus chunks of your anatomy unless we can escape from this predicament," Oric snapped, thoroughly irritated.

"How dare you speak to me so rudely? I shall have you thrashed upon our return to Bayersby Manor."

Oric ignored Guwain's threats and dragged the dagger out of his boot. He jabbed the pointed blade through the sack and sawed it back and forth until he cut a hole in the fabric large enough to push his hands through.

"If we are to escape with our lives we must help each

other. Tell me, Master Guwain, are you trussed up in a sack?"

Oric's authoritative tone finally got through to Guwain. "Yes, I am," he replied petulantly.

"Lie on your side and hold your arms out behind. Keep the cloth as taut as you can. I have a knife and I will try to cut your hands free."

Back to back the boys struggled, Oric cutting, Guwain doing his best to avoid being slashed by the dagger. Their contortions continued until the rope fell away from Guwain's hands. Guwain seized the dagger and hacked the sack away from his upper torso.

"Hurry, Master Guwain. Cut me free now."

Released from his sack, Oric retrieved his dagger and slashed the ropes that bound their feet. "Come on," he urged. "We must run away before the kidnappers return."

"No!" Guwain sat with his legs dangling over the back of the cart. "I intend to remain here. The rogues have robbed me of my horse and I have no desire to crash about the countryside on foot in the dark." He tossed his head confidently. "My father will rescue us very soon. In the meantime, boy, gather some bracken and make me a comfortable bed."

"If you will hear me out, you may want to change your mind." Not giving Guwain a chance to answer, Oric hurried on. "Earlier today Master Ichtheus discovered a ransom note tacked to his medicine chest. It described in vivid detail the body parts those villains intend to chop from your person if your father fails to come up with substantial ransom monies by first light tomorrow."

Guwain leaped from the cart as if it had suddenly grown red-hot. "They would not dare!" His tone failed to carry the conviction of his words and he needed no further encouragement to follow Oric.

No moon lit their way, and heavy clouds obliterated the stars. The boys blundered on, putting distance between themselves and the cart. Each time Guwain tripped and fell, Oric stopped to help him. When Oric stumbled, Guwain kept on running.

A light wind sprang up and every rustle caused Guwain to jump like a startled rabbit. He ran in any direction oblivious to Oric's calls.

The blows Oric had received hurt and his lungs felt as though they would burst. In the end he grabbed Guwain's wrist and called a halt.

"'Tis too dangerous to travel any further; we could stumble into a bog or run into a wolf's lair. I am going to find a safe place for us to spend the night."

The bole of a large tree provided suitable shelter and, afraid to carry on alone, Guwain lay down without protest.

Oric awoke at first light. He sat up and explored his stomach with gentle fingers. His lower ribs were intact and his innards felt better than they had the day before. A stream chattered nearby, and Oric realised that he was parched.

Guwain stirred. He heard the running water, too. "I have a fierce thirst. Go and fetch me a drink, boy."

"How do you propose I carry liquid without a pitcher?" Oric asked, trying to hide his exasperation. "If you want to quench your thirst, you will have to accompany me to the water's edge."

Grumbling all the way, Guwain followed Oric. They knelt beside the stream, cupped their hands, and slaked their thirst with cold water. Somewhat restored, Oric rested back on his heels and took stock of his surroundings.

Guwain paced up and down. "My word, boy, you have succeeded in getting us thoroughly lost. When my father learns of your inefficiency, you will be punished."

"Listen to me!" Oric roared, grabbing Guwain's tunic and yanking him forward so that they stood nose to nose. "'Tis not *I* that will be punished but *you*, for running away in the first place. And, whilst we are about it, let us have a little less of this 'boy' business. My name is Oric."

Oric's flash of temper evaporated as quickly as it had ignited. He let go of Guwain, and stepped back. "Now," he said in a normal voice, "I suggest we put our heads together and find the best way out of our predicament. My instinct tells me to follow the stream. What say you, Master Guwain?"

But Master Guwain had an attack of the sulks and said nothing at all.

By mid-morning the boys were ravenously hungry, and Guwain crumpled into a miserable heap. "I am weak from lack of nourishment," he bleated. "You will have to carry me for I cannot walk another step."

"Use your legs and give your tongue a rest," Oric snapped, near the end of his tether.

Reaching the edge of the forest, Oric looked for familiar landmarks. The view lifted his spirits beyond measure. Across the valley Bayersby Manor glowed in the afternoon sunshine.

"Look at that!" Oric cried in delight. "We are almost home."

Lethargy forgotten, Guwain ran down the hill toward the manor.

Chapter Sixteen

Figg Foiled

Entering through the compound gates, Oric could barely comprehend what he saw and heard.

Guwain, thumbs hooked into his belt, expounded his adventure to a small audience of serfs. "Had I not done some quick thinking, I would not be here to tell the tale. Risked life and limb to rescue the apothecary's apprentice from the villains," he stated smugly. "Not only did I save his miserable life, it was *I* that found our way home."

Oric shook his head in disbelief, and took himself off to the kitchen. Famished, Guwain followed.

Mother Morghan's jaw dropped when she caught sight of the Bayersby heir.

"Catching flies, are we?" said Guwain, snapping her mouth shut with his finger under her chin. "Start cooking, woman, my belly feels as though it is banging on my backbone!"

With self-preservation in mind, Mother Morghan hid her agitation in the production of food. Guwain's unexpected return suggested that something had gone seriously wrong.

Ye gods! What sort of gormless cur was Figg? He could not organise a church meeting, let alone a kidnapping.

Mother Morghan banged bowls of sloppy gruel down in front of Guwain and Oric. "Where in creation have you been?" she demanded, her three chins wobbling like a tub full of calves' jelly. "The entire manor is out looking for you."

Guwain attempted to walk away, but Mother Morghan grabbed his arm. "You stay right here, young master, whilst I give the good news to your mother. The poor lady has been in her chamber bawling ever since Master Ichtheus found the ransom note."

After a fruitless night searching for his son, Sir Edred returned to Bayersby Manor. He had, in his infinite wisdom, decided not to place a penny piece in the hollow oak tree, choosing instead to leave three heavily armed men hiding nearby to catch the culprit. Now, in the cold light of day, he agonised over the imminent delivery of his son's body parts. Sliding down from his horse, he threw the reins to a stable boy and, accompanied by Sir Oswold and Ichtheus, he lumbered into the kitchen.

Sir Edred's relief upon seeing Guwain, seated unharmed at the table, was plain for all to see. In a few strides he crossed the room and crushed the boy in a mighty embrace. Without a backward glance he bore his son into the great hall in vociferous search of Lady Myferny. The expression of smug satisfaction that Guwain cast over his father's shoulder was not lost on Oric.

Dian also observed Guwain's behaviour, and her dislike of him deepened. She set aside the bowl of bread she was kneading and crossed the kitchen to where Oric sat with his head in his hands. Gently patting his shoulder she said, "Take no notice of Master Guwain, I am sure Sir Edred will not blame you."

"I hope you are right," Oric replied tiredly. "If he thinks I am at fault, my life will not be worth living. After hearing what I have to say, you will also be angry with me, Master Ichtheus."

"Go on. Lad, you had best tell me what happened," said Ichtheus.

Oric faced his mentor. "Shortly after you left with Sir Edred's search party, Mother Morghan reappeared. So rather than remain here, I took your donkey and cart to collect Sir Oswold's armour. But someone had already removed it. Rather than return home empty-handed, I went to collect the plunder that Dian and I found in the hovel the night we were out searching for Lady Myferny's cat." Oric ran agitated fingers through his hair. "Not only have I failed to bring back any plunder, Braccus has vanished and the cart is abandoned somewhere deep in Scraggswood forest."

"The cart is of secondary importance," Ichtheus soothed. "I am grateful that you and Master Guwain are both still in one piece." His whiskery face cracked into a smile. "As for Braccus, that wily donkey has already returned home of his own accord."

Relieved not to be in his master's bad books, Oric spooned up Mother Morghan's sloppy gruel.

"What sort of ghastly concoction is that to feed a hero?" Ichtheus exclaimed. "Yon housekeeper is the freezing limit." He whipped the bowl away and passed it to Dian. "Would you please make the lad something more substantial, my dear?"

Oric dropped a dollop of honey into the freshly cooked oats that Dian proffered. As he stirred it into the thick porridge, he recounted his hair-raising story.

"You did well, young fellow," Sir Oswold congratulated Oric. "Were it not for your presence of mind, Master Guwain would have lost his ears at the very least. I shall make sure that Sir Edred hears of your brave deeds."

Ichtheus slammed his fist on to the table, making everyone jump. "It is imperative that we stop these rogues. If we fail to find them, God knows what heinous crime they will attempt next."

-oOo-

Secure in the knowledge that the hostages were safely restrained, Rastus made his way back to St Griswald's Church.

At the sight of his grinning henchman, Figg ceased scratching figures on a piece of parchment and carefully laid down his quill pen. "Where did you deposit our victims?"

"No need to worry, Master Figg, I threw them in the apothecary's cart and used Master Guwain's horse to drag them deep into Scraggswood Forest." Rastus leered confidently. "I assure you, those lads are going nowhere." He made eager washing motions with his hands. "By gum! I hope Sir Edred takes his time to deposit the ransom. I shall enjoy hacking off a few chunks of Master Guwain's tender flesh!"

Hard-hearted though he was, Figg's stomach roiled at the sight of his horrible henchman, and he redoubled his determination to dispose of the sickening reptile the moment he ceased to be of use. Figg averted his eyes and rolled up his parchment. He secured it with a length of red ribbon, and locked it away in a chest. "Let us be on our way," he growled. "The time has come time to collect Sir Edred's gold."

At the designated oak, Figg hid and sent Rastus to investigate. If Sir Edred had set a trap, he had no intention of getting caught.

Rastus had no cause to worry. Cold and miserable, Sir Edred's guards had each guzzled a bladder of mead. The men lay in a drunken heap, snoring like a trio of warthogs.

Bent from the waist, the elder Horzefell brother grovelled inside the tree's hollow trunk. Coming up for air, he indicated that he could find nothing there. "Methinks Sir Edred had best look out for a severed ear or two," he wheezed gleefully.

Driven beyond reason, Figg broke cover and kicked his henchman hard. "Take me to the place you left the brats."

In a dither of apprehension, Rastus remounted Guwain's horse and led the way into Scraggswood Forest. "Here we are, Master Figg," he said, pretending a confidence he was far from feeling. When he saw the cut ropes and two empty sacks in the cart, his heart all but stopped beating.

Chapter Seventeen

The Secret Door

Every part of Rastus' body throbbed from the beating Figg had inflicted with a broken branch. "You can rob day and night for all I care," Figg had screamed, glassy-eyed with fury. "Kill your victims if necessary. But do not show your face until you have made up the ransom money you have caused me to lose."

Rastus limped along the track. If he had half a brain he would cut his losses and run away, but wherever he went Master Figg would seek him out. So here he was, about to perform more dirty deeds in the name of Esica Figg.

-oOo-

Deveril's key remained safely concealed in the box that Ichtheus kept hidden under Braccus' stall. To safeguard their secret, Oric readily volunteered to muck-out the stables whenever necessary. Whistling merrily, he shovelled a winter's worth of dung into a pile near the well that provided the manor's drinking water. In due course, the gardener would use the manure to improve the vegetable patch.

A brown egg in Dian's hand felt warm and smooth. She collected several more from the straw-filled nesting boxes in the hen-house and added them to the others in her basket. As she reached for the last egg, her eyes were drawn to a knothole in the back of the box. She peeped through to see Guwain hunkered down behind the coop.

Initially Guwain had thought the apothecary's apprentice unworthy of attention. To his astonishment, the youth had received many accolades. To make matters worse Sir Edred had meted out punishment in the form of restricted privileges and had threatened Guwain with a severe thrashing if he ever disobeyed orders again. Guwain blamed Oric for his misfortune, and constantly sought sneaky ways to get the apprentice into trouble.

The mucking-out completed, Oric pushed a barrow-load of fresh straw into the stables.

Guwain seized his chance and ran from his hiding place behind the hen coup. He gathered up buckets full of the horse manure and tipped the excrement into the well. Intent upon his mission, he failed to see Dian dart from the chicken run.

Moments later, a kitchen serf arrived to draw water from the well.

Oric pushed his wheelbarrow back into the yard as the serf approached Sir Edred with a bucketful of contaminated water.

A volatile man, Sir Edred lost his temper. Confronting Oric, he bellowed, "It seems you are not as trustworthy as I thought. Your sloppy carelessness may well poison every person in the manor." To teach the apprentice a lesson, Sir Edred seized a pitchfork and jabbed, stopping the thrusts just short of the boy's chest.

"Have a care, sir," Oric shrilled, crossing his arms to protect his torso. "You will run me through at this rate."

His wicked prank accomplished, Guwain slipped away.

Eggs forgotten, Dian ran into the kitchen. "Master Ichtheus! Master Ichtheus! Come quickly!"

"What is it, now?" the apothecary snapped. "Can you not see how busy I am?" He had arranged a meeting to discuss the current crime wave with his friends in Kilterton and, afraid that he might forget some important point, he was scribbling down notes to jog his memory.

"Sir Edred is attacking Oric!" Dian screamed.

"Oh, my sainted aunt!" Ichtheus dropped his notes and galloped into the yard. He lunged toward Sir Edred and clung like a leech to the pitchfork shaft. "Please, sir, allow *me* to deal with this stupid boy!"

Sir Edred wrenched the fork from Ichtheus' grasp. "Very well, but see that he cleans the well first." He flung the implement on the ground and strode away.

Oric pleaded innocence, Dian supported his story, and Ichtheus believed them. Nevertheless, the job of cleaning up the mess fell to Oric. He climbed over the well's rim and stepped into the leather bucket used for drawing water. White knuckled, he clung to the creaking rope as Ichtheus wound the bucket down the gloomy shaft.

The further Oric descended, the more anxious Dian became. "For goodness sake, take care," she called, willing him to hold tight.

Oric glanced down the black tube that fell away below him, and his stomach lurched. "I fear there is a fair way to go yet. You had best keep winding, Master Ichtheus."

Many agonising heartbeats later, the bucket splashed into the water and a cold wave gushed over Oric's feet. "For pity's sake stop winding, Master Ichtheus, I am up to my ankles in water." His voice echoed eerily, adding to the strangeness of the situation.

Ichtheus secured the rope and sent an empty bucket rattling down.

Extreme discomfort lent speed to Oric's endeavour and he soon returned a bucket of manure to the surface. He swivelled around and, about to start filling a second bucket, he noticed a small doorway in the wall.

Intrigued, he used his dagger to prize the door open. A powerful smell of mildew belched out. Oric dragged himself closer and stuck his head into the aperture. A narrow tunnel disappeared into inky blackness; to explore any further would require a lantern. He clicked the door shut and returned to the job in hand. Scooping up all that he could see of the muck, he prayed that any residue he might have missed would sink to the bottom of the well.

Safely returned to ground level, Oric gabbled about his discovery. "I want to explore the passage as soon as possible."

Dian gasped at the very idea. "Are you sure? Might it not be too dangerous?"

"The lass is right," Ichtheus agreed. "It would be unwise to venture into unknown territory until we have some idea of where the passage leads." Inclined toward caution and with an ulterior motive in mind, he went to find Sir Edred.

Ichtheus found his quarry in the paddock. "We are finished our task, my lord. Would you care to inspect the well?"

His flash of temper forgotten, the Lord of Bayersby shook his head. "I am sure you have the matter in hand, Ichtheus." He trusted his apothecary and much preferred to school his favourite charger rather than to grovel around in a well.

To promote conversation, Ichtheus praised his lord's choice of horseflesh. Always eager to discuss his favourite subject, Sir Edred launched into an animated lecture on the horse's finer points. Ichtheus listened politely for a while, and then insinuated the topic of secret tunnels into the conversation.

Sir Edred guffawed. "There were many feudal skirmishes in my grandfather's time. Rumour has it that he installed an escape route when Bayersby Manor was first built." He shrugged dismissively. "Though God knows if there is any truth in the story." Bored with the subject, he whipped up his charger, cleared a small hedge, and galloped off across the fields.

Ichtheus scurried back indoors and was assailed by a rich farmyard smell. "Od's blood! Is it you that stinks, Oric?"

"Huh! I am not the only one that pongs," Oric parried indignantly. "With respect, sir, I suggest you sniff your own attire."

"Hang it all!" Ichtheus exclaimed in dismay. "I must bathe and change my clothes before I inflict myself upon others. No doubt that will make me late for my meeting in Kilterton." He dropped his cloak and shed his boots. "If you wish to accompany me, Oric, you had best do the same."

Chapter Eighteen

Mistress Malla Saved

Despite the chilly weather, Ichtheus decided to bathe outside. "If we are quick about it, lad, we should come to no harm."

"What do you mean, *we*?" Oric was convinced that too much bathing sapped a man's strength. "I never agreed to bathe. *I* had a good clean-up last quarter moon." Smiles wreathed his freckled face. "Nevertheless, if you are determined upon this folly, Master Ichtheus, I am happy to assist you."

With his recent foray involving buckets and ropes uppermost in his mind, Ichtheus had a brainwave.

"Has Master Ichtheus taken leave of his senses?" Dian asked as she helped to skewer a leather bucket with sharp spikes.

"I think he might have," Oric replied, wondering gleefully what sort of fool his master was about to make of himself. "Even an idiot would know that a container full of holes is neither use nor ornament."

Doing as he was bid, Oric set a cauldron of water upon the fire to heat. He sent a serf with a ladder to hang the prepared bucket from the branch of an apple tree that grew in a quiet corner of the compound. "I should stay and watch if I were you," Oric grinned at Dian. "This could be an interesting exercise."

The water boiled and Oric poured it into a large pitcher. Following his master's instructions, he carried the pitcher outside, and teetered up a ladder propped against the tree branch.

Stripped to his loincloth, Ichtheus dithered below.

"Are you ready, master?"

"Yes, boy!" snapped Ichtheus, his temper beginning to fray. "For goodness sake get a move on. I am freezing to death."

Oric streamed hot water into the suspended, perforated bucket.

"*Or-i-i-i-i-c!*" Ichtheus leapt aside as if shifted by some supernatural force. You halfwit! I am scalded." He glared up the ladder. "Do I have to explain even the simplest of instructions *word* by *word*?" Frozen and boiled at one and the same time, Ichtheus continued at full volume. "For pity's sake, go and mix some cold water with the hot."

A few of the household serfs joined Dian outside to see who might be on the receiving end of this latest bout of shouting. At the sight of the dithering apothecary, they hooted and made ribald comments at Ichtheus' expense.

Hanging on to what remained of his tattered pride, Ichtheus awaited Oric's return with the tempered water.

A short while later, bathed, dried and dressed, Ichtheus rewarded Oric with a sadistic smile. "Now, lad, 'tis your turn for a good scrub."

-oOo-

The midday meal was eaten and the platters cleared away. Dian tidied the kitchen then begged leave to accompany Oric and Ichtheus to Kilterton. She had not visited her parents' since before Yuletide, and she longed to see her siblings. Much to Mother Morghan's annoyance, Lady Myferny gave the maid permission to go.

"Take a basket of foodstuff with you," Lady Myferny urged. Aware of Eadbald and Frida's poor parenting abilities, she imagined that the Cole children would be hungry.

"We shall leave Parzifal at home this time," Ichtheus stated. "I could do without the responsibility of looking after him for once.

Riding pillion upon Otty, Dian clung to Oric's back. Oric whistled a lively tune, feeling ten foot tall.

Ichtheus followed a short distance behind with Braccus and a borrowed cart. He observed the two youngsters and smiled. After a rocky start, they seemed to be forming a firm friendship.

Without Parzifal, the first part of the journey passed without incident and they soon arrived at the Roxdale Beck. Otty, having overcome her fear of water, splashed across the ford without turning a hair. On the other side, however, she began to buck and toss. Dian clung to Oric for dear life.

"Steady on, you skittish beast," Oric cried, holding tight to Otty's bridle. "Can you see anything that might have spooked her, Dian?"

A heap of dead leaves in the middle of the pathway was the cause of Otty's discomfort and she flatly refused to walk through them. Oric dismounted, swished through the leaves, and was appalled to discover a semi-conscious woman. But for Otty, they would have ridden roughshod over the body.

The silver-haired woman groaned, and struggled to sit up. "Thank goodness you arrived when you did," she murmured groggily. "A man accosted me and stole my pony. Had he not heard your approach, I am sure he would have killed me and made off with all my possessions."

Dian slid down from Oric's donkey and rushed to the lady's side. "Oh, you poor soul," she soothed. "Let me help you up."

Under his mentor's guidance, Oric probed for broken bones. "You will be pleased to hear that you are in one piece, mistress, though I suspect you will be black and blue by tomorrow." He produced a powder of Solomon's-seal from a travelling pack he had taken to carrying and handed the jar to Dian. "Smooth some of the medicament onto areas most likely to bruise. It will help to dispel blood that might congeal under the lady's skin."

Ichtheus noted that the woman's clothes, though torn and muddy, were of good quality and a sizeable canvas bag lay nearby. "Where are you going, madam? Perhaps we can escort you to your destination?"

"I am bound for Kilterton," the lady replied. "I intend to stay at the inn until I am able to find more suitable accommodation."

Curiosity over-rode Ichtheus' good manners. "May I enquire as to your name and your purpose for visiting Kilterton?"

"Mistress Malla, midwife and herbalist," said the lady inclining her head.

Genuinely delighted, Ichtheus offered Mistress Malla his hand. "Welcome. I am Ichtheus, overworked apothecary of Bayersby and Kilterton. The presence of another healer will surely lighten my workload."

Oric and Dian gladly relinquished Otty to Mistress Malla, and they set off once again.

Daylight was gone by the time Ichtheus led his small

group into the stable-yard behind the inn. He assisted Mistress Malla down from the donkey's back, and delivered her into the capable and sympathetic hands of the landlord's wife.

Rather than face a return trip in the dark, Ichtheus suggested they stay overnight. "The inn is clean, the landlord serves good ale, and the landlady is an excellent cook. What more could a body ask?"

Oric walked Dian to her parents' cottage, wishing her goodnight on the doorstep.

"Thank you, Oric," Dian smiled. "Sleep well but be sure to collect me before you return to Bayersby Manor in the morning."

Frida Cole was happy to receive Lady Myferny's basket of provisions, though she was not quite so pleased to see her eldest daughter. Dian's fresh appearance and fastidious habits made Frida feel uncomfortable. On the other hand Eadbald Cole could not have cared less. He had run out of funds, and was sleeping off his latest alcoholic binge in a corner of the single-roomed cottage.

The welcome Dian received from her siblings compensated for her parents' indifference. Returning the youngsters' hugs and kisses, she answered their eager queries. "What is it like, working for a lord and lady?" they demanded as they delved into the treats Lady Myferny had sent. Keeping their voices low for fear of disturbing their father, they marvelled at the descriptions Dian gave of her life at Bayersby Manor.

"Enough of this nonsense," Dian laughed. "Unless I start cooking, there will be no supper this evening." She placed a pot of water on the fire and threw in chopped cabbage, several onions and a large marrowbone.

Dian left the food to cook, and tackled her siblings' lice-infested hair. At Oric's suggestion she had brought a pot of olibanum and barrow grease – an effective way to kill the pests, and one that would not damage the children's brains. Dian pasted each child's scalp with ointment and then, instructing them to strip near naked, she washed them from top to toe. That night the Cole children went to bed clean and with their bellies full. Gathering up their filthy clothes, Dian grabbed a lantern and hastened to the village pond. She spread the garments on a flat rock prior to giving them a good scrub. She returned to her parents' cottage, and hung the clothes out to dry. Tired after her exertions she curled up with two of her little sisters to sleep.

Half way through his first pot of ale at the inn, Oric received a mighty whack between his shoulder blades. "Hah! Lazing away your life, as usual, I see!" Egglebart guffawed at his own joke.

"Lazing?" Oric glowered at the tall, red-haired man. "You have no idea of the day I just endured."

Uther, the Kilterton boot maker, followed Egglebart into the inn and handed over the new pair of boots that Ichtheus had ordered. "I hope these are to your liking, my friend," he said, nodding to one and all. He collected a pot of ale, made a beeline for the fire that blazed on the central hearth, and lowered his wiry frame onto a stool.

The Kilterton butcher was last to arrive and he ran the good-natured gauntlet of his crony's taunts. "It seems my daughters' needs are more important than keeping an eye on me," Tewdric joked. Although the men made light of the matter, they were heartfelt glad that the shrewish Helled Bascoomb had not accompanied her husband.

The inn swiftly filled with thirsty locals and, to avoid eavesdroppers, Ichtheus directed his group to the far end of the room. Before commencing the meeting, they made short work of several rabbit pies and washed the food down with quantities of the landlord's excellent ale. When everyone had finished, Egglebart seized the opportunity to issue invitations to his forthcoming nuptials. Satisfied that his friends were happy with his arrangements, he belched, wiped his greasy beard on his sleeve, and waited expectantly for Ichtheus to call the meeting to order.

"I am sorry to bring a sombre note to such an auspicious occasion," said Ichtheus, "but the time has come to discuss a most serious matter." He described the crimes that had taken place throughout the district and told of Master Guwain's close call with death on his way home from Roxbrough. "To add insult to injury, the boy has recently escaped a vicious kidnap attempt. And, on our way here this very evening, we saved a lady from some evil villain's clutches," Ichtheus concluded.

Tewdric Bascoomb sowed the first seeds of an idea. "We should become vigilantes and meet regularly." Tewdric imagined that membership of such an important group might allow him a valid escape from his wife from time to time.

Uther Tidwall immediately guessed the reasoning behind the butcher's suggestion. "Aye, well, a vigilante group might work if we can stop Mistress Bascoomb from joining in. If she gets wind of what we are about, she will want to take over."

Tewdric's rosy complexion paled and his breath came in short bursts. "But she must not be told!" It would be too awful if his new-found freedom were to end before it began.

Since Tewdric had traded bones for potions with Oric, Ichtheus had avoided Helled Bascoomb. Filled with apprehension, he faced the butcher. "Please tell me your wife does not know it was I that made up those purges."

Tewdric had the grace to look ashamed. He had

administered the potions in an attempt to flush out his wife's ill humour, telling her that Master Ichtheus' medications would enhance her beauty. She had swallowed the lot. The medication failed to produce the effect Tewdric desired, and Helled had felt unwell for two days. Her looks had not improved, nor had her temper. Now she had retribution in mind, and Ichtheus had good cause to feel nervous.

Ale flowed and the threat of Helled Bascoomb diminished. At midnight the friends unanimously agreed to entrap those felons who were striking fear and trepidation into Kilterton's citizens. Ichtheus declared the meeting over whereupon everyone retired to their allotted sleeping places.

Chapter Nineteen

Into the Tunnel

"Mother Morghan, Mother Morghan. Are you there?"

Dragged from her slumbers by the insistent voice, Mother Morghan arose from her comfortable chair in the kitchen and cursed Ichtheus. The old man's absence had already caused her extra work, and now she was in danger of losing sleep as well.

Lady Myferny stood at the top of the stairs. "I am sorry to disturb you in the middle of the night," she said, "but I need you to take a look at Master Guwain. He seems to have developed some kind of malady."

Mother Morghan glared at Guwain's pasty face. *The only malady the stupid boy suffers,* she thought *is brought on by over-indulgence.* "I shall give him a purgative, my lady. A good clean-out will make him feel better."

Throughout the night, Guwain disgorged the contents of his stomach on to his bed, the floor, and Mother Morghan. Finally, when the young lord's innards had nothing more to offer, she left him in a deep sleep.

As dawn filtered into the kitchen, Mother Morghan cast

off her soiled apron. She had done her duty. If anyone else fell ill, they could fend for themselves. In need of fresh air, she threw a shawl over her shoulders and set out to visit Hersica Horzefell at St Griswald's Church.

With nothing of interest to report, Mother Morghan prayed that Esica Figg might be out and about his business elsewhere. Her worst fears were realised when she bumped into him at the church door.

"Do you have fresh information for me?" Figg snapped.

"By gor, Master Figg, 'tis a cold day, and no mistake." Mother Morghan chafed her hands together in an attempt to put off the moment of truth. "Have you got a little drop o' summat to warm the cockles of a poor old woman's heart?"

"You get nothing from me until you prove your worth," Figg snarled.

"Truthfully speaking, Master Figg, I ain't got much to report."

"Then why waste my time, you stupid woman?" Figg lashed out with the flat of his hand. At the current rate of non-progress, he imagined that he might grow too old to overthrow Sir Edred. Thoroughly depressed, he saddled his horse and departed for his shop in Kilterton.

Over time an uneasy truce had developed between Hersica Horzefell and Mother Morghan. Nevertheless, each was aware that the other would save her own skin should circumstance force a choice. Today, however, Hersica was not on the receiving end of Figg's short temper, and smug relief enabled her to take pity on Mother Morghan.

"Pay no attention to yon moneylender," Hersica soothed. "He will get over his tantrum soon enough." Observing Mother Morghan's discomfort, she continued swiftly, "Since his high and mightiness has taken himself off, why not stay and share a drop of ale with me? A little drink might help to calm your nerves."

"*He* may well get over his ill humour, but *I* will not," hissed Mother Morghan, placing her hand over the livid finger marks that Figg had imprinted upon her cheek. "Yon reptile has slapped me once too often." She took a long pull from the flagon of ale that Hersica proffered and wiped her mouth on the corner of her shawl. "Esica Figg will regret getting on the wrong side of me, of that you may be certain."

Another flagon of ale followed the first and the two women quaffed, gossiped, and commiserated with each other on their unfortunate lot in life. They lost all sense of time until Mother Morghan glanced up the crypt stairway and noticed that the light of day had faded. "Lawks," she cried, struggling to her feet. "The day is almost done. I must away back to Bayersby Manor."

-oOo-

The Kilterton Inn loft provided a comfortable sleeping place, and Oric awoke feeling none the worse for his night of indulgence. Ichtheus was not so lucky. The sight of Oric wolfing down a platter of jugged hare in the landlady's kitchen turned his delicate stomach.

Finished with his own food, Oric polished-off Ichtheus' untouched breakfast for good measure. Smacking his lips, he winked at Egglebart. "Worry not, my friend, *I* will be back for your wedding in two days' time." He glanced cheekily at Ichtheus, "Though I am not sure my honourable mentor will be fit enough!" He laughed, and ducked to avoid Ichtheus' good-natured swipe.

With plenty of chores to complete around her parents' cottage, Dian arose at dawn. Josh had kept the fire going all night, and the washed garments strung about the room were almost dry.

"Keep quiet and get dressed," Dian whispered as she shook each child in turn. "If father wakes and sees you out of your clothes, he will sell them for money to spend at the inn." She would rather the youngsters wore damp garments than none at all.

Hefting the stew pot back on to the fire, Dian added water and a handful of barley to the leftover gravy. The liquid was thin, but it was better than nothing. Whilst she waited for her concoction to heat, she swept the dirt floor. She gathered ashes from the hearth and threw them into the yard to soak up the mud.

The broth bubbled; Dian spread fat on chunks of rough bread, and called the children to eat. Forgetting their sleeping parents, the youngsters squabbled noisily over who had the biggest portion of food.

"Ye gods, can you lot do nothing quietly?" Frida Cole rolled off her pile of straw and scratched herself vigorously. She eyed her husband, who was beginning to stir. "You cause nowt but trouble," she snapped, staring balefully at Dian. "The sooner you clear off, the better."

A loud rap on the cottage door halted Frida's tirade. "Whoever that is, get rid of them," she hissed. "I am in no mood for callers."

Dian opened the door to a cheerful Oric. "Good morning," he beamed.

"I dare not invite you in," Dian mouthed. "Mother does not want any visitors today. My brothers and sisters are misbehaving," she added in lame explanation.

A small face pushed in between Dian and the doorpost. "Ma says you have to clear off, and to shut the door when you leave." The youngest member of the Cole family reached up for a hug, wishing her big sister did not have to go.

On the return journey to Bayersby Manor, Oric brought up the subject of the secret tunnel. "I am game to explore it," he offered cheerfully. "But to keep our discovery secret, I think we should wait until everyone is abed."

"I am not happy about winching you down the well again," said Ichtheus. "Though I admit my curiosity is getting the better of me."

Parzifal greeted the trio at the manor door. He wagged his tail forlornly and pointed his nose suggestively at his empty bowl.

Ichtheus collared a passing kitchen serf. "Did I not leave instructions for Mother Morghan to feed the dog whilst we were absent?" He patted Parzifal sympathetically. "For goodness sake, give the beast his dinner." Ichtheus' eyes darted around the kitchen. "And, just as a matter of interest, where *is* the housekeeper?"

Elbows bent, palms out, the serf shrugged his shoulders. "I ain't got no idea where the old boiler has gone. She's been missing since first thing this morning. Yon harridan is a law unto herself." Disgruntled, the serf shambled off in search of scraps for the dog.

Dian beckoned Oric to come close. "I suspect Mother Morghan is up to no good. Perhaps we should keep an eye upon her in future."

"Aye!" Oric agreed. "The woman is missing from the manor all too often, but there is naught we can do about it. 'Tis Lady Myferny's place to discipline her housekeeper."

The fire had burned out, and Oric fetched some kindling. He soon had a merry blaze crackling upon the inglenook hearth. Dian chopped turnips and dropped them into a cauldron with three pig's trotters. Setting the heavy vessel on a trivet over the fire, she added a handful of beans and a bouquet of dried herbs.

Later in the day, Dian called Oric and Ichtheus to the table. Oric proclaimed her stew the best he had ever tasted.

"We shall make the most of Mother Morghan's absence," Ichtheus stated, tossing his empty dish into a bucket for washing. He wiped the tabletop clean and set out books, pestles and mortars. "When you are ready, Oric, I will instruct you in the making of some new herbal remedies."

Oric worked throughout the day to take his mind off his forthcoming trip down the well. Evening arrived with still no sign of Mother Morghan. One by one the Bayersby inhabitants drifted off to their beds, and the manor reverberated with snores. Oric and Ichtheus waited for a while before they stepped out into a dark, moonless night. Dian insisted upon accompanying them. If anything went wrong, she wanted to be on hand to help.

Oric peered over the well's rim. "Now I am faced with the reality, I am not quite so enthusiastic," he admitted.

"There is no need for you to go," Ichtheus replied quickly, offering his apprentice the chance to withdraw. "After all, the tunnel may lead nowhere."

"Master Ichtheus is quite right," Dian quivered with apprehension. "You might endanger your life."

"I appreciate your concern," said Oric bracing his shoulders. "However, if I fail to investigate now, I will spend the rest of my life wondering."

Resigned to his departure, Dian handed Oric a length of rope. "Fasten this around your waist. I will secure the other end to one of the well's posts. If you fall out of the bucket, the rope will save you from drowning."

Oric's first trip down the well during daylight hours had been scary enough, but darkness introduced new terrors. In the light of his flickering oil lamp, the walls seemed to close in upon him. Drips from the bottom of the bucket plopped eerily into the water far below. Oric shivered. He squinted up at the dark circle of sky above his head and thought, melodramatically, that even the moon had deserted him.

To avoid getting his feet wet again, Oric watched his descent carefully. He held his lamp over the side of the bucket until the water, black and slick, loomed close. "You can stop winding now, Master Ichtheus!" he called. "I am abreast of the tunnel."

The bucket creaked to a stop.

Oric pulled his dagger from its scabbard and prised the door open.

The tunnel retained its strong mushroom smell and was barely high enough to crawl along. Oric untied the rope from around his waist and left it trapped in the door, ready for his return. An unpleasant thought struck him. What if there was no return? Quelling his maudlin speculations, he moved slowly forward.

-oOo-

Mother Morghan crashed tipsily along the overgrown track back to Bayersby Manor. She hated walking, but it was her only way of getting about since neither Sir Edred nor Esica Figg saw fit to supply her with her a donkey. "Huh! 'Tis all very well for that pair to ride about the district," the housekeeper grizzled, "but I has to hobble everywhere on me poor, old feet."

Upon entering the manor compound, a movement caught Mother Morghan's attention. She ducked into a nearby stable and peeked over the open half-door. Some daft fool was going down the well! Intrigued, she continued to watch as the apothecary's apprentice climbed into the bucket and

Master Ichtheus began to wind. Mother Morghan wheezed with subdued laughter. Yon numbskull apprentice certainly had guts. *Fancy putting his life in the hands of that skinny old fool,* she thought.

The new kitchen maid also hung over the rim of the well. Mother Morghan narrowed her eyes speculatively. She would need to watch the little hussy, for the girl was getting altogether too thick with the apothecary's apprentice. Time dragged on but the apprentice remained down the well. The apothecary and the kitchen maid continued to peer over the rim.

Bored with the lack of action, Mother Morghan tiptoed out of the stable, and crept unsteadily into the kitchen. She threw more logs on to the fire, lit a pair of candles, and kicked off her boots. Dropping into her sagging chair, she stretched and yawned. One thing was for sure... Master Figg would get no more information unless he paid up first.

-oOo-

Oric crawled slowly along the tunnel, trying to ignore the weird shapes his flickering light cast upon the walls. His heart raced, and he gripped the lantern's handle until his fingernails indented half-moon crescents into his palm.

A scuttling noise caused him to stop. Rats! Dozens of them ran at him, their eyes glowing red in the lamplight. Hundreds of little feet passed over him as the creatures scampered down the tunnel. Oric gritted his teeth to stop himself from screaming. Of all the animals in Christendom, he hated rats the most.

All sense of time deserted him. His hands and knees became sore from contact with the tunnel's rough floor but curiosity drove him on until he sensed a slight change of direction. Quite suddenly the small tunnel joined a larger passageway. Holding his lantern high, Oric saw that the new tunnel went to both left and right. He straightened up, flexed his cramped muscles, and wondered which way to go next. Following his instinct he turned left. Soon he came to a flight of steep, rough-hewn steps and counted them as he climbed. He reached number twenty before his head made contact with the roof. Disappointed, he wondered if he had come to a dead end. He sat down on the top step wondering what to do next, for he did not fancy returning whence he had come.

On to the last drop of oil, his lantern spluttered and went out. Blackness enveloped everything and Oric looked around in panic. A hand's breadth above his head he saw the outline of a dimly illuminated square. Maybe it was a trap door. He put his shoulder to the roof and pushed. A narrow crack opened up.

Something wet and warm made contact with Oric's cheek. Startled, he jerked his head back. A grey, whiskery muzzle poked down through the lighted space, followed by Parzifal's bright eyes and floppy ears.

"Od's blood!" Oric exclaimed, "What are you doing here, old lad?"

Parzifal was exactly where he preferred to be on a cold night; curled up in front of the hearth in the Bayersby Manor kitchen.

Oric eased back the flagstone and climbed out whilst Parzifal jumped around in happy greeting.

The sudden activity attracted Mother Morghan's attention, and her face became a study of puzzlement. *The apprentice must have come out of the well and sneaked back indoors.* Too sozzled to give the matter any further thought, Mother Morghan fell into a deep sleep.

Beside the well, Dian fought back her tears. "Oric has been gone too long," she gasped. "Something dreadful must have happened."

Almost beside himself with worry, Ichtheus hung further out over the well's rim. "I should never have allowed Oric to go down in the first place. What sort of coward am I to let a mere boy do such a thing? I should have gone in the lad's stead."

Ichtheus' concern paled into insignificance compared to his reaction when Oric tapped him on the shoulder.

In the nick of time, Oric grabbed his master's legs to prevent him from falling head-long down the shaft. "Oops! That was a near thing. I am sorry, Master Ichtheus. I did not mean to give you such a fright."

"Damn and blast, boy," Ichtheus breathed deeply to slow his wildly pounding heart. "I was nearly out of my skull with worry."

Dian flung her arms around Oric's neck. "Thank goodness you are safe. Where on earth did you spring from?"

In a fever of excitement, Oric described his adventure and explained how the other part of the tunnel veered off in a different direction. "With the entrance directly beneath my bed, I no longer need to go down the well, Master Ichtheus. From now on we can gain easy access and explore underground any time we like."

But the opportunity for further exploration would not arise until after Egglebart's wedding.

Chapter Twenty

Wedding Celebrations

The haunting call of a cuckoo wakened Ichtheus early. Keen to greet the day, he left his bed and went outside for a stroll. Rays of pale sunshine sparkled droplets of morning dew with rainbow colours, and a soft breeze filled with the scent of wild flowers wafted from the valley. Ichtheus inhaled appreciatively. *Yes indeed,* he thought, *'tis a perfect day for a wedding.* His euphoria came to an abrupt end when Oric and Dian tottered into the compound with a heavy pannier that contained Egglebart and Etheldrida's wedding gift.

Ichtheus ran to lend a hand. "For goodness sake, be careful!"

"Worry not," Oric replied cheerfully. "We can manage, can we not, Dian?" On the count of three they hefted their burden on to Braccus' back.

Ichtheus had concocted a range of herbal remedies for the bride and groom. The finished products were contained in brown jars, which he had purchased from the Kilterton potter. All were packed within the basket that Oric and Dian were so casually strapping down.

"Have you properly secured the donkey's saddle?" Ichtheus shoved the youngsters aside and tested the girth strap for himself. "I do not want my gift smashed before it reaches its destination." Satisfied that Oric and Dian had done a good job, Ichtheus stepped back. "Oh, my sainted aunt!" he gasped, looking his apprentice up and down. "You surely are not proposing to attend Egglebart's wedding in that filthy state?"

"Filthy? What do you mean? I bathed not long since," Oric exclaimed defensively. Thrusting out his grubby hands, he inspected them front and back. Dian raised her eyebrows, and Oric groaned regretfully. "Maybe I do need a bit of a clean-up." He filled a bucket of water from the well and lugged it into the stables.

Oric reappeared dressed in the brown homespun tunic and britches that Lady Myferny had given to him at Yuletide. A dark-green hood with a short cape attached completed his ensemble. Since apprentices were forbidden to wear grand clothes, Oric's new, simple apparel proved ideal for the wedding.

"My word, Oric, you look smart," said Dian, twirling into the kitchen to show off her own blue kirtle.

Guwain ogled the kitchen maid and, with his mind firmly set upon getting to know her better, he pestered his father for permission to attend the wedding. Sir Edred acquiesced, but not until he had extracted Oric's promise to keep Guwain out of trouble. The Bayersby heir hurried away to change. He strutted back a short while later clad in a magnificent outfit of crimson and gold. Oric hoped it would be as easy to keep Guwain out of mischief as it would be to keep him within sight.

The betrothed couple had chosen Kilterton's new priory to celebrate their nuptials. To be there in time for the afternoon celebration, the Bayersby party left the manor after breakfast. They reached their destination as a group of excited villagers gathered outside the priory to await the arrival of the bride and groom.

Egglebart was the first to appear, looking magnificent in blueberry-coloured robes. He had tamed his red hair with liberal applications of oil, and his beard was plaited in two long braids secured with black ribbons. A bronze torque encircled his muscular neck. Egglebart's awe-inspiring appearance belied his nervous state and, after entering the priory, he glanced repeatedly over his shoulder.

"You don't suppose Etheldrida has changed her mind, do you, Oric?" he whispered, his face crumpled with anxiety.

Oric's reply was lost amidst the sound of blaring horns and bellowing beasts as a large cart, drawn by two magnificent oxen, rumbled to a halt in front of the priory. The bridal party had arrived.

"Look at that voluminous green cloak Etheldrida is wearing," whispered a village-woman to her neighbour. "Fancy surrounding such a big person with all those entwined leaves and flowers, too; she looks like a cabbage in a vegetable patch."

"Aye," replied the other woman, "but I do like the silver chain that holds back her hair. Mind you," she added spitefully, "if I had that many chins I would want to hide them."

Aided by four handmaidens, Etheldrida vacated her nest in the cart. She waved and nodded graciously to the crowd, laughing uproariously when a group of urchins made remarks about her generous proportions. Absolutely nothing could spoil her day.

One small boy ran ahead to let the minstrels know the bridal party was on its way and the Kilterton bell-ringers clanged into action. The congregation sang. A priest intoned a prayer or two, and the betrothed couple exchanged vows. After the short ceremony, Egglebart kissed his bride with a resounding smack.

Pink and flustered, Etheldrida shoved him playfully. "Behave yourself! 'Tis not proper to behave like that before all of our guests."

"And why not?" Egglebart thundered. "Now that you are my wife, I can kiss you whenever I like." His one blue eye twinkled wickedly. "If the fancy takes me, I shall beat you, too."

Ichtheus smothered a chuckle. Egglebart beat his new spouse? Hah! That would be the day. How he wished he could say the same for the Bascoombs. Seated beside Helled, Tewdric's black eye and martyred expression spoke volumes.

Outside the church, Ichtheus nervously bid Helled good day. He breathed more easily when she failed to mention the purgatives that Tewdric had dosed her with. However, observing her frigid expression, Ichtheus had a nasty feeling he had not heard the last of the unfortunate incident.

Helled's face softened as she gazed at her twelve-year-old twins, Lunette and Novena, and thanked God the girls took after her side of the family. Helled glanced at Tewdric, comparing him to her father. How different the two men were. Her plain and portly husband butchered meat for a living; her handsome sire had died a hero on the battlefield. Barely old enough to fend for herself, Helled had married the first man to offer her a home. Tewdric Bascoomb had money, but he could not hold a candle to her father. Helled's mother remained a mystery, for the girl had disappeared shortly after she gave birth to her baby. Brought up by housekeepers, none of whom stayed long, Helled had received little affection during her formative years. Quelling waves of resentment, she ushered her girls toward the inn. As long as she had breath in her body, Helled determined that her daughters would never suffer the degradations that she had experienced. "Come along, my treasures. Let us join in with the jollifications." Helled was in a hurry, for she had a score to settle with Ichtheus.

Oric and Dian entered the inn and were immediately enveloped in the rank odour of unwashed humanity.

"Ye gods!" Oric buried his face in his cape. "If the folk herein can stomach this pong, they are in serious need of my beetroot nasal wash."

Ichtheus laughed. "Hark at the kettle calling the pot black," he shouted above the din. "Not so long ago it was you that required cleansing. You had best get used to the smell, lad, for you stand little chance of changing folks' habits of a lifetime."

Hardened by similar conditions in her parents' cottage, Dian seemed unperturbed by the inn's claustrophobic atmosphere. Seeing several village girls seated at a table by the door, she asked if she could join them. At Ichtheus' nod, she hurried across to her friends to catch up with the latest gossip.

The innkeeper's wife, supplied with a generous purse from Egglebart, had excelled herself. A roasted hog provided the centrepiece. Two trestle tables groaned under the weight of pies, stewed rabbits, eels, herrings and sweetmeats. Liquor flowed freely and stories of past battles were trotted out.

After dark someone lit a bonfire in the village square. Soon the wedding party spilled out doors. A harp was produced, and the newly-weds danced to the instrument's melodious twangs.

Egglebart whirled Etheldrida around and around until she shrieked in mock terror. Undaunted Egglebart danced on and sang at the top of his voice.

More members of the wedding party joined in the dance, and the market square became full of whirling bodies. Having no desire to join the noisy revellers outside, Ichtheus, Tewdric and Uther remained in the inn, hogged the fire, and talked.

Guwain made a nuisance of himself, showing off in front of Dian and her friends. The girls batted their eyelashes, giggling self-consciously. Soon bored with their foolish twitters, Guwain wandered off to find food.

In the heartbeat of time it took Oric to pick up a bite of supper, Guwain disappeared. Oric left the inn, pushed his way through the crowded square, and climbed the steps of Kilterton's central monument. He chewed on a pork shin-bone whilst he kept a watchful eye open for his missing charge.

There was nothing like a drunken crowd to boost earnings, and one of Figg's young thieves had enjoyed a lucrative day. His hopes were raised further when the Bayersby heir strode into the alley Ned had chosen to operate from.

Ned jostled Guwain against the wall as he picked the young boy's pouch. "You look bored to death, young sir. Is there owt I can do to cheer you?"

Not realising he had just been robbed, Guwain pointed to Oric. "See that fellow over there? He follows me everywhere. I gave him the slip, but he will not rest until he finds me again. I would like you to get rid of him."

Still smarting from his loss of face at Oric's hands during the chestnut game, Ned was happy to oblige. He palmed the two silver coins he had extracted from Guwain's pouch and smiled slyly. "Come – we shall teach the fellow a lesson he will not forget."

Intent upon sucking marrow from his bone, Oric failed to see the two shadowy figures that crept up the monument steps from behind.

Ned leaped on to Oric's back, knocking him down the steps.

"Hold him down!" Guwain squealed. "I shall give him

a good kicking."

Caught off-guard, Oric was slow to react. The unseen bully thrust him down in the dirt and pinned his arms behind his back. "You spineless worm!" Oric yelled. "Have you not the courage to fight me face-to-face?"

In his element, Guwain avoided Oric's wildly thrashing legs and planted a hefty kick to his temple.

Oric saw stars that had nothing to do with the night sky.

Guwain raised his foot again, but he had no chance to deliver a second blow.

"Stop, for pity's sake, stop!" Josh Cole yelled as he burst from the crowd. "If you carry on at this rate you will kill Oric."

Distracted, Guwain swung away from his prey. Given a moment to think, he realised that the peasant-boy was right.

Oric seized his chance, freed one arm from Ned's grasp and whacked his assailant with the hog's shin-bone. Ned rolled away, clutching his jaw.

Eager to witness a fight, the youths of Kilterton chanted their disappointment when the two protagonists retreated.

"I will get you for that, Josh Cole!" Ned's parting words were enough to curdle blood. "No one crosses me and gets away with it."

Thwarted, Guwain sloped back to the inn.

"Are you all right?" Josh asked anxiously, helping Oric to his feet. "By heck, Master Guwain is a cowardly mongrel. I would expect such behaviour from Ned, for he knows no better, but never from the son of the lord of the manor."

Oric grinned wryly and brushed himself down. "Ned has been brewing for a fight ever since I trounced him at chestnuts. Perhaps now he might leave me alone." He rubbed his eye, which was beginning to swell. "But 'tis hard to believe that Guwain and I both hail from the same household."

Ichtheus also had problems. Feeling nauseous, he went

in search of water to drink and came face to face with Helled Bascoomb.

"Good evening, Master Ichtheus. I trust that I find you in *good* health." Helled's voice seemed to drift up from the bottom of a bucket and Ichtheus shook his head to clear a mist that suddenly blurred his eyes.

"Judging by your pallor, I suspect you have imbibed something that has disagreed with you." Helled's oily concern was strangely out of character.

An iron fist gripped Ichtheus' belly, confirming his suspicion that Helled had paid him back with his own potions. He raced outside to the midden and remained there for some time. He eventually tottered back inside the inn, feeling as though his innards were turned inside out.

"Ah, Ichtheus – I would like to introduce you to this delightful lady," said Sir Oswold, indicating a small woman at his side. "She tells me that she plans to settle hereabouts."

"Well, bless my soul!" Ichtheus exclaimed, prising his furry tongue from the roof of his mouth. "No introduction is necessary, for Mistress Malla and I are already acquainted." He smiled wanly and bowed over the lady's hand. "I am delighted to see you so well recovered after your misfortune." Ichtheus wished he could say the same for himself.

"This is the gentleman I was telling you about." Malla explained to Sir Oswold. "But for his well-timed intervention, I may not have lived to tell the tale." She dazzled Ichtheus with a smile. "I am indebted to you, kind sir."

Oric followed Guwain into the inn. "If you step outside without me again, I will report you to your father when we return to Bayersby."

Guwain wobbled his head defiantly. "I shall remain indoors, but not at your behest." He jerked his thumb at

Dian. "Yon kitchen maid is in need of some company and I am just the fellow to provide it."

Oric's heart sank. *What chance did a mere apprentice stand against a member of the landed gentry?*

With no particular destination in mind, Oric stepped outside to wander listlessly along the street. Abreast of Esica Figg's moneylending shop, the same wheezy voice Oric had heard during his kidnap at the hovel brought him to an abrupt halt. Curious to see who the voice belonged to, Oric slid behind the trunk of a nearby chestnut tree. He did not have long to wait. Within a few heartbeats two men left the shop, mounted horses and rode away in different directions. Gooseflesh prickled Oric's skin, for Esica Figg was one of the men. In a state of high excitement, he hastened back to the inn to seek out his mentor.

Ichtheus scowled at Oric's dishevelled appearance, "Kindly explain your state of disarray!"

"You may well ask, Master Ichtheus," Oric brushed aside his skirmish with Ned and Guwain and dropped his voice to a whisper. "I believe it was Esica Figg who kidnapped Guwain and me."

"Are you sure?"

"Yes, I am sure," Oric nodded vigorously and recounted what he had seen and heard.

Ichtheus smashed a fist into his palm. "But we have only your word against his. We need more proof to get him arrested."

They re-joined their friends beside the fire, and Oric repeated his story.

Uther rubbed his jaw. "If what you say is right, young fellow, 'tis time we did summat about yon money-grubbing worm. I proposed that we form a Council of War." Everyone raised their hands in enthusiastic agreement and, in the couple's absence, Egglebart and Etheldrida's farm was chosen as the ideal place to meet.

"They will be most accommodating, I am sure," said Ichtheus. "But courtesy dictates that we allow the newly-weds a few days' respite before we descend upon them."

"Aye," Tewdric agreed. "If the new bride is like my Helled, a day or two of peace is all that Egglebart has left. Once the novelty wears off, she will surely give the poor beggar a run for his money." Recalling his own unhappy marital state, Tewdric changed the subject. "Since we are not actually going to war, I reckon we should call ourselves a Council of Law." He grinned enthusiastically, "If we band together we should soon put a stop to Esica Figg's wickedness."

Ichtheus doubted the task would be that simple, for he believed Esica Figg to be smarter than a sack-full of rats. "Come on, Oric," he urged, "'tis time we left. Round up Dian and Guwain – we have a long ride ahead of us."

Chapter Twenty One

Into the Tunnel Again

The day after Egglebart's wedding, Oric awoke with a spectacular black eye. Ichtheus swabbed the swollen area with a decoction of bugleweed, offering his apprentice scant sympathy. "'Od's blood, boy! What *am* I going to do with you?"

Oric winced and ducked his head. "*I* obeyed Sir Edred's orders, 'tis not my fault that Master Guwain is so petty."

Ichtheus continued to dab at Oric's bruised face. "Say what you like, lad, Sir Edred must be informed of his son's disgraceful behaviour. Guwain cannot be allowed to ride rough-shod over whomsoever he pleases."

"Nay, Master Ichtheus, let it be," Oric begged. "Blood is thicker than water, and I have no desire to upset Sir Edred. I will sort Master Guwain out in my own good time." To change the subject, he suggested that they explore the tunnel after breakfast. Always on the lookout for clues that might throw light on Master Deveril's warning and the double-knot key, Oric was keen to investigate the unexplored underground territory.

Ichtheus shrugged unenthusiastically. His guts remained in an uproar after drinking Helled's evil potion, and he had spent a sleepless night thinking about Esica Figg. What if Oric was right? Perhaps the moneylender was responsible for Guwain's kidnapping, but where was the proof? Oric had not actually set eyes upon the culprit. "Before we descend into the bowels of the earth, I suggest we tell Sir Oswold where we are going." Ichtheus advised "We must also wait until the serfs have gone about their business – we do not want every Tom, Dick and Harry to know about the tunnel."

By the time Mother Morghan finally left the kitchen for the woman's quarters, and the last serf had dawdled away about his daily chores, Oric's patience was all but spent.

"Come, Master Ichtheus, let us be gone before anyone reappears." Oric slid back the flagstone that hid the tunnel entrance. "Now, pass me the shovel, ropes, and lanterns that I brought from the tool shed." Secretly hoping the tunnel might contain information pertaining to Deveril's mysterious key, Oric was keen to get started.

Dian peered at the top of Oric's head as he hurried down the dark flight of stairs. "Wait for me! Master Ichtheus is not well, I shall take his place. He can stand guard in the warm kitchen instead of Sir Oswold."

"You will do no such thing!" Oric exclaimed, afraid for Dian's safety. But his protests fell on deaf ears for she followed him anyway.

With excitement squeezing her stomach into a tight knot, Dian climbed down the stars with a lantern in her hand.

"If you encounter the least hint of danger, turn back immediately," Ichtheus warned. He held on to Parzifal and squinted down the stairwell until the lanterns' glow disappeared. Replacing the slab over the hole, he settled down beside the dog to wait.

-oOo-

Oric paused where the small tunnel branched off to the well. He had given some thought to its situation and he believed the well was too near the manor to be of use as an escape route. He surmised that the well shaft had probably been used to remove earth dug from the larger tunnel.

Catching up, Dian gave Oric a shove. "Go on! Keep moving, I am dying of curiosity."

Cocooned in his own small bubble of light, Oric lost touch with reality. He trudged on into the darkness, and was thankful when nothing remarkable happened. Dian followed at slower pace, hampered by her overlarge boots and the rough going.

The tunnel sloped gradually downward and, rounding a slight curve, Oric experienced bitter disappointment when he came upon a dead end. "The passage cannot stop in the middle of nowhere," he stated. "What would be the point of that?" He shouted to Dian, who had fallen behind again. "I think the roof has fallen in and caused a blockage."

Dian caught up with Oric. "Since we have come this far we should try to find a way through. If more debris tumbles down, we can always go back the way we came."

They worked to clear away the rubble until, without any warning, another section of the roof collapsed. Blinded by dust, Oric and Dian clutched each other nervously. An eerie silence ensued, broken only by small rivulets of earth that trickled down from above their heads.

-oOo-

Inside his cave, Rastus leapt from a bed of dry bracken. Were those voices he had heard? He put his ear to the wall. Now he could hear scraping sounds. A cloud of dust issued from a crack in the roof, filling his eyes with grit. Terrified that someone was about to enter the cave, Rastus abandoned his stash. If he were caught with stolen goods he would be hung, drawn and quartered for sure. He ran outside, mounted his donkey and hastened away as fast as the animal would trot.

-oOo-

Oric held his lantern high. "It seems all the loose stuff has come down," he said. He poked the area with a shovel to make sure, and a shaft of gloomy daylight filtered through a narrow fissure near the roof. Oric began to dig for all he was worth.

"Do be careful," Dian cautioned. "Goodness knows what you might find on the other side."

Oric laboured until he made a hole big enough to wriggle through, and rolled down a bank of shale into a sizeable cave. Sweeping aside a curtain of vines at the cave's entrance, he shaded his eyes against the sun's glare. *What a superb escape route,* he thought. *Whoever dug this tunnel knew what he was doing.*

Dian followed Oric. "Do you know where we are?" she asked.

"If I am not mistaken, that is the start of Scraggswood Forest," Oric replied, pointing to a wood on the other side of a brook.

Dian viewed the broken bushes and fresh tracks outside the cave. "It looks as if someone has been here recently," she said, keeping her voice low.

"A band of pilgrims, most likely," Oric replied, depression

settling upon him like a heavy cloak. The tunnel had failed to reveal a single clue as to the secret of Master Deveril's key. Where next could he look?

"Oric!" Dian's excited voice echoed from within the depths of the cave. "Come back inside."

"I am not entering that tunnel again," Oric stated. "We will return to Bayersby Manor across the fields."

"Never mind the tunnel, look what I have found." Dian indicated a pile of armour, "And, as far as I can make out, there are many more items stashed around the cave."

Oric recognised the scarlet dragons emblazoned upon the breastplate and helmet, and his depression lessened. Master Deveril's key remained a mystery, but they had found Sir Oswold's missing possessions.

Upon her return to Bayersby Manor, Dian received a lambasting that ruined all her feelings of euphoria. "Where have you been, you wretched girl?" Mother Morghan screeched. "I have been seeking you all afternoon." She thrust a bucketful of vegetables into Dian's hands, and threw four brace of rabbits on to the table. "If folks are to eat supper tonight you had best get skinning and chopping." Giving Dian a vicious jab, the housekeeper continued her tirade, "And there is wool to spin, eggs to gather, not to mention all the cooking pots that need scouring. If you skulk off again, I shall report your absence to Lady Myferny."

Dian set about the task of preparing supper. She did not want to lose her position and be forced to return to her parents' cottage. Perhaps, for a little while, she had better not accompany Oric on any jaunts.

Chapter Twenty Two

Council of Law

Dian bid Oric and Ichtheus farewell, wishing she could accompany them to Rookery Farm. She comforted herself with the idea of spying on Mother Morghan. If the woman could be caught out in some wrongdoing, it would be the housekeeper who left the manor, not the kitchen maid.

Gimlet-eyed, Mother Morghan watched over Dian as she scoured out a large iron pot with sand. On her knees and covered in soot, the girl still looked as if goose grease would not melt in her mouth. Mother Morghan longed get rid of the fancy little piece, but the workload her absence would create did not bear thinking about.

-oOo-

Egglebart and Etheldrida had no idea that their home was to be the venue for the new Council of Law. Feeling somewhat embarrassed, Ichtheus arrived at Rookery Farm well before the designated meeting time. The least he could do was to warn his friends of the pending influx of people.

Rookery Farm had been in a state of disrepair and the land neglected when Egglebart purchased the property from Sir Edred a few weeks before he married Etheldrida. Since then the couple had worked wonders. A new thatch roof topped sturdy walls, and a pen for newborn lambs was tacked on the southern side of the house. Several fat cows grazed in a green pasture, an adjoining field was already sown with barley.

At the front of the dwelling, Etheldrida hoed between rows of vegetable seedlings. She gave a cheery wave in response to Ichtheus' shouted greeting, and propped her hoe against the house wall.

"Egglebart is in the bottom paddock, but I am expecting him back at any moment. She pointed to a patch of lush grass. "Tether your donkeys over there, Oric, they can eat their fill." Kicking her muddy boots off at the door, she invited Ichtheus inside. "Would you care to join us for a bite to eat?"

"Dear lady, I have a confession to make," said Ichtheus, looking shamefaced. "After your wedding celebrations several people were invited here to form a Council of Law, and today is the day. I sincerely apologise for any inconvenience this may cause."

Etheldrida raised and dropped her plump hands. "Master Ichtheus, stop your worry, do. I shall be glad of the company."

At Etheldrida's invitation, Ichtheus settled himself in a chair. From his comfortable perch, he viewed Etheldrida's home appreciatively. The walls were freshly limed and the stone floor was scrubbed clean. Two more chairs and a pair of benches stood beside a long timber table, and a pitcher on the tabletop held colourful wild flowers. A well-scoured pot on a trivet over the fire emitted delicious smells, and a freshly baked loaf lay on the hearth to keep warm.

"Ho, my dove, what culinary delights have you concocted for your husband today?" Blinded from the bright sun outside, Egglebart failed to see Ichtheus seated beside the fire. He grabbed his chortling lady around her ample waist and twirled her around the room.

"For goodness sake, Egglebart," Etheldrida admonished breathlessly, "We have a visitor. What must he be thinking?"

"I am thinking what a lucky man is Egglebart," said Ichtheus with a chuckle.

Etheldrida struggled with suppressed laughter, patted her hair into shape, and smacked her apron straight. "Make yourself useful, husband! Go tell Oric that food is on the table."

-oOo-

On the journey to Rookery Farm, Ichtheus had suggested that Oric tell Egglebart and Etheldrida about Deveril's key. Convinced that the couple was trustworthy, he was keen to have another opinion on the subject, and he stared pointedly at Oric. "Methinks 'tis time to share your secret, lad."

Oric mopped up the remainder of his broth with a chunk of bread and, swallowing his last mouthful, confronted his friends. "Before Master Ichtheus appointed me as his apprentice, I was employed as serf at Dunburton Manor. I narrowly escaped a dawn raid and returned to find the house on fire. Master Deveril, the alchemist, lay on the floor in the great hall. I rushed to his aid, but I could do nothing for him. Moments before he drew his last breath he pressed a key into my hand, promising that it would unlock the secret to great wealth. He also warned that untold disasters might occur if the key were to fall into evil hands."

"Good gracious!" Egglebart exclaimed. "What kind of

disasters? And where is the wealth you speak of?"

"I asked the same questions." Oric gulped unhappily. "But Master Deveril died before he was able to tell me. I have no idea what the key might open. The only clue I have is the double knot engraved on the key's shaft."

"'Tis my guess the symbol has something to do with a family crest." Egglebart suggested. "Rest assured, lad, now that we know of your dilemma we shall leave no stone unturned in our efforts to unravel Master Deveril's mystery."

Further discussion was prevented by the arrival of Sir Oswold and Mistress Malla. Battling his emotions, Oric excused himself and went to tether their horses.

Uther Tidwall, next to arrive, doffed his cap as Etheldrida welcomed him.

Tewdric Bascoomb was not quite so welcome when the group saw that his wife accompanied him. Tewdric had not wanted to bring Helled, but she had browbeaten him into submission. Better in health than temper, she barely nodded as she planted her skinny behind on the end of the bench.

Horses tethered and his emotions under control, Oric returned to Etheldrida's noisy kitchen.

"Order! Order!" Ichtheus yelled, banging a dagger handle upon the table top. A hush descended as eight pairs of eyes regarded Ichtheus expectantly.

"I have called this meeting to discuss the formation of a Council of Law. Our objective is to stop the appalling upsurge of crime in the district. Although we believe Figg is involved with most of the robberies, we have no proof of his misdeeds. If anyone has any suggestions as to how we can trap him, please speak up."

"If you ask me, 'tis nothing to do with us," Helled stated peevishly. "I fail to understand why my husband is involved with this ill-assorted group of blundering windbags."

Horribly embarrassed, Tewdric retorted. "Well, no one is asking you! If you have nothing more sensible to say, kindly remain silent."

"I will speak the truth since no other fool is game." Helled encompassed everyone with a sweep of her arm. "The likes of you will be lambs to the slaughter and I want nothing to do with your ridiculous Council of Law." Her eyes glittered like shards of polished jet as she jerked her head at Tewdric. "If he knows what's good for him, he will follow my example."

"Yon shrew needs bridling," Uther remarked laconically.

Stung into action, Helled leapt to her feet. Egglebart, sitting on the other end of the bench, was tipped to the floor.

Etheldrida rushed to her husband's assistance, "You horrible little creature," she shrilled at Helled. "What in heaven's name has made you so sour?"

Ichtheus put his head in his hands. Helled Bascoomb had created mayhem yet again.

Gratified by the discord she had caused, Helled wandered over to the hearth and began to trace patterns in the ashes with her booted toe.

Ichtheus drew in a steadying breath and looked pleadingly at Sir Oswold. "I would be honoured to hear your opinion, my friend."

"Firstly I wish to propose a vote of thanks to Ichtheus and Oric for recovering my armour. As a result of their diligence, several other folk have also been reunited with their missing possessions." A crafty look replaced Sir Oswold's smile. "The villains who stole the goods in the first place will be keen to recoup their losses. We need bait to draw them out. Next market day I propose that someone brags about the valuables he is carrying." Sir Oswold tapped his nose knowingly. "Such talk will attract any rogues that may be in the vicinity. When our victim leaves the market to travel home, the robbers will surely follow."

Ichtheus immediately volunteered.

"Well done, my friend!" Sir Oswold boomed. "Now let us refine the details."

Oric wondered if he had heard right. "You do realise that you may be putting your life at stake, Master Ichtheus?"

Ichtheus nodded.

"If you insist upon this folly, I shall accompany you," said Oric.

"You have nothing to fear, dear boy," Sir Oswold reassured. "Egglebart and I will follow you at a safe distance. When the felons strike, we shall break cover and arrest them."

"I reckon Oric should hide in the cart for the duration of the market," said Uther, gazing over his steepled fingers. "You never know what he might overhear if he lies low." Ignoring Helled's expression of ridicule, he challenged Tewdric. "You and I should keep a weather eye open throughout the day for anyone behaving suspiciously."

The motions were put to the vote and each Council member, bar Helled, said aye. They congratulated themselves on the success of the meeting, and Ichtheus promised to approach Sir Edred for his support; however, Ichtheus did not have to wait to approach the Lord of Bayersby.

A commotion outside heralded the arrival of Sir Edred accompanied by two of his knights. Rumours about a Council of War had brought the lord from his manor to take charge of the action. "Hah! 'Tis a fine state of affairs when any humble citizen thinks he can organise a skirmish," he bellowed, swinging down from his charger. "What sort of place is this to host a Council of War?"

Ichtheus cringed as he listened to Sir Edred's bluster. The lord had many virtues, but sensitivity was not one of them.

Egglebart stepped forward and bowed low. "Pray come inside, my lord, and partake of some refreshment."

Slightly less aggrieved, Sir Edred entered through the low doorway into Egglebart's home and seated himself before the fire. Etheldrida offered a pot of ale, which he graciously accepted.

More ale, plus a good deal of subtle flattery convinced Sir Edred that no one threatened his authority. Persuaded that the Council was to be one of law, not war, he agreed to sit in judgement upon any miscreant the Council members managed to apprehend. With a brusque word of thanks for his host's hospitality he strode from the house, mounted his horse and led his knights out of Etheldrida's garden.

"Thank goodness we have acquired Sir Edred's blessing," said Ichtheus, greatly relieved that he had been spared the task of approaching the volatile lord by himself. "Now we can go straight ahead with our plans. If we stick together, I am convinced that we shall be successful in our endeavours."

Helled threw her cloak over her shoulders. "If this ridiculous farce costs money, Tewdric Bascoomb, I shall take it out on your hide. Now let us away home to our girls, for I have little faith in the childcare abilities of the new maid you employed.

"Wait, my turtle dove!" Tewdric called. "Surely we can come to some agreeable compromise." Ducking his head in farewell, he scuttled after his wife.

"Go untether our donkeys, Oric," said Ichtheus, feeling utterly exhausted. "We have caused our good friends sufficient upset for one day."

Etheldrida chuckled good-naturedly, "Nay, Master Ichtheus, think nothing of it. When I left my bed this morning, I had no inkling of the interesting day that lay ahead. Now, away with you before it gets too dark to see your way home."

Chapter Twenty Three

Sir Oswold's Plan in Action

Ichtheus usually looked forward to Kilterton market, but on this occasion he felt dismally apprehensive. Not so much concerned for his own safety, he agonised over the well-being of his friends. How could he ever forgive himself if anything untoward happened to any of them? Worried sick, he wished he had not agreed to Sir Oswold's dangerous scheme.

The one-armed knight strolled into the compound to see Oric and Ichtheus off. "Have no fear, my friends, Egglebart and I will watch over your return from the market this evening." Sir Oswold grinned wickedly. "You may not be aware of our presence, but rest assured we shall be there." He harrumphed enthusiastically, "Mark my words; we shall see heads on spikes before the month is out."

At the compound gate, Dian thrust a parcel into Oric's hands. "I made up a batch of your favourite honey cakes to eat along the way." She regarded him from eyes the size of small platters. "You will be extra careful, will you not?" She attempted to laugh off her anxiety. "It seems I am always telling you to take care these days. I will be glad when all the villains are captured."

Heavy overnight rain had turned the moorland pathway into a river of mud, and Braccus struggled to pull the cart. To lighten the donkey's load, Oric and Ichtheus climbed down and walked alongside. Slate-coloured clouds boiled up over the horizon and thunder rumbled in the distance.

Ichtheus glowered at the threatening sky. "Huh! A storm is all we need."

The words had barely left his mouth when the cart lurched sideways and Ichtheus fell headlong into a ditch along with several packages. A wheel rolled past and came to rest a little further down the track. Parzifal chased after it, and stood guard.

"Oh dear, oh dear, 'tis a bad omen" Ichtheus muttered as Oric helped him back on to the path. "If we had any sense at all, we would turn around and go back home."

"Aye maybe so, Master Ichtheus, but we both know you are made of sterner stuff."

They barely had time to re-affix the wheel and retrieve the spilled merchandise before a cloudburst sent them scrambling for shelter beneath the cart. Terrified of thunder, Parzifal forced his way between the two people he loved best. He pushed his head under Oric's arm and lay in a dither for the duration of the storm. Poor Braccus laid back his ears and braved the downpour.

The storm soon passed, and warm rays of sunshine teased wisps of vapour from the wet ground. Thankful to see clear weather ahead, Oric and Ichtheus continued with their journey. They stopped a short distance from Kilterton to allow Oric to climb into the back of the cart.

Ichtheus covered his apprentice with sacks. "Keep your wits about you, boy. Do not fall asleep, for my life may depend upon your ability to remain alert."

"Aye, Master." Oric's voice was muffled. "I will try."

Nervousness made Ichtheus irritable. "No use just trying boy! For pities sake, *succeed*!"

It seemed that every man and his dog had turned out to swell the market crowd. Kilterton high street throbbed with life. Travellers Ichtheus had never seen before set up stalls of exotic merchandise in every spare nook and cranny. Charlatans, he surmised, hoping to bleed money from innocent country folk. Farmers brought livestock for barter, and piles of steaming dung added a pungent odour to the smell of wet fish, ripe cheeses and unwashed bodies. Further down the street, a blacksmith displayed honed axes alongside hand-tooled farm implements. His buxom wife parried customers' saucy remarks and, with her shiny, apple-red cheeks, she looked as polished as one of her man's newly-forged tools.

Arriving at his usual site in front of Tewdric's shop, Ichtheus struggled to unload his merchandise.

"Have a care for your back, Master Ichtheus," Oric tittered from beneath his nest of sacks. "It would be a crying shame if you caused yourself an injury."

"Be silent, you insolent boy, or you will ruin our plans," Ichtheus hissed. Muttering unintelligibly, he backed the cart out of the way and tethered Braccus to a tree.

Around mid-morning, Tewdric put the first stage of the Council of Law's plan into action. He shouted at Ichtheus as if he were stone deaf, "How goes trade with you today, Master Apothecary?"

Ichtheus loudly proclaimed that he was doing very well. "In fact, my dear Tewdric," he crowed, "I have not enjoyed such excellent takings for many a long month and we are not yet halfway through the day." Ichtheus was not exaggerating. For once he had received a steady flow of coinage instead of the many cumbersome exchanges he was often obliged to drag home.

"I, too, am having a most rewarding day." Tewdric tilted back his cap and scratched his bald pate. "In fact, this is the busiest market I have seen in many a long moon. The extra takings should certainly put a smile on my Helled's face."

Ichtheus doubted it. He glanced around nervously, "Be careful what you say, Tewdric. We know not who might be listening and you have no protection for your journey home."

Esica Figg was also doing a roaring trade. Quantities of currency changed hands, always in the moneylender's favour.

To Ichtheus' dismay, Figg left an underling in charge of his stand and sauntered across the square. Such was his presence, people moved aside to allow him free passage.

"Good day to you, apothecary," Figg's thin lips stretched into an unpleasant smile.

"What can I do for you?" Ichtheus growled, noting with distaste Figg's lank hair.

"'Tis not what you can do for me, apothecary." Figg indicated Ichtheus' depleted stock. "'Tis what *I* can to do for *you*." He stared at Ichtheus from opaque, grey eyes. "Perhaps you could use a loan to help increase your stock."

"I do not need your money," Ichtheus snapped, bristling at the condescending cheek of the man. "My medicaments are created from herbs and roots that I gather from the countryside." Suppressing a shudder, he imagined that a forked, viper-like tongue might dart from between Figg's bloodless lips at any moment.

"Please yourself!" Figg shrugged, mildly disappointed. The collection of repayments from the apothecary would have provided a legitimate reason to visit Bayersby Manor on a regular basis. Never mind, there were always Mother Morghan's reports to fall back on. And, if everything went according to plan, his dream would soon become Sir Edred's nightmare. Smiling a secret smile, Figg wandered off to watch the butcher sell his meat as fast as he could cut it up.

The day grew warmer. Lying under his layer of sacks, Oric fought a losing battle with sleep. Giggles from behind the cart suddenly jarred him awake. He peeped out to see a buxom woman plant a kiss upon a young squire's lips. A coin changed hands and the couple parted company. Moments later, the same woman returned with a different fellow. She delivered another kiss and palmed a second coin. Several more visitations occurred, and Oric surmised that the woman had devised this scheme as a way of boosting her income.

At midday the inn swiftly filled with hungry folk. Tewdric left his wife and daughters to mind the shop, and joined a queue for food. He bought two pigeon pies and sneaked one to Oric. Sighing contentedly, Tewdric sat on the ground with his back against the cart's wheel. About to take his first bite, the pie was kicked from his grasp.

Arms akimbo, Helled glared down at her husband. "So this is where you are, you sneaky weasel! I suspected you were up to no good."

Tewdric scrambled to his feet, looking puzzled. "Whatever do you mean my turtle dove?"

"I have been watching the disgraceful comings and goings behind this cart all morning." Helled continued with her tirade. "I take my eyes off you for one moment and where do you slope off to?" She whirled around as if looking for some other person. "To this den of iniquity, that is where! She fetched her husband two hefty swipes and screeched into his ringing ears, "Is the blacksmith's wife so short of funds that she has to sell her kisses to other folks' husbands?"

Perplexed, Tewdric stared as his wife's retreating back. What was the woman raving about? He had simply brought food for Oric and sat down to enjoy his own pie.

Helled brought Lunette and Novena from the shop and hustled them on to their father's cart. "You had best get back to work," she yelled at Tewdric. "We are returning to Diggitdow Farm! You can make your own way home when the day's trading is done."

Buried under his pile of sacks, Oric listened to the furore. He peered out of a narrow gap between the planks in the cart's side, and watched as Ned and Joe approached.

"That swine's nowt but a money-grubbing bloodsucker."

Oric recognised Joe's voice. He lay still, intrigued to discover who the bloodsucker might be.

"I worked the crowd well this day and the pickings were good," Joe continued. "But Figg said my haul was poor and then he beat me."

Ned snorted. "Aye, he battered me an' all … see!" He pulled up his tunic to display several purple welts across his back. "I am sick of risking my life to fill that villain's coffers and then get nowt but abuse for my trouble."

Joe nodded his agreement. "Yon shyster is so tight he would charge for the stink from his fart."

Grinning at his friend's remark, Ned pulled a small dagger from his belt. "Here is one item I intend to keep for myself." His smile widened, "I lifted this from a fellow so engrossed in arguing over the price of a turnip, he never felt a thing." Ned stroked the blade lovingly. "One of these days I shall plunge this little beauty into the moneylender's ribcage." To illustrate his point, he jabbed the knife down into the cartful of sacks.

The honed blade nicked the end of Oric's nose. Horribly shocked, he sprang up. Bloody, festooned in sacking, and howling like a wounded beast, he presented a fearsome sight. At the same moment Ichtheus approached, with his arms full of fresh produce. In their haste to escape the gory monster, Ned and Joe knocked Ichtheus to the ground. Fruit and vegetables rolled in all directions.

"You skittering rascals," Ichtheus yelled after the two boys. "If I set eyes on you again, I will skin the pair of you." As he scrambled to his feet, his gaze fell upon Oric's bloody face. "Ye gods, what has happened to you?"

Ichtheus staunched Oric's flow of blood. "The wound is superficial. I doubt you will sustain a scar."

Dabbing at his nose with a rag, Oric gathered up the spilled vegetables and loaded them on to the cart along with a few remaining items from his master's stall. He untied Braccus and whistled Parzifal to heel. With his cover blown, he volunteered to drive Ichtheus home.

Tewdric rushed out of his shop to wish them luck. Apart from the fracas with his wife, he admitted to seeing nothing untoward.

Uther, having spent the entire day in his shop taking orders for new boots, had nothing to report either. He raised a hand with crossed fingers as Ichtheus and Oric drove past.

Bit by bit, a crimson sun slipped down the sky. The purple twilight that followed seemed filled with menace. Egglebart and Sir Oswold's invisible presence should have been comforting, but it was not. Oric's skin crawled as he anticipated an axe blow or dagger stab at every heartbeat.

"I overheard an interesting conversation between those two young fellows that knocked you down earlier today," said Oric, trying to shut out his worries.

"Indeed," replied Ichtheus. "Pray enlighten me."

"They said they had been thieving for Esica Figg." Oric looked hopeful. "Could we not report them to Sir Edred and have all three arrested?"

Ichtheus chewed on his lip. "We have no real proof, 'tis only your word against theirs. Sir Edred would never condemn any person on such slender evidence." Aware of his bulging pouch of silver, Ichtheus omitted to put into words the hazards he imagined might lie ahead. His worries were groundless, for they arrived back at Bayersby Manor unscathed.

In a foul humour Sir Oswold followed Oric and Ichtheus into the compound. He crashed down from his charger, and bellowed his displeasure. "What a wasted day! We kept to the edge of the forest, but we saw nothing untoward. Halfway home, I sent Egglebart back to his wife. No point dragging him all this way for no good reason."

Oric, too, felt dejected. The day had, indeed, been a total failure, and he was still far from finding Deveril's treasure.

Chapter Twenty Four

The Robbers Strike

Thanks to Helled's early departure with the horse and cart, Tewdric faced a long trudge to Diggitdow Farm on foot. The day's trading had been exceptional, and he lugged two coin-filled pouches. A hopeful glow warmed his heart. Surely Helled would welcome him home when she saw how well he had done.

-oOo-

Egglebart clopped through Kilterton in the dark. Market stallholders had long since packed up and gone, leaving the main street strewn with litter and dung. Judging by the noise coming from the inn, Egglebart surmised that many of them were squandering their day's takings, making merry. The aroma of food and wood smoke drifted on the still night air, and his mouth watered. Etheldrida would be preparing a tasty supper at Rookery farm, and Egglebart could barely wait to get home.

A cloud swallowed the moon as Egglebart entered the forest south of the village. He travelled cautiously, using instinct rather than sight. *Not far now,* he thought, longing for his cosy farmhouse.

A wolf howled, sounding perilously close. Egglebart's flesh crawled with apprehension and he tightened his grip upon his axe shaft. At the Diggitdow Farm turning, the noise intensified.

"Whoa, old lad," Egglebart gentled his horse's neck. "That cry does not sound like a wolf." He dismounted and led his horse a short way down the track.

The howls ceased.

Something dripped onto Egglebart's neck. Thinking it a roosting bird's dropping, he swiped at the mess with the flat of his hand. A moonbeam escaped from behind the clouds, illuminating a sack that hung from a branch above his head.

The sack wriggled and moaned.

Another sticky glob dripped on to Egglebart's upturned face. He wiped it off and saw that it was blood.

Shinning up the tree, Egglebart wriggled cautiously along the branch that held the sack. He cut the plaited horsehair that suspended the bundle and eased the load to the ground. His heart thudding against his ribcage he jumped down from the tree, and gently peeled back the sacking. Tewdric Bascoomb's battered face stared out.

Egglebart suspected that Tewdric would receive cold comfort from Helled and, in the spur of the moment, he decided to take his friend home to Etheldrida. He hoisted the butcher onto his horse and held him tight to keep him from falling. By the time Rookery Farm loomed out of the dark, the injured man was unconscious. "Etheldrida!" Egglebart roared. "Come quickly, I need your help."

Etheldrida's bulky form appeared in the doorway, outlined by a welcoming glow from the fire. "Whatever is wrong? Are you hurt?"

"No, no, I am fine!"

"The Lord be praised," Etheldrida cried. "You were gone so long I feared something had happened to you." She hurried toward him, her arms flung wide in welcome. She dropped them to her sides when she saw the still form clasped to her husband's chest. "Oh, my sweet heaven!" she gasped. "What do you have there?"

"'Tis Tewdric Bascoomb," Egglebart replied. "And he is in a bad way."

"Whatever has befallen the poor little man?" Etheldrida asked, as she helped to carry Tewdric indoors.

"I don't know," Egglebart replied.

They lowered the butcher onto their feather bed and Etheldrida fetched a bowl of warm water. Whilst she gently bathed Tewdric's face, Egglebart explained what had happened.

"How could anyone be so cruel?" Etheldrida demanded angrily. "The poor fellow is almost dead."

Tewdric moaned and prised open his swollen eyelids.

"Hush now, rest yourself," Etheldrida soothed. "You are safe with Egglebart and me." She raised Tewdric's head and held a horn of water to his lips. He swallowed a few drops and managed a pathetic smile.

"Thank God you happened along when you did, Egglebart" he croaked, "Or I would have surely died."

Egglebart knelt beside the bed. "Can you remember what happened?"

"Only that I was walking home with the day's takings." Tewdric sipped more water. "Helled took our daughters home early with the horse and cart." He sighed, "She can be difficult, can my Helled." After a moment's rest he carried on. "I was almost home when robbers set about me with a cudgel. They laughed like they were enjoying themselves." A ragged sob escaped him. "I suppose all my money is gone."

Egglebart nodded sadly. "Aye my friend, I am afraid it is."

"What am I to tell my Helled?" Tewdric struggled to sit up. "She will be furious with me."

Egglebart and Etheldrida exchanged telling glances. They persuaded Tewdric to lie back down, and he quickly lapsed into a deep sleep.

"After supper, I will ride over to Diggitdow Farm." Egglebart spoke between mouthfuls of spit-roasted chicken. "Helled must be told what has happened."

"You will do no such thing," Etheldrida admonished. "That madam could not care less about her poor husband. All she will worry about is the missing money." She picked a strand of chicken skin from between her teeth. "Let the vixen stew until daylight."

"I suppose you are right, my love." Egglebart suddenly felt bone weary. The day had ended badly, and he blamed himself for not being there when Tewdric needed him.

-oOo-

Rastus trailed back to Kilterton, clutching Tewdric's two bags of silver. If he were not so afraid of Figg, he would run away. But his life would never be safe if he did. A vindictive man, Figg always pursued and killed those who crossed him.

Rastus regretted his swift departure from the cave. Perhaps if he had waited, he might have rescued his stash. A wave of bitterness engulfed him. As a result of his cowardice he was a pauper again and, for the foreseeable future, he would have to share accommodation in St Griswald's crypt with his mother, Ned, Joe, and any other unsavoury rogue that Figg chose to thrust upon him. For two sticks he could burst into tears. Resigned to his fate, Rastus entered Figg's shop to relate of his encounter with the butcher. Finished his tale, he dropped Tewdric's pouches of silver on the moneylenders counter.

Figg dismissed his henchman without a word of thanks. In the gloomy depths of his shop, he trickled the butcher's silver coins through his fingers. Rastus had done well. Figg sniggered as he visualised Tewdric Bascoomb dangling upside down from a tree branch. *Serve the pompous little butcher right,* he thought.

Figg's delight was marred by the arrival of his two chief warriors. They reported that the army was building well at Scutterskiff Keep, but they were far from happy about the calibre of volunteers.

Figg failed to understand Rafe and Cadoc's worries. "So what if the soldiers lack quality?" he snapped. "Quantity is all that I require to win my battle for Bayersby Manor."

Chapter Twenty Five

Fishing Expedition

Ichtheus awoke before dawn and clambered out of his truckle bed. Rubbing his aching knees, he made a mental note to gather some monkshood. The plant was poisonous, but the juice rubbed into his sore joints might ease his pain.

On the other side of the inglenook fireplace, Oric sprawled and snored.

"Stir yourself, lad." Ichtheus dug his apprentice in the ribs with his toe. "We have a busy day ahead of us."

"Master! 'Tis not light, yet." Oric yawned and knuckled his eyes, "Are we seeking rogues again today?"

"Indeed we are not! Yesterday was a complete waste of time. Before we embark upon any further investigations, the council needs to devise a better plan." Ichtheus smoothed pork dripping onto a chunk of coarse bread. "Today, my boy, we are heading for Dunburton, and we shall be away from Bayersby manor for a few days."

Memories of his unhappy childhood and the untimely death of Master Deveril flashed before Oric's eyes. "Must we go there?"

Ichtheus noted Oric's agitation, "I understand that it may be difficult for you to return to Dunburton, but there is no longer anything to be afraid of."

"Aye, so you say." Oric was not convinced. Village folk that survived the raid had moved on, and Oric had heard that itinerants often made use of the vacant cottages. "Mark my words," he grumbled, "Dunburton has become a dangerous place."

"Nay, Oric, you worry too much." Ichtheus smiled encouragingly, "We are going to the Meeting of the Waters and shall bypass the village.

Once a year, hundreds of salmon leaped upriver to spawn. Ichtheus liked to hook a few fish to eat straight away, but the bulk of his catch he dried for consumption during the winter months when fresh food was scarce. Recently, one of Sir Edred's villeins had taught him how to tickle trout, and Ichtheus was keen to put his new skill into practice. "Bring a spear along, Oric. You can improve your own fishing skills." Hoping to cheer the lad up, Ichtheus suggested that Dian might like to join them. "Mother Morghan will grumble; nevertheless, I shall convince her that we need the kitchen maid to gut our catch."

Excited by her forthcoming outing, Dian followed Oric into the stables. Otty, the female donkey, shifted uneasily and made little snickering noises. "See how her belly bulges?" Dian fondled the animal's soft nose. "I suspect she may soon drop her foal."

Oric gave the little jenny an encouraging pat. "Aye, by my reckoning, she is about due." Feeling better, he entered the neighbouring stall and led Braccus out into the pink dawn of a new day.

Outside the compound, bloom-laden hawthorn bushes hosted several pink chaffinches. The rosy little birds fluttered amongst the sweet-smelling flowers in search of insects, and the paean call of a lone cuckoo echoed from the valley below. Oric grinned at Dian. It was a good-to-be-alive sort of day.

Ichtheus battled through the kitchen's outer door, clutching an untidy jumble of fishing equipment. Suspecting that some new adventure was afoot, Parzifal capered around the old man's legs, exacerbating his irritation.

"You seem to be in a right pickle, Master Ichtheus," Oric laughed. "If I may say so, you should have attended to those lines before you put them away."

"No, you may not say so." Ichtheus hurled knotted twine and several rusty hooks on to the back of his cart. "Since you are so clever, you may untangle the mess as we drive along." He snorted with disgust, "'Tis the last time I lend my property to Master Guwain if this is the state in which he returns it."

Oric lifted Dian onto the seat beside his master and retreated to the back of the cart. He made a place for himself amongst the provisions and bedrolls, and began to untangle the mess of fishing lines. Ichtheus slapped the reins against Braccus' rump and they were off.

-oOo-

Egglebart left Rookery Farm before dawn. On his way to Bayersby Manor to enlist Ichtheus' help for Tewdric, he turned into the track that led to Diggitdow Farm. After all, he reasoned, it was only fair to let Helled know what had happened to her husband.

At the sound of Egglebart's arrival, Helled hastened into the yard. "If you have come to make excuses for my husband, save your breath," she screamed. "My only concern is for our day's takings."

Egglebart dismounted. "Listen to me, Helled! Tewdric narrowly escaped death last night…"

"Narrowly escaped death?" Helled beetled her dark brows together, "Hah, what sort of fool do you take me for? We both know that Tewdric spent the night carousing around town. No doubt he used our takings to buy ale for his cronies, including yon blacksmith's hussy." She jabbed Egglebart's arm with a sharp fingernail, "Let me tell you, when the rat does return home, he *will* narrowly escape death." Without further ado, she stalked into the farmhouse and slammed the door.

The unpleasant confrontation with Helled remained in Egglebart's mind, and he wished he had not wasted his time. Worried about Tewdric, he rode hard. He arrived in the Bayersby Manor compound dishevelled and sweaty. Serfs stared, round-eyed, as the wild apparition leaped down from his horse.

"Ichtheus!" Egglebart hollered, "Where are you, man?"

Mother Morghan lurched upright in her chair. "Lawks, man, you gave me a fright! The apothecary ain't here. He and his half-wit apprentice left the manor at dawn."

Sir Oswold strode into the room, clad only in his nightshirt. "Good morning, Egglebart. What brings you this far from home so early in the day?"

Egglebart described the night's occurrence and explained his need to enlist the apothecary's assistance for Tewdric.

"Ichtheus has taken Oric and Dian to the Meeting of the Waters on a fishing expedition. However, Mistress Malla is well versed in the application of medicinal herbs. I am sure she will administer to Tewdric's wounds." Sir Oswold strode towards the kitchen door, "Give me a moment to dress and I shall accompany you to Kilterton."

Egglebart paced the compound whilst he waited for Sir Oswold. What on earth was Ichtheus thinking of? The Meeting of the Waters lay perilously close to Dunburton. Perhaps the old man was unaware that dangerous itinerants had taken up residence in the derelict village.

Chapter Twenty Six

Close Encounter

The journey to the Meeting of the Waters took Ichtheus, Oric and Dian past St Griswald's Church. Bathed in bright sunshine, the old building seemed less sinister, and Oric convinced himself that the ghostly apparitions he had seen before Yuletide were naught but tricks of the moonlight.

They journeyed on without incident, and spent a pleasant night in a forest glade. The following day they came to the section of Roxdale Beck that flowed past Dunburton. "Just look at the place! The marauder's left the place almost uninhabitable." Oric exclaimed. "I heard the village had deteriorated, though I never imagined it would be so bad.

"It is certainly dilapidated," Ichtheus agreed. "What a dreadful pity."

"Let us be on our way," Dian begged. "The place looks scary."

Past the northern tip of the village, Roxdale Beck and Nidderdale Brook merged to become the Roxnid River. White water rushed in joyous tumult over time-smoothed boulders, and pink salmon glistened as they leaped in their annual migration upstream.

Oric had not used a spear for some time, and he could not wait to start. He jabbed the weapon into the water several times before he managed to impale a fish. Not a dog to miss out on any action, Parzifal hurled himself into the water, yapping and snapping at fish as they flew past his nose.

With supper caught, Oric and Ichtheus set up camp; Dian made a fire and cooked Oric's fish. Their bellies full, they bedded down for the night.

Next morning Dian set out oatcakes and apples. After a hearty breakfast, Oric returned to the river. He soon improved his technique and caught another fish. Two more followed in swift succession. "Quick, Dian," he yelled. "Drag them up the bank before they wriggle back into the water." Parzifal proved no help at all. He dashed about between the stranded fish, repeatedly tossing one of them into the air.

Dian pushed Parzifal out of the way, and grabbed the salmon. She honed her knife on a flat stone, tested the blade's cutting edge with her thumb, and gutted Oric's catch.

Ichtheus left the trio to their noisy pursuits, and retraced his steps to where the beck curved peacefully around Dunburton. The current's flow had eroded away the bank, creating a perfect pool. Gossamer-winged dragonflies flitted across the water's surface and an iridescent kingfisher eyed them hungrily from his perch on a branch. Bathed with a sensation of utter peace, Ichtheus lay down upon an overhanging ledge. Keen to tickle a trout, he rolled up his sleeves and submerged his bare arms in the chilly water. With luck a trout would investigate his dangling fingers before the cold numbed all sensation.

-oOo-

Esica Figg would rather not have returned to Dunburton, nevertheless, his visit was a necessary evil. Situated halfway between Scutterskiff Keep and Bayersby Manor, the deserted settlement offered an ideal pre-battle mustering point for his mercenary army.

Many moons had passed since Figg's narrow escape from a dawn raid upon Dunburton Manor. Had he not taken refuge behind a wall tapestry on that fateful morning, he would have met his maker along with everyone else. Despite the passage of time, the memory remained unnervingly fresh in his mind.

Figg took a steadying breath, and entered the burned-out hulk of Dunburton manor. Always on the lookout for anything worth stealing, he inspected a row of alcoves. The sleeping platform inside one of them seemed higher than the rest. His curiosity aroused, Figg swept away piles of charred debris to discover a door set horizontally into the top of the stonework.

The door was locked.

Figg recalled the Dunburton alchemist's last words about a key that was supposed to unlock the secret to great wealth. Greedy for more riches, he conveniently forgot that danger might be involved.

Breathing deeply in an effort to curb his excitement, Figg wondered if the wealth Deveril had mentioned lay beneath the door. If so, he needed no key. He removed his dagger from its sheath and set about picking the lock. The sturdy mechanism refused to budge. Time was running out; his henchmen would arrive at any moment and Figg did not intend to reveal his discovery to any of them.

In desperation, Figg abandoned his dagger. He ran outside to where he had left the cart and seized an axe. Back in the manor, he hacked at the door. Sweat stung his eyes, but he kept up the onslaught. At last the hinges broke and he dragged the door open. A large iron chest, emblazoned with a double-knot emblem, lay in the cavity beneath the platform.

Figg used all his strength to drag the heavy container from its hiding place. It landed on the floor with a resounding crash. A padlock the size of Figg's fist secured the chest lid. Spewing expletives, he ran to the manor door to make sure there was no sign of his men. Nothing stirred, so he applied his axe once again.

The padlock snapped, and Figg eased open the lid.

Small nuggets of gold gleamed in a shaft of sunlight. Jewel-encrusted coronets, brooches, torques and two silver candelabra were protected by layers of musty clothes. At the bottom of the chest lay several waterproof pouches. Figg removed one of them and tipped out the contents. His imagination took flight as fine black powder trickled through his fingers. It stank, and Figg turned his head away. If the chest had belonged to the alchemist, perhaps the substance might be the raw material for making gold. A crumpled parchment beneath the pouches increased Figg's excitement, but his euphoria was short-lived. He suspected that the words were Latin, a language he had not learned. Convinced that he had found the instructions for making gold, he rolled up the parchment and tucked it inside his tunic. Perhaps he could obtain a translation without arousing curiosity, but he knew no one to ask.

Discarding the empty chest, Figg stuffed the treasures into sacks and secured them to his cart. He tied the pouches of black powder to a belt, which he fastened around his waist beneath his tunic. Until he ascertained exactly what the substance was, he had no intention of letting the pouches out of his sight.

-oOo-

Ichtheus' peace was shattered by several loud clangs, and he scrambled to his feet. The ledge overhanging the river fell away and, too late to save himself, Ichtheus plunged head over heels into the water. Coughing and spluttering, he fought his way back to the surface. As he dragged silver tendrils of hair from his eyes, he heard shouts and clopping hooves. He peered over the bank to see who had arrived in Dunburton, and his cry for help died on his lips. Sliding back into the beck, he dragged himself hand over hand through the reeds. In a wooded downstream area he crawled on to the bank. His mind in turmoil, he squelched back to the Meeting of the Waters as fast as his sodden clothes would allow.

Oric waded out of the River Roxnid shallows, thinking his catch sufficient for the time being. Unaware of the drama that was about to unfold, he complimented Dian on her expertly gutted fish.

"Oh dear, oh Lord!" Ichtheus puffed. "I have had a terrible fright."

Oric ran to his master's aid. "Calm yourself before you take a turn." He gently pushed the old man down on to a large rock. "Sit awhile and catch your breath. What happened? Did you tumble into the river?"

"I certainly did!" Ichtheus' face was the colour of old parchment. "I nearly froze to death, but the river gave sufficient cover for me to escape."

"Escape? Escape from what?" Dian asked.

"I heard loud clangs followed by hoof beats and shouts from the village. I hauled myself up the bank to take a look." Ichtheus sucked in his breath, "To think, I almost cried out for help. Hah! You can imagine the sort of assistance I would have received."

Impatience overtook Oric's concern. "What are you talking about, Master Ichtheus?"

"If you will cease interrupting me, boy, I will tell you." Ichtheus closed his eyes and summoned up a mental image. "Two men built like oxen, warlords I suspect, rode into Dunburton." Ichtheus blew out his cheeks, "Foof! I should not like to fall foul of those battle-scarred fellows. And who do you suppose accompanied them?"

"For pity's sake, tell me," Oric snapped, his patience spent.

"The Horzefells, mother and son," Ichtheus rolled his eyes toward the heavens. "Another male person sat beside them and a fifth man, who looked uncannily like Hersica, rode beside the cart on a horse."

Oric's eyebrows disappeared up under his fringe. "With respect, Sir, I did mention that itinerants had taken over the village. Without doubt the Horzefells have moved into Dunburton, and I will bet my boots they are already involved in more law-breaking."

"Yes, yes! I take your point." Ichtheus snapped. "Now, cease wasting time and load the salmon into the cart." He changed into dry clothes, wrung out his bonnet and rammed it back on to his head. "Do you realise, Oric, this is the first time I have set eyes upon the Horzefells since they attempted to end my life? They must be captured as soon as possible, and I shall not rest until justice is done. Since no-one expects us back at Bayersby Manor for a few days, we shall travel to Rookery Farm and inform Egglebart of my discovery."

Oric tied Parzifal to the cart and assisted his master aboard. Dian climbed onto the driving bench. Oric jumped up beside her and, seeing that his master was in no fit state to drive, he seized the reins.

"Avoid confrontation by keeping to the woods," Ichtheus mumbled through his chattering teeth. "Then take the moorland track past Rigg Farm. Perhaps we can recruit Nathaniel. The more folk we can muster to our cause the better. When we reach Kilterton, we shall collect Uther," Ichtheus continued, thinking aloud. "We must get as many council members together as we can."

They travelled for the rest of the day, stopping only for a few hours to rest. Fed and watered, Braccus soldiered on until he brought his passengers safely to Rigg Farm.

Oric expected Nathaniel to be out tending his flock, and he was relieved to find the shepherd at work in the home paddock.

"Good day to you." Nathaniel beamed his delight. He flared his nostrils and snorted noisily. "See how well I breathe. I sniffed up juice of beetroot as you suggested, Oric, and have never fared better."

"Never mind that now!" Ichtheus flapped his hands, "We have far more important things to deal with."

Nathaniel listened and promptly asked if he could join the Council of Law. At Ichtheus' nod he put away his tools, and whistled his two dogs to heel.

In Kilterton, they found Uther repairing boots in his shop. Keen to support his friends, the cobbler grabbed a wood-chopping axe, stuffed a dagger into his belt, and shut his up his premises.

"Hold hard!" Egglebart's booming voice reverberated down the street. "Where are you all going in such a hurry?"

"What a stroke of luck!" Ichtheus exclaimed, feeling better by the minute. "We are on our way to Rookery Farm to find you, Egglebart."

"And I have been seeking you, my friend," Egglebart replied. "Sir Oswold has taken Mistress Malla to assist Tewdric in your absence, Ichtheus."

Ichtheus gave Egglebart a wry look, "And what injury

has Helled inflicted upon the poor man, this time?"

"For once, Helled is not to blame." Egglebart related how Tewdric had been trussed in a sack and left to die.

A terrible fury welled within Ichtheus as he visualised the butcher suspended head down from the tree. "That kind of cowardly attack is exactly how the Horzefells operate! I shall not rest until those vile wretches are apprehended." As they rode, Ichtheus told Egglebart how he had almost run into Hersica and Zebediah at Dunburton.

They arrived at Rookery Farm to find Tewdric propped up in bed. Lady Malla had administered to his wounds and, feeling better, he was relating his misadventure to Sir Oswold.

The Council of Law, thankfully minus Helled, faced each other over Etheldrida's kitchen table.

"The Horzefells must be punished!" Uther shook his fist. "If I had my way, I would tear them all limb from limb."

Sir Oswold looked thoughtful. "Suppose the Horzefells are not responsible for Tewdric's misfortune? We cannot ride into Dunburton hacking and chopping until we make sure they truly are the culprits."

"I will eat my bonnet if they are not," Ichtheus promised. "And remember – they did try to kill me a while back."

"We shall allow them to account for themselves," Nathaniel chimed in. "Then we will chop them to bits."

"Two wrongs do not make a right." Ichtheus turned his back to the fire, and hitched up his tunic to let in the heat. "We are obliged to run a fair trial. If the Horzefells are found guilty, it is up to Sir Edred to mete out their punishment."

Oric paid attention to Ichtheus' wise words for, although he was keen to see swift retribution, he had no desire to sink to the level of a common felon by taking the law into his own hands. The council members swiftly came to the same conclusion, and everyone voted to capture the rogues with as little blood-letting as possible.

"Kilterton Inn has a cellar," suggested Dian. "I am sure the innkeeper would lock up the prisoners until a trial can be arranged."

Tewdric swung his legs out of bed and swayed dizzily as he stood up. "If I may borrow a horse, I shall join you in your endeavours."

"Have some sense, man," Egglebart boomed. "In your present state you would be more of a hindrance than a help." He urged Tewdric back to bed. "This is one occasion where you must allow your friends to wreak vengeance in your stead."

"Battles are not won on empty stomachs," Etheldrida announced. "No one shall leave my house hungry." She enlisted Dian's help and the two women bustled around the room, serving everyone with a generous platter of mutton stew.

Mistress Malla remained at Rookery Farm to care for Tewdric, but Etheldrida insisted on accompanying her husband.

"If Etheldrida is going," Dian stated, "so am I."

Oric was horrified. "No! I will not allow it! The situation is far too dangerous."

"And what, may I ask, is it to do with you?" Dian asked, tossing her head.

"Well said, lass!" Etheldrida chuckled and gave Dian a hug. "We shall make it our business to deal with the Horzefell woman." She made neck-wringing motions with her hands. "Yon scrawny piece will be no match for us, eh, Dian?"

Armed with his trusty sword, Egglebart offered farm tools to those Council of Law members that had no weapons. Carrying an assortment of pitchforks, axes knives and daggers, they set off for Dunburton.

Chapter Twenty Seven

Dance with Death

Heavy clouds blew in from the coast, and the Council of Law saw no sunset as thin rain turned into a soaking downpour. Glad to be doing something positive, Ichtheus and his friends ignored their discomfort. At the Diggitdow turning, they branched off the main thoroughfare to take the road through Tewdric Bascoomb's land. They passed by the farmhouse as quietly as possible, nevertheless, the door cracked open. "Clear off!" Helled screamed. "I know not who you are, nor do I care." Fiercely protective of her two daughters, she would set the dogs on any person that endangered the girls' safety.

"What yon harridan lacks in charm she certainly makes up for in volume," Uther muttered, urging his donkey to go faster.

The farmhouse door opened wider to reveal four snarling dogs on chains. "I warn you, I shall let these beasts loose unless you are gone by my count of ten. One! Two! Three!" Helled counted too fast for comfort and it became clear that no-one would escape without a mauling.

"For God's sake, woman," Egglebart yelled. "We are friends, not foes!"

"Oh, 'tis you, is it?" Helled recognised her neighbour's voice and, in the nick of time, she pulled her dogs back inside. "Why are you sneaking across my land?"

Helled listened to Ichtheus' explanation. Not giving a thought for her husband's misfortune, she horrified everyone by announcing that she would accompany the Council of Law to Dunburton. Her motive was not philanthropic. She intended to use Tewdric's unsuspecting friends as bodyguards whilst she searched for her lost takings. She instructed her maid to look after Lunette and Novena, donned an oiled cloak, and stepped out into the rain.

The would-be law keepers travelled on until darkness shadowed the countryside. They set up a make-shift camp for the night, but were back on the road by first light.

Another day almost done, they dismounted and tethered their horses on the outskirts of Dunburton. Mist rose from the river marshes and, grateful for the cover it afforded, Egglebart led his group into the weed-choked village. Deserted by the original inhabitants, most dwellings were in a state of disrepair. However, smoke issued from the roof hole of one larger-than-average building, and a faint glimmer of light showed through the closed shutters.

"Hush!" Egglebart put a finger to his lips. "Our situation will be strengthened if we know exactly what we are up against. Take cover whilst I investigate." Without further ado, he dodged across the open square and disappeared behind the cottage. Moments later, he re-joined his friends.

"A gap in the shutters afforded a clear view inside the cottage," Egglebart reported. "An old crone is preparing supper and five fellows are lolling around a table. I doubt the men will put up much of a fight, for I believe they all have a skin-full of ale. But a sixth man is not drinking." Egglebart paused to gain maximum effect. "And that man is Esica Figg."

Ichtheus clenched his fists in anger. "I knew that oily cretin was involved in evildoing. God willing, we will have him this time."

"I am eager to discover why Figg is associating with known felons," Egglebart grasped Sir Oswold's arm. "Are you ready to smash down the door, my friend?"

Sir Oswold flexed his bicep. "I am ready. Lead me into the fray."

Egglebart beckoned Oric and Nathaniel forward. "There are two shuttered window openings, one at the back of the building and one at the side. At my shout, break the shutters and enter the dwelling from the rear. Ichtheus and Uther, you cover the opening at the side. Make sure no one escapes."

"What are Dian and I supposed to do?" Etheldrida demanded, not wanting to miss out on the action.

"Remain in hiding, my dear." Egglebart instructed his wife. "Break cover only if the Horzefell woman attempts to escape." He stared pointedly at Helled, "If Mistress Horzefell becomes troublesome, I expect you to help Etheldrida and Dian to restrain her." Shifting his attention to the men, he continued gruffly. "Please refrain from any unnecessary heroics. The less blood we spill the better, especially if it is our own."

One powerful blow from Sir Oswold's battle-axe broke down the cottage door. At Egglebart's command, the assembled group leapt into action.

Dian had no intention of missing out and, giving Etheldrida the slip, she sneaked around to the back of the cottage. Oric and Uther were climbing through the window and Dian prepared to follow them.

Inside the dwelling, the astonished villains were caught off-guard. Egglebart swung his broadsword, flat-side down, on Zebediah Horzefell's skull. Rendered semi-conscious, the victim pitched forward onto the table. Another wily fellow used the diversion to grab up a spear. He jabbed it repeatedly at anyone that came near. Uther sneaked up behind the man and pinned down his arms in a bear-hug. Seizing the opportunity, Egglebart trussed up the prisoner with a length of rope. Parzifal, jowls drawn back in a ferocious snarl, stood guard.

Keen to save her own skin, Hersica Horzefell jumped out of the window just as Dian was about to jump in. Dian grabbed Hersica's lank hair and pulled. "Ha! Thought you would escape did you? Well, let me tell you …" Dian got no further.

Used to defending herself, Hersica sank her claws into Dian's arm. With the fingers of her other hand she jabbed at the girl's eyes. Dian snapped her head back, and Hersica seized the chance to run away.

Two battle-scarred individuals took on Oric and Nathaniel. One pulled a dagger from his belt, the other used an axe. Nathaniel's two sheepdogs snapped at the warrior's heels. The men fought on regardless but, full of ale, they flailed their weapons recklessly. Oric blocked several brutal thrusts with a pitchfork shaft then, swiftly turning the implement, he skewered his assailant with the prongs. The man wrenched the tines from his thigh, bellowing like an angry bull.

An axe bit deep into Nathaniel's forearm as he fought desperately to avoid the wild slashings of his foe. Blood spurted forth, but he battled on bravely.

Egglebart pushed the shepherd out of harm's way without taking his eyes off two warriors. "You black-hearted devils!" he bellowed. "Let us see how you measure up against someone your own size." Sir Oswold pitched in, wielding his battle-axe with surprising efficiency.

The four warriors fought as if the devil drove them. The villains' drunken thrusts, born of desperation, were ill-aimed, and Egglebart and Sir Oswold soon cornered their opponents. The younger of the two war dogs threw his weapon to the ground and begged for mercy.

Ichtheus followed Uther in through the side window. Slowed by age, he was unable to prevent Rastus Horzefell from grabbing his arm and twisting it just short of breaking point. "One false move and this old fool dies!" To back his threat, Rastus thrust the point of a dagger against Ichtheus' throat.

"Seems we have reached stalemate," countered Egglebart, placing the tip of his sword beneath the grovelling war dog's chin. "I offer you this worm's life in exchange for the life of the old man."

"Why should I care about him?" Ichtheus' captor hissed. "To save his own skin he would slit my gizzard without a qualm." Forcing Ichtheus through the window, he yelled, "If you want to see this bag-of-bones again, I advise you not to give chase." Holding his dagger steady, Rastus twisted a handful of Ichtheus' hair around his hand and yanked. "Run, you old goat."

Rastus held tight to his hostage until they forded the river and entered the forest. Under cover of the trees, he loosened his grip on Ichtheus so suddenly that the old man stumbled and fell.

"If you imagine that I will spare your life, you are sadly mistaken." Rastus bared his teeth. "Ending your life will prove most rewarding."

His strength sapped, Ichtheus bowed his head and awaited the deathblow. Nothing occurred. He opened his eyes to see that a spear protruded from his aggressor's neck.

Rastus gurgled and clawed frantically at the weapon embedded in his throat. Blood gushed from his mouth, his legs buckled and he dropped like a stone.

Oric crashed through the bushes, "Are you all right, Master Ichtheus?" He helped the old man to his feet. "The light is so poor that I hardly dared to hurl my spear for fear of striking you. When the fellow released you I took my chance." He glanced at the body upon the ground. "Thank God my weapon found its mark."

Ichtheus leaned on his apprentice. "Thank you, Oric. This is the second time you have saved my life; I sincerely hope that the occurrence does not need to become a habit."

Chapter Twenty Eight

The Mysterious Iron Chest

Figg sidled around the edge of the room, keeping well away from flying fists and flailing weapons. If he could keep his wits about him he might just escape. Taking a last look to make sure no-one was watching, he flipped through the window at the rear of the cottage.

The cart, with its precious load, remained outside Dunburton manor where Figg had left it. He leaped aboard, whipped the donkey across Roxdale Beck, and disappeared into the forest.

Hersica Horzefell also made her bid for freedom. In her haste, she ran full tilt into Etheldrida. "Let go of me, you great tub of goose-grease," she shrieked, wriggling ineffectually in Etheldrida's powerful grip.

Etheldrida shoved the woman to the ground and sat on her chest. "Cease squawking, you old boiler!"

To save her friend from a thorough kicking, Dian launched herself on to Hersica's flailing legs.

"Where have you been, you naughty girl?" Etheldrida's sparkling eyes belied her sharp tone, for the Horzefell woman would surely have escaped had Dian not acted so bravely.

Helled emerged from the depths of the cottage empty-handed. Angrily disappointed, she sidestepped the trio of wrestling women.

"Hey! Mistress Bascoomb," Etheldrida yelled. "Where are you going? Come back here and give us a hand with this madam."

Helled reluctantly helped to tie the Horzefell woman to Etheldrida's cart, and then stormed off about her own business.

Sir Oswold rounded up the villains' mounts. The animals would bring a good price at the next Kilterton market. Any funds they raised could be used to compensate the robbers' victims.

Oric and Ichtheus dragged Rastus' body out of the forest. At sight of his dead sibling, Zebediah screamed abuse. Egglebart restrained him and lashed him to the Horzefell cart along with the two defeated warriors.

"Forget any idea of escape," Egglebart pointed to Nathaniel's two sheepdogs and Parzifal. "These beasts are killers. They will savage you at a single command."

"We ain't done no wrong!" Hersica countered, seemingly unaffected by the death of her eldest son. "Yon poxy moneylender is the one you should be after."

Etheldrida gave the leather thong that tied Hersica to the cart a savage yank. "Save your breath for running," she snapped, and encouraged the donkey to trot faster.

Winded and seriously worried, the captured villains fell silent. At best, their punishment would mean the loss of a hand. The worst did not bear thinking about.

Travelling past Dunburton Manor, Oric requested a last look at his old home. "I doubt I shall ever visit here again, but I would like to show Dian where I spent my childhood."

Oric led Dian into the blackened remains of the great hall. "Master Deveril was the only person who showed me any kindness when I was young. He also taught me how to read and write." Oric turned away to hide his tears, and collided with an iron chest. He rubbed his eyes, and ogled the double knot emblazoned upon the chest's lid. The emblem was a larger version of the knots that embellished Deveril's key.

Oric raced for the door. "Master Ichtheus! Come and see what I have found."

Dian stared at the shabby iron chest, wondering why it should cause Oric such agitation.

Cloak flying, Ichtheus flapped into the hall. "What is it that so excites you, boy?" His wound throbbed and he was in no mood for frivolities.

Oric pointed to the knots on the chest. "They are the same as the ones on Deveril's key," he whispered.

Even though the chest was empty, Ichtheus was glad that Oric had found something that might once have belonged to Deveril. "Lift the chest on to the cart, lad. We shall transport it back to Bayersby."

Not only did Oric want the chest for sentimental reasons, he was also intrigued by some black powder that coated the chest's base.

-oOo-

The Council of Law arrived in Kilterton, and manhandled their prisoners into the inn's cellar.

The burly landlord locked the rogues up and secured the key to a belt around his waist. "I will keep the villains incarcerated until justice is done," he promised.

Despite his fatigue, Ichtheus insisted that he search

Figg's moneylending premises. Leaving Dian at the inn, Oric followed his master to make sure that the old man came to no harm.

In a room at the back of Figg's shop, Ichtheus unearthed several items that he believed to be stolen property. Irrefutable proof that Figg was a thief did nothing to lift Ichtheus' sombre mood, for the villain had yet to be apprehended. The moneylender was slipperier than a barrel of eels, and it would be no easy task to catch him.

The Council of Law members pledged to give back all stolen items to the rightful owners and, on a first come, first serve basis, Helled demanded the equivalent of Tewdric's lost takings. She left the inn with a large pouch of silver coins in her hand and a satisfied smirk upon her face.

The group's only injuries were sustained by Nathaniel and Ichtheus. Oric pasted their wounds with balm of primrose leaf from the pot he carried in his pouch. "Your arm will heal in a few days," he assured Nathaniel. "Keep it dry and rested." Turning his attention to Ichtheus, he asked sympathetically, "Is your neck causing you much pain?"

"Aye, lad, it does hurt." Ichtheus sighed and placed his hand on the wound. "But the discomfort is bearable."

Back in his normal environment, Oric was suddenly overwhelmed by the fact that he had killed a man. In a state of shock, he began to babble about a medicinal recipe he had recently concocted. "Just the smell of the mixture is enough to make a patient feel better." He gazed with troubled eyes at his mentor. "I am a healer, not a killer, Master Ichtheus."

Ichtheus understood the boy's torment, and he patted Oric's shaky hands. "Sometimes we have no choice. Sometimes it's kill or be killed, and I am profoundly grateful for what you did."

-oOo-

Figg skulked around St Griswald's crypt, mulling over the disastrous day. The apothecary had bested him again and the knowledge stuck in his craw. Now that he was a marked man, the collection of debts from his legitimate customers would be difficult. Every righteous peasant in the district would be on the lookout for him, but not to repay the money they had borrowed. Figg thanked providence that he had already removed the bulk of his wealth from St Griswald's Churchyard to a safer place.

Across the lake from Scutterskiff Keep, Figg had discovered a shack. Hidden from the water by a copse of trees, the old building made an ideal hideout. He implemented repairs to the building, and made use of rocks from the lake's edge to construct a cavity at the back of the fireplace. To disguise the false wall, he added a cowl that jutted out over the hearth and a chimney above to dispose of the smoke. The cavity now housed most of his wealth.

Fatigue dragged Figg's eyelids down and he stretched out on his bed of hay in St Griswald's dismal crypt. Now he had become a wanted man, the church was a mite too close to Bayersby Manor for his comfort. Within the next few days he planned to take his plunder from the churchyard gravesites, and the contents of the chest he had found at Dunburton Manor, to the shack. However, until he obtained a translation for Deveril's gold-making recipe, Figg resolved to keep the parchment and the black powder hidden under his tunic.

Chapter Twenty Nine

Payback

The news that Figg's three henchmen were incarcerated in Kilterton travelled around the district like wildfire. A belligerent crowd gathered outside the inn and, under pressure, the innkeeper relinquished his key. He stood back as the irate villagers surged down his cellar steps.

Zebediah Horzefell and his two fellow miscreants were shown no mercy, for they had inflicted misery upon almost every family in the district. Kicking and screaming, the scoundrels were dragged into the depths of Kilterton Forest. As the first rays of morning sun kissed the treetops, their life of wrongdoing came to a gruesome end.

Meanwhile, the village women locked Hersica Horzefell into the stock. She sat in a miserable heap with her feet protruding through holes in the cross planks, whilst passers-by hurled rubbish at her. The stock, situated immediately outside Tewdric's shop, was soon piled high with rotting vegetation, and the stinking mess buzzed with flies.

At the end of each day, Tewdric paid a youth to shovel away the debris. In the evening, after the villagers had returned to their homes, he fed Hersica scraps of food and drizzles of water.

"Yon old biddy needs finishing off, not nurturing," Helled snapped when she saw what her husband was doing.

Tewdric had not fully recovered from his beating and he remembered what it was like to stare death in the face. He felt sorry for Hersica and, upon her release from the stock, he took her home to Diggitdow Farm.

Helled was abusive, but Tewdric could, on occasion, be stubborn. "Clean her up and feed her," he said, thrusting the swooning Horzefell woman into the arms of his wife. "She can earn her keep working here at the farm." Without giving Helled chance to say another word, he limped off to attend his livestock.

Food and a few days' rest revived Hersica, and Helled put her to work. Thus the mistress of Diggitdow Farm gained a free slave, but Hersica did not remain cowed for long.

-oOo-

Hersica soon tired of fetching and carrying for her disagreeable mistress. In the quiet of night she arose from her palette of straw in a corner of the Bascoombs' stable, and sneaked across the dark farmyard. Used to the woman's comings and goings, the farm dogs barely raised their heads. A window Hersica had opened earlier in the day remained unlatched and she climbed through.

Snores reverberated from the Bascoombs' bed, and the twins remained fast asleep inside their own curtained alcove.

Helled's chatelaine dangled from a hook in the wall above her head. Hardly daring to breathe, Hersica eased it on to a broom handle. If she dropped the bundle of paraphernalia now, she would be done for.

Tewdric snorted in his sleep and rolled on to Helled.

Hersica froze to the spot.

Without opening her eyes, Helled rammed a sharp elbow into her husband's ribs. "Shift," she mumbled.

Tewdric grunted and moved back to his own side of the bed. Unaware of the intruder, the pair slumbered on.

Hersica crept away from the sleeping place with the chatelaine in her hand, and approached the chest in which Helled kept her valuables. The first two keys Hersica tried failed to open the padlock. A third slid easily into the keyhole and the lock clicked open. Rusty hinges squeaked as she raised the lid.

Dead to the world, the Bascoombs snored on.

Hersica helped herself to a pouch of coins. She deliberated over a suit of chain-mail and a helmet, but decided the items might make too much rattle if she shifted them. Besides, Helled's jewellery and spare kirtle proved far more appealing. Hersica placed her spoils in a cloth bag, and laid the chatelaine with the keys at the bottom of the chest. She closed the lid, and eased the padlock shut. Nervous as she was, she had trouble not laughing. When Tewdric Bascoomb's 'turtle dove' eventually found her missing keys and the loss of her possessions, Helled's fat little husband would likely need the services of a bone setter.

A huge moon hung low in the sky, and Hersica hurried away from Diggitdow Farm as fast as her legs would go. She regretted the loss of her two sons but, often more trouble than they were worth, she was probably well rid of them. Master Figg had promised her the position of housekeeper when he took over Bayersby Manor and, with a team of serfs to do her bidding, a new life of luxury beckoned.

Chapter Thirty

Figg's Fright

A few nights after his escape from Dunburton, Esica Figg braved a clandestine visit to Kilterton to retrieve the last few items of value from his shop. But they had disappeared. *Some thieving piece of filth has stolen them,* he thought. Thankful that he had already removed his most prized possessions, Figg crept away from the village.

Ned and Joe sneaked out of St Griswald's crypt, hoping to avoid a confrontation with their master, but he was already striding through the churchyard gate.

"What time do you call this?" Figg demanded, squinting at the dawn sky. He lashed out with his horsewhip and caught Ned a smarting blow across the shoulders. "It will soon be daylight – get off about your business before I thrash the pair of you."

Ned fingered his dagger. One of these days he would stab the blade into Master Figg's evil heart. Running back into the crypt, he pulled two chunks of stewed hare from Hersica's cauldron. He picked a place behind the churchyard wall, and handed Joe a hind leg. "Here, eat some breakfast.

We ain't thieving for Master Figg with nowt in our bellies."

For the hundredth time Figg stared at the parchment he had found alongside the pouches in Deveril's box. Thus far he had failed to obtain a translation, which irritated him beyond measure. Convinced he held a recipe for making gold, he stuffed the crumpled page back inside his tunic for safekeeping. With the crypt deserted for the day, Figg decided to risk a few experiments with the powder anyway.

The eight pouches weighed heavy around Figg's waist, and he unbuckled the belt with a sigh of relief. Pulling open one of the pouches, he poured a small amount of powder into his palm. It stank like rotten eggs! He shook the powder into a bowl and mixed in a few drops of water. An unimpressive slurry formed. Figg scratched his head. Perhaps heat might transform the substance into gold. He formed a well in the centre of the hearth, and dropped a handful of dry powder onto the smouldering logs.

VAROOOMPH – BOOM!

The force of the blast knocked Figg off his feet. Stunned and blinded by the demonic flash, he cowered in a crumpled heap on the floor.

Ned dropped his greasy bone on the ground. "Ye gods! What was that?"

Joe jumped to his feet. "Gawd knows! But I ain't hanging around to find out."

"Wait a bit!" Ned grabbed Joe's ankle and hauled him back down. "We ain't running off just yet. Not till we see what has happened." Easing himself up, Ned peeped over the wall and was hard pressed not to guffaw. He gently side kicked Joe. "Take a look at this."

Figg was a wrecked man. Minus eyebrows and lashes, he staggered out of the church. Most of his hair and newly grown beard were singed and his clothing hung in blackened tatters.

"He looks a bit worse for wear." Ned tittered.

"Why is he waving his arms about?" whispered, Joe.

"Looks like the silly beggar cannot see!" Ned prepared to vault over the wall. "Now might be a good time for us to finish him off."

"Nay!" Joe's face turned pale with fright. "If we get caught, we will hang. Why put ourselves at risk? Figg is a hated man; 'tis only a matter of time afore somebody else does the deed."

"Aye, maybe you are right. But I ain't going to Figg's aid. Let the worm suffer," said Ned.

The blast had temporarily robbed Figg of his sight. His ears rang, his burned flesh zinged, and he wondered what kind of devil had he unleashed. In his blind state, Figg failed to see the precious parchment flutter out of his tunic. Nor did he see Ned creep forward to scoop it up.

The multi-coloured flashes behind Figg's eyelids gradually faded and by midday his sight had returned. He stared at the blackened mess that surrounded the hearth, and shuddered. He was lucky to have escaped with his life. It was clear that the alchemist had invented something far more powerful than gold, but Figg could not find the parchment. It was unlikely that he could produce more black powder without the recipe, but he would put the volatile substance to good use.

Chapter Thirty One
Meeting at Diggitdow Farm

Ichtheus lay sleepless on his truckle bed, his thoughts darting from one subject to another. The black powder from Deveril's chest remained a mystery and he resented the time he and Oric had wasted upon it. He rolled on to his back and yawned. If the powder was his only problem, he would be a happy man.

The capture and demise of the Horzefell mob had failed to stem the tide of crime. In fact, the attacks and robberies had increased. If Figg was the culprit, he must have recruited a whole brigade of new villains. It was just as well the Council of Law members were gathering together on the morrow to discuss the dreadful situation.

The meeting was to be held at Diggitdow Farm to spare Tewdric, still not fully recovered from the beating he had suffered, an unnecessary ride. Ichtheus prayed that Helled would be in a good mood, or better still… absent altogether.

A log shifted on the hearth and the flames cast weird shapes across the kitchen's vaulted ceiling. Mother Morghan sprawled in her chair. With her eyes shut and her mouth open, she emitted the same noises as a porker with its nose in a bucket of swill. At this rate, Ichtheus lamented, he would get no sleep at all. He shut his eyes and tried to clear away all troublesome thoughts, but the image of Bayersby's empty medicine chest immediately filled his mind. The winter season of coughs and sneezes was just around the corner and he needed to replenish his herbal stocks. Instead of returning to Bayersby Manor after the Council of Law meeting, he decided to journey to his old shack on the shores of Lake Brinwath. An ample supply of plants, roots and berries could be gathered along the way. Too many moons had passed since his last visit to the lake, and a few days' spent away from Mother Morghan would provide a welcome respite. On these more pleasant thoughts, Ichtheus finally drifted off to sleep.

-oOo-

"A few days!" Mother Morghan screeched. "How dare you leave me on my own for so long – I cannot cope, I tell you, I cannot cope!"

"You will have to manage as best you can," Ichtheus hissed, "for go we must."

A drinking horn whistled past Ichtheus' ear and, if looks could kill, he would have dropped down dead.

Oric and Dian spluttered into their breakfast oats. Some of the exchanges between the apothecary and the housekeeper were hilarious.

"I have your measure, indeed I do, Master Ichtheus," continued Mother Morghan not yet finished with her tirade. Her triple chins wobbled as she shook a large ladle. "You and yon halfwit apprentice slope off on useless forays to avoid pulling your weight, and the way you grovel to obtain Sir

Edred's permission turns my stomach!"

Bottles and pots rattled as Ichtheus slammed his fist on to the table. "Hold your tongue, woman! I am not interested in *your* opinion. Furthermore, I *never* grovel." He turned his back to discourage any further discourse and gave Oric a shove. "Go! Harness Braccus to the cart. I will inform Sir Edred of our forthcoming excursion." He glared at Mother Morghan spitefully. "And I shall ask Lady Myferny's permission for Dian to accompany us as far as Kilterton. 'Tis a while since the lass paid her family a visit." In the kitchen maid's absence, Ichtheus knew that the housekeeper would be obliged to work instead of issuing orders from her chair – *and serve her right,* he thought.

Coping with excess chores was not Mother Morghan's only concern. She had informed Esica Figg if he failed to come up with decent rewards, she would no longer act as his spy.

"Is that right?" Figg had replied, his voice laced with oily menace. "I am sorry you think that way, but the choice is yours."

As it turned out, the choice was not to Mother Morghan's liking. Figg informed her that if she failed to do exactly as he ordered, he would instruct one of his bully boys to wring her neck.

To save her skin, Mother Morghan intended to obey Figg. But how was she supposed to get away from the manor with the apothecary missing for days on end?

The outer door crashed open and Oric hurtled back into the kitchen. "Dian! Master Ichtheus! Come outside," he shouted.

"What now?" Ichtheus hardly dare to imagine what new disaster could have occurred.

During the night, Otty had given birth to her foal. The little jack staggered on gangling legs and thrust his velvet nose into Ichtheus' outstretched hand. Ichtheus felt as though his heart would melt. "Ah, me," he muttered. I am becoming soft in my old age."

-oOo-

Pale sunshine warmed Ichtheus' back as he drove Braccus along at a leisurely pace. Oric and Dian sat on the rear of the cart with their legs dangling over the edge. Late September had produced some exceptional weather, and Dian drew Oric's attention to the crimson, copper and gold hues of autumn. "Everything is so beautiful at this time of year," she breathed. "I just wish it would last." She pulled her shawl close about her shoulders, "I dread the winter cold."

"Aye," Oric nodded his agreement. "And I dread the sickness caused by bad weather and poor food."

Parzifal dashed hither and thither, stopping often to cock his leg against a tree or to roll in a pile of smelly dung. Every journey he took the dog seemed to run twice the distance, and Oric wondered where he found his energy.

In Kilterton, Ichtheus stopped outside the Coles' cottage, and Oric helped Dian to carry the hamper that Lady Myferny had sent. "Enjoy your visit with the family," he said as they set the basket down at the cottage door. His voice lacked enthusiasm, for he would miss Dian's company.

Dian was immediately surrounded by her younger siblings. "What has your fine lady sent for us this time?" The children were generally famished and, seizing Lady Myferny's basket of food, they spat and clawed over the contents like a litter of half-starved kittens.

Frida Cole, beaten down by the daily grind of survival, was in no mood for socialising. Nor did she want any of Lady

Myferny's food to go down her eldest daughter's gullet. She seized the basket and swung it away from the children. "Nice of you to call," she snapped at Dian. "When are you leaving?"

Utterly dejected Dian left the cottage, and ran after Ichtheus and Oric. "Please may I come with you? Mother does not want me to stay at home."

Josh Cole followed his sister and fell into conversation with Oric. "I ain't seen hide nor hair of Ned and Joe since our dispute on Egglebart and Etheldrida's wedding day," Josh grinned. "Perhaps we scared them off."

"I doubt it," Oric replied. "Those two lads have hides thicker than wild boars. It will take more than a scuffle to get rid of them."

Josh watched enviously as Dian climbed on to Ichtheus' cart. The lass had fallen on her feet and he was happy for her. He waved her off, wishing he could find work at Bayersby Manor.

Oric, Ichtheus and Dian continued along the high street until they came abreast of Uther's shop. At the sight of his friends, the boot maker put up his shutters. A few moments later he reappeared from behind the building astride an elderly donkey. Together they set off for Diggitdow Farm.

Nearing the Bascoombs' farm, the sound of Helled's shrill voice echoed down the track.

"Seems yon hell-hag is at it again," Uther remarked, hunching inside his cloak. "How Tewdric puts up with her is beyond me."

Helled glared at the new arrivals. "*I* did not invite anyone. Did you, Tewdric?"

"Um! Well – yes, dearest. I asked them to visit," Tewdric grasped his wife's elbow and propelled her toward the house. "Would you excuse us for a moment?" He said with a sickly grin. "My dear wife and I seem to be in the midst of a small crisis."

Helled wrenched her elbow from Tewdric's grasp. "*A small crisis!* How dare you refer to the disappearance of my family's jewellery, three days takings, and my best kirtle as a *small* crisis?

"Are you sure everything has gone, turtle dove? Perhaps, have you mislaid your valuables?"

"God's teeth, man, do you take me for a complete fool? Of course I have not mislaid them! In the absence of a key I had to break into my chest. Everything except my father's chain mail and helmet has gone and, surprise, surprise, so has the Horzefell woman."

"We shall place the retrieval of your possessions on top of the Council's agenda," Ichtheus pledged in an attempt to calm Helled's tantrum.

The other council members arrived, and everyone entered Helled's kitchen. Etheldrida eyed the grubby rushes on the floor, the piles of ash that surrounded the hearth, and the soot-encrusted cobwebs that hung from every rafter. Helled Bascoomb was clearly a lazy housewife.

Seated around the table, everyone began talking at once.

Ichtheus produced his notes, and banged for silence with his dagger handle. "We meet once again to discuss the escalation of crime in the Bayersby and Kilterton districts." He looked expectantly at the eight faces around the table. No one, he noticed, rested his or her arms upon the food-encrusted planks.

"I would like to see the villains' heads hacked off and displayed on spikes," Egglebart stated.

"I wholeheartedly agree," Sir Oswold chimed in. "But how can we chop off heads until we find the bodies to which they belong?"

Egglebart flexed his sword arm. "If punishment were left to me I would disembowel the culprits and throw their innards to the rooks." He slapped his hand down upon the table and instantly wished that he had not. Scraping a glob of rancid fat from his palm he roared, "'Od's blood, what is this filth?"

"Egglebart!" Etheldrida admonished in shocked tones. "Must you be so outspoken?" Looking flustered, she shrugged apologetically.

"Order! Order!" Ichtheus called in desperation. "Unless we proceed with the business at hand, we shall be here all day." A hush settled over the council members. No one wanted to remain under Helled's roof a moment longer than was necessary. Ichtheus battled on. "The last few robberies were similar and extremely well planned. I suspect that one clever person is at the root of all the trouble."

"Odd how the only folk robbed always have something worth stealing," Mistress Malla remarked softly. "It seems to me that the villains know in advance what their victims carry. Perhaps there is a spy in our midst."

"Aye!" Uther cried angrily "Several of my tanned hides disappeared the other night, not to mention some of my best tools. The thieving swine must have been watching my every movement, for I am not often out. By God, had I been in my shop I would have run the blaggard through."

"Thank Heaven you were not!" Tewdric retorted, still feeling weak from his altercation in the woods. "'Tis more than likely you would be the one stabbed to death."

A short, tense silence followed. Then everyone began to shout again. The loudest, most strident voice belonged to Helled.

"Where is all this twaddle leading us? Ye gods, there is not half a brain between you!" Jumping up from the table, Helled stomped out of the room.

Ever practical Etheldrida interjected. "We are not going to get anywhere until we capture a suspect."

Maybe we should begin with Mother Morghan," Dian piped up. "Even though she is supposed to stay at the manor when Oric and Master Ichtheus are out, she often disappears. It might be a good idea to find out where she goes."

"Nay!" Ichtheus snorted derisively, "The woman has less brain than a flea, and she is bone idle to boot. I doubt she would have the ability, or the inclination, to involve herself in serious crime." Seeing Dian's crushed expression, he added hastily, "Nevertheless, my dear, please keep an eye on her."

"Esica Figg is the person that springs to my mind," said Oric. "I reckon he might have banded together with the Horzefell woman again."

"You might be right," replied Ichtheus "Let us make Figg's whereabouts our first priority." He wagged his finger in warning, "But no single person must approach him for he is a dangerous villain. Once he is located, we shall organise a group to arrest him. If you all agree, say aye."

Every person answered in the affirmative, and Ichtheus closed the meeting.

Helled did not reappear, no supper was served, and the council members hastened outside to say their farewells.

Uther clambered on to his donkey. "Would you care to join me for a bite of supper before you ride back to Bayersby, Sir Oswold?"

"Kind of you to ask, Uther, but I shall not be returning to the manor." Sir Oswold reached for Mistress Malla's hand. "Perhaps, my dear, the time has come to make our announcement."

Malla beamed and nodded.

"I have leased Cowslip Cottage from Sir Edred." Sir Oswold continued, "And, early this morning, in a private ceremony at Kilterton Priory, Mistress Malla did me the honour of becoming my wife."

Dian rushed to give the elderly couple a hug. "How romantic," she cried.

Ichtheus took little persuading to stay overnight at Rookery Farm. Seated around Etheldrida's spotless table, the five friends made short work of pickled fish and rye bread, washed down with pots of home-made cider. With the meal finished, Etheldrida and Dian took the dirty platters outside to swill them off beside the water butt.

Ichtheus stared hollow-eyed at Oric and Egglebart. "I'm afraid Helled was right! This afternoon's Council meeting was a waste of time."

The cottage door opened and a gust of cold wind followed Etheldrida and Dian back inside.

No one had an inkling of the terrors the next few days would bring.

Chapter Thirty Two

The Lakeside Shack

Etheldrida's food hamper proved heavier than Oric expected. He manhandled the basket into the yard and paused to gather his strength. Dian ran to his aid and they hefted the load onto the cart.

"Are you looking forward to our adventure?" Dian asked.

"Yes, indeed," replied Oric fervently delighted to have Dian's uninterrupted company for the duration of the excursion.

"And I am glad to get away from Mother Morghan for a while. She often blames me for her own misdeeds," said Dian indignantly. "If Lady Myferny were not so tolerant, I would be in constant trouble. As it is, the mistress must think I am a simpleton." Dian's expression hardened. "But most of all, I will not miss Master Guwain."

Oric's heart lurched. "You do not care for the Bayersby heir?"

"Care for him? I cannot stand him!"

Amazed, Oric expressed his disbelief. "Truly? I thought you were flattered by his attentions."

Dian's face flushed an angry red. "I cannot imagine what gave you that idea."

Etheldrida arrived in the yard, her arms full of more supplies. She noted Dian's flushed face and Oric's animated gesticulations and chuckled. Perhaps the youngsters were developing more than a passing interest in each other. *Time will tell,* she thought, *time will tell.*

Eager to get started Ichtheus urged Dian and Oric to climb on to the cart. He bid his hosts a fond farewell, whistled for Parzifal, and set Braccus off at a smart trot.

On a gently sloping hillside, a farmer tilled his land with an ox-drawn plough. Curls of umber earth folded back alongside the wooden blades with each new furrow. A flock of red-shanked gulls wheeled against the pale sky, their beady eyes trained upon the ground in search of newly exposed worms. The faint smell of wood smoke drifted on the still air, and Oric sniffed appreciatively. He stole a glance at Dian, feeling happier than he had for many a long day.

Daylight faded, and Ichtheus called a halt. They dined on delicacies from Etheldrida's generous hamper and, after supper, they crawled under the cart to sleep. Parzifal pushed in and snored all night.

Toward the end of their second day away from Rookery Cottage, the travellers caught their first glimpse of Lake Brinwath. In the evening light the surface of the water looked slick and cold. An isthmus jutted out from the western shore. At the far end of the narrow strip of land stood a castellated tower.

"What is that place?" Oric asked, standing up in the cart to get a better view. "Can we take a look?"

"That is Scutterskiff Keep," Ichtheus explained, "built during the Norman invasion. As far as I know, the building has remained uninhabited for many years. There will be time aplenty to explore it at a later date." He pointed across the water. "My old shack lies over there, hidden from view by the trees. To reach it requires a considerable trek around the shoreline."

"Is that a faint light in the tower?" said Dian. She shivered, and pulled her shawl more tightly around her shoulders. "Let us keep going, this place scares me."

"Nay, you are mistaken, lass." Ichtheus smiled, hoping to jolly Dian along. "The light is naught but a reflection from the lake."

It was dark by the time Oric, Ichtheus and Dian reached the shack on the water's edge. Oric lit two lanterns, and Dian unpacked what they needed for the night. There would be time aplenty to stow away their possessions on the morrow.

Many moons had passed since Ichtheus had last visited his shack, and he was astonished to find that someone had implemented several repairs. Whoever it was had gone to some trouble, for they had constructed a cowl and a chimney over the old, open hearth. Funny thing was … the fireplace and the inside of the chimney stack were both soot free. In the absence of any personal belongings, Ichtheus surmised that whoever was responsible for the renovations must have moved on before the onset of winter.

Oric set light to a bundle of kindling on the hearth and added a handful of dry leaves. Smoke belched out into the room.

"What in heaven's name have you done to the fire, boy?" Ichtheus spluttered.

Oric held a rag to his face and peered up the chimney, but he could see nothing amiss. Defeated he fetched a bladder of water from the lake to douse the flames. *So much for enjoying a comforting blaze,* he thought.

Tired after their long day, the trio shared another of Etheldrida's pies followed by some goat's cheese Ichtheus had brought from Bayersby Manor. Feeling sleepy and relaxed, they spread out wolf pelts, and lay down to sleep.

Ichtheus awakened early, surprised to see that Oric and Dian were not in the shack. About to go in search of them he was almost bowled over when they burst through the doorway. Parzifal, sopping wet from a swim in the lake, leaped up and deluged Ichtheus with muddy water.

"Heaven preserve us," Ichtheus quavered. "Shut the brute outside until he dries off."

"Good morning, sleepyhead," Dian laughed. "You have missed a glorious sunrise." She thrust several bunches of herbs into the old man's hands. "See how busy we have been whilst you slept."

The autumn morning was pleasantly warm and they ate breakfast outside. Not a ripple disturbed the lake's surface and trees ablaze with russet and gold leaves reflected upon the still water. Mountains in the far distance thrust skywards, purple and mysterious.

"If you have nothing important for me to do," said Oric, his chin sprinkled with crumbs from Etheldrida's oatcakes, "I would like to try out my new invention." In his spare time, he had assembled a few fish traps from willow branches woven together with horsehair.

Enamoured with the idea of a fish supper, Ichtheus readily gave Oric permission to go. "I left an old raft moored at the end of the jetty last time I was here. Have a look, it might still be there. Take care, though, 'tis a long time since I used the vessel, and the boards on the jetty are sure to be rotten so watch your step." Ichtheus slung a sack over his shoulder. "Meanwhile, I shall away to the woods to collect valerian and thyme. Whilst I am at it, I will seek mushrooms to complement your catch."

Oric had already unloaded their supplies from the cart and Dian stowed everything away inside the shack. She shook out their bedding, swept the floor, and cleaned up the hearth. Thrusting her head inside the inglenook she could see that a twiggy crow's nest blocked the top of the chimney. Before they lit another fire, Oric would need to climb up and clear the outlet.

Whistling merrily, Oric clattered along the wooden jetty. The noise he made disturbed a paddle of ducks. The birds flapped up in ragged take off, leaving behind trails of water as they gained the safety of the air.

Parzifal lumbered after the ducks, woofing with delight. Too late to catch one, he leapt into the water anyway. Oric shook his head and left the dog to amuse himself.

The raft was in better shape than Master Ichtheus had described, and the jetty also showed signs of repair. Oric wondered if the old man had visited more recently than he remembered. Giving the matter no further thought, Oric boarded the vessel and secured his fish traps. He took an almighty swipe at the water with the sculling oar, missed, and fell on his back. Feeling foolish, he glanced around to make sure no one was watching.

In the distance, Scutterskiff Keep reared up from its rocky peninsular. Master Ichtheus had paid scant attention to the light Dian had described; nevertheless, Oric was keen to investigate. Once he mastered the raft, he determined to scull across the lake and take a closer look at the Norman keep.

A swift learner, Oric manoeuvred the cumbersome vessel into deeper water. He tossed his baited traps overboard and watched as small air bubbles floated up from the lake's brackish depths. Above each trap bobbed a branch with a small flag attached, identifying its location. He recalled Guwain's derisive remarks during the assembly process and felt justifiably smug. Sir Edred's son was not as knowledgeable as he pretended. Best of all, Dian's lack of interest in the Bayersby heir caused Oric's heart to sing.

Bored with swimming, Parzifal yapped non-stop from the shallows. Oric sculled back to the shore with all the speed he could muster. Unless he stopped the foolish mutt's noise, the fish would all be scared away. As Oric approached the jetty, Parzifal took a flying leap at the raft. Unstable at the best of times the vessel heaved under the impact. Oric lost his balance, grabbed a jetty post, and waited for the rocking motion to ease. The more he pulled the raft in, the further out it floated. With his body almost touching the water, Oric glanced down to see his own strained grimace reflected back.

Unsettled by the craft's rocking motion, Parzifal sat on Oric's back.

"Get off me, you ill begotten hound!" Oric yelled.

Parzifal did as he was told and launched himself back onto the jetty.

Oric plunged head-first into the cold lake. His boots filled with water and he sank like a stone. At the lake's muddy bottom, he gave an almighty upward push with his feet. Floundering wildly, he grasped at a jetty post.

Dian ran to help. "Oh, dearie-me," she laughed. "You are festooned with pondweed."

Back in the shack, a large pool of water gathered around Oric's feet and he shivered disconsolately. "I shall *never* take Parzifal fishing again." He kept his word. Before retrieving his traps later in the day, he tied the dog to a tree.

A mild night followed a blood-red sunset and, rather risk another smoky session indoors, Oric lit a fire in the open. He changed into dry apparel, spread his wet clothes out to dry, and upended his wet boots near the blaze. He gutted the perch he had caught, skewered the fish onto sticks and placed them on the hot embers. Dian unearthed a skillet and cooked the mushrooms Ichtheus had picked. After dinner they threw the discarded pile of fish bones onto the flames and lay back to stargaze.

The fire burned low, and Ichtheus shivered. "Come on," he said, struggling to his feet. "Methinks 'tis time for bed."

About to follow his master, several small lights on the lake's far shore arrested Oric's attention. "Come and look at this!" he called softly. "Something is floating on the water. What do you suppose it could be at this time of night?"

Ichtheus strained his eyes to see. "Whatever it is seems to be heading for Scutterskiff Keep."

"I told you yesterday that I saw a light in the keep." Dian's tremulous voice indicated her concern. "Do you suppose something sinister is going on?"

Oric gathered up his nearly dry clothes and boots, doused the lanterns and made sure the fire was properly extinguished. If he could see lights on the lake, whoever it was would be able to see lights on the shore. He was not exactly afraid, but he had a strong premonition that all was not well.

Chapter Thirty Three

Spying on Scutterskiff Keep

Oric awoke early, disturbed by a relentless *drip, drip, drip.* He threw on his cloak, jammed his feet into his damp boots, and went outside to investigate. Mist, dank with moisture, drifted from the lake and teardrops of water from overhead branches plopped intermittently on to the shack's roof. In a few short strides Oric became hopelessly disorientated.

"Hey! Master Ichtheus," he cried, hoping his mentor was not still asleep. "I have lost my sense of direction. Call out and guide me back to the shack."

Ichtheus' fruity cackle rattled through the damp air. "Mind how you go, lad. It would be a crying shame if you fell in the lake again."

Hair and lashes beaded with moisture, Oric materialised in the shack's doorway. "This weather may be uncomfortable, but I reckon it is heaven sent."

"Heaven sent!" Ichtheus exclaimed. "What are you talking about?"

"I think we ought to investigate the keep." Oric reached for the cloth that Dian proffered and rubbed his wet hair.

"These misty conditions will provide us with perfect cover."

A long walk around the lake's edge held no appeal for the apothecary, and Oric suggested they scull across the water instead. Worried that Parzifal would bark and draw attention to their whereabouts, he asked Dian to restrain the dog inside the shack. Glad of an excuse to remain behind, Dian readily accepted Oric's suggestion. She wrapped herself in her shawl and prepared to spend a long, lonely day.

The sturdy raft moored beside the jetty bore no resemblance to the makeshift vessel that Ichtheus remembered. Some unknown person had also repaired the jetty. Ichtheus' body prickled with gooseflesh; something untoward was surely afoot.

"I will scull," Ichtheus stated when Oric joined him aboard. "You paddle with the small scoop up front, and for pity's sake keep the bank in sight. If we lose our way we could spend the entire day floating around in circles."

Oric concentrated on the shoreline. "I wish this mist would thin out a bit," he grumbled, rubbing his red rimmed eyes.

"Perish the thought, lad." Ichtheus pushed the paddle rhythmically back and forth. "If that were to happen we would be exposed like a pair of sitting ducks."

As if conjured by magic, the keep loomed out of the mist.

Ichtheus hastily back paddled. "Heaven preserve us! Another few strokes would have propelled us directly under the battlements."

Near the bank, the raft swished gently onto the lake's muddy bottom. Oric leapt ashore. He dragged the vessel into a cave of weeping willow branches and secured it to the tree trunk.

Encompassed by swirls of mist, Oric and Ichtheus made their way along the isthmus. Scrubby bushes gave them added cover and they soon arrived at the base of the keep.

An iron-studded gate, protected by a portcullis, gave access to the ground-floor bailey and guard house.

"How clever those Normans were," said Ichtheus, scrutinising the hazy outline of the square, five-storey tower. "With those gates shut tight, the keep is virtually impenetrable. Invaders arriving by boat, or on foot, would need to scale the walls to get inside." He stretched his head back to view the top of the keep. "The inhabitants would make things more difficult by shooting arrows from the battlements and, no doubt, they would also upend nasty substances upon the attackers' heads."

A string of commands issued from inside the keep brought Oric and Ichtheus to an abrupt halt.

"Tighten up your shield wall, you brainless oafs! An infant could break through that milksop defence you are attempting to form."

Ichtheus shoved Oric beneath a flight of stone steps that led to a small door on the first floor. Behind the door two people were engaged in noisy conversation.

"How many men are ready to fight, Cadoc?"

"Fifty! Sixty maybe," answered a gruff voice.

"Argh! Is that the best you can do? Does that number include the new recruits that crossed the lake by boat last night?"

Blood drained from Oric's face, "I am sure that is Esica Figg!"

"Ssh!" Ichtheus placed a finger to his lips. "Listen."

A hint of insolence crept into the first voice. "What do you expect? You have not endeared yourself to folk hereabouts. The new recruits have come from further afield and, judging by the shield wall they just formed, their fighting skills are poor."

A strangled oath failed to deter the speaker.

"You can curse all you like, but the paltry purse you offer for mercenary soldiers attracts only scum."

"Damn your eyes!" the man who sounded like Figg shouted. "Despite what you think, Cadoc, victory will be mine. Yon Bayersby peacock has done naught but play at battle for years. His knights are so decrepit we shall wipe them out before they draw their swords. Plus we have the element of surprise on our side."

"Sir Edred is no fool!" retorted the man called Cadoc. "Mark my words; the wily old dog will give us a run for our money."

"Not so! 'Tis the Bayersby knights who will run in swift retreat. How much time do you need to bring your wastrels to peak fighting form?"

"Six days, maybe seven. After that, all the training in the world ain't going to improve this raggedy-arsed lot."

Under the stairs, Oric and Ichtheus continued to strain their ears, but they heard nothing more save the clash of weapons. Thoroughly alarmed, they crept back along the causeway.

"Hurry up, lad!" Ichtheus urged as Oric eased the raft away from the bank. "We must return to Bayersby Manor immediately. Sir Edred must be warned that he is about to face a challenge."

"If that was Figg, and I sincerely believe that it was, does he truly intend to depose Sir Edred?" Oric assailed his master with more questions. "How can we stop him? Has Sir Edred got the manpower? Will we get back to Bayersby in time to give everyone sufficient warning?"

Ichtheus struggled for breath as he pumped the oar back and forth. "I cannot answer all your questions, but I believe that Sir Edred will put up a good fight. I also agree that the fellow in the keep sounds like Esica Figg. He is an evil toad, but I never imagined he would dare to challenge Sir Edred." Fearing a seizure of the heart, Ichtheus slowed his sculling. "Take a turn with the oar, dear boy, I need to recover my breath."

A brisk wind dispersed the mist. Only a few wisps of cloud remained to wreath the distant mountains and, in clear view of the keep, Ichtheus knew it was only a matter of time before someone spotted the raft.

-oOo-

Figg longed to dispose of his insubordinate master at arms, but, for the time being, Cadoc remained indispensable. Figg stamped up the spiral stairway to his top-floor room and, needing a breath of air, he threw open the shutters and stepped out on to the ramparts. In the middle of the lake two figures paddled a raft as if pursued by the Devil.

Figg leaped down the stairs four at a time. "Launch the boats," he screamed. "Someone is attempting to escape."

Several mercenaries had already deserted their posts, and Figg was not about to let another two depart. This time he intended to make an example of the culprits. No one would dare to run away after they saw what happened to cowards.

The first vessel was launched, but the boat capsized almost before it floated away from the rocky wall of the isthmus. In a second craft, the oarsmen pulled at different times and in opposite directions. More boats were launched, but the offenders in the middle of the lake were now too far away to catch. "Saddle the horses, Figg yelled. "We may be able to apprehend the escapees at the far side of the lake.

-oOo-

"Scull harder, lad!" Ichtheus yelled. "We have been spotted."

White caps whipped up by the wind made the lake choppy. Arms pumping the steering oar, Oric pitted his strength against the weather. "No need to worry, Master Ichtheus. We are too far away to be recognised and we have a head start." Oric glanced back at their pursuers and laughed, "The rate yon oarsmen are going, they will still be rowing come Yuletide."

Reaching the lake's edge, Ichtheus scrambled ashore. "Leave everything behind," he called as he ran to unhitch Braccus. "We have no time to pack and the cart will slow us down. Figg will not give up. As we speak he is probably on his way, here, overland."

Dian collided with Oric in the shack's doorway. "What is all the fuss about?"

"Grab enough food to keep us going for a couple of days, leave the rest behind." In his panic, Oric squeezed Dian's upper arms hard. "Figg's men are after us. If we are to stay alive, we must run."

Chapter Thirty Four

Sir Edred's Troops

Ichtheus led Braccus through the woods, Dian followed, and Oric brought up the rear with Parzifal on a leash. They walked through the night and all the next day. Another night went by with only a short stop to eat and rest. Exhausted and bedraggled, the trio entered the Bayersby compound as dawn broke on the third day.

"There had better be good reason for dragging me from my slumber at this ungodly hour," Sir Edred grumbled.

"Indeed there is, my lord," Ichtheus assured. "And when you hear what I have to say, you will have no desire to return to your bed."

Ichtheus revealed Esica Figg's conspiracy and Sir Edred's face twisted with rage. "How dare that scheming bastard challenge me?" Sir Edred slammed a clenched fist into his palm. "Rest assured, the moneylender's mercenaries will prove no match for my fighting forces."

Oric wondered what fighting force Sir Edred had in mind. "Perhaps I should ride to Rookery Farm and inform Egglebart of the impending battle."

"Aye," Sir Edred nodded his permission, "We could use the old warrior's expertise. Get him to enlist every able-bodied man in Kilterton. Meanwhile, I shall muster our Bayersby men."

Roused by the to-do, Guwain entered the kitchen and made straight for Dian.

Sure of his ground, Oric stepped between them. "Leave her be, Master Guwain. Your advances are not welcome."

"You insolent cur," Guwain thrust out his chin, "I will speak to whomsoever I choose."

Irritated by his son's interest in the lowly serving wench, Sir Edred gave Guwain a sharp nudge. "Go with Oric! Perhaps he can find something useful for you to do."

Moments into the journey, Guwain urged his horse into a canter and raced past Oric. "You will be disappointed if you imagine that I shall trot meekly along behind," he yelled.

Here we go, thought Oric, heeling the horse Sir Edred had loaned him. "Full tilt to Rookery Farm and both animals exhausted by the time we get there."

Ichtheus stood no chance of keeping up with the boys. He waved Oric past, "I will collect Nathaniel from Rigg Farm and Uther in Kilterton. We will wait at the inn until you arrive with Egglebart."

Guwain attempted to turn the journey into a challenge. To save the horses, Oric refused to rise to the bait. Nevertheless, the animals were lathered by the time they arrived at their destination.

Guwain burst through the farmhouse door to find Egglebart halfway through his mid-day meal. Oric apologised for the interruption and explained the reason for their visit.

"Cease your prattle, boy!" Guwain stood straddle-legged, his thumbs hooked into his belt. "As Sir Edred's envoy, it is my place to do the talking." He stared pointedly at

Egglebart, "And, in the presence of your betters, you should stand to attention."

Egglebart ignored Guwain. He remained seated, and chewed on his last mouthful of food.

Guwain fidgeted under Egglebart's one-eyed glare.

"When you have earned my respect, I will treat you accordingly," said Egglebart. "If you continue to behave in this arrogant manner, I shall inform your father."

"Please yourself!" Guwain suspected that his father would back the old warrior and, to save face, he stalked outside to wait whilst Egglebart gathered his battle gear together.

A chilly dusk ended another long day. It was too dark to achieve a great deal, so Oric and Egglebart joined Ichtheus and the other Council of Law members at the inn. Guwain sat well away from the group, drowning his sorrows with ale.

The inn filled with customers and, encouraged by Ichtheus, they swapped stories of Figg's treachery.

Niall, the smithy, had borrowed money for equipment and Figg's henchmen had browbeaten him into paying back far more than he owed. Kilterton's potter was heavily in debt to the same source. So, too, was Dian's father, who had financed his drinking habit with some of Figg's money.

"That piece of filth has filched plenty from me, too," hollered Helled Bascoomb

Ale from Tewdric's tankard slopped on to the landlady's table as he banged down his pot. "Good God, woman! How much did you borrow?" He looked hurt and embarrassed. "Do I not allow you sufficient funds for your needs?"

"I did not borrow, you stupid butcher, I invested! Yon devil's spawn talked me into a scheme whereby my money would treble in six-quarter moons, *so he said*. And, like a fool, I believed him!"

"Remarkable!" Tewdric snapped at his wife. "For the first time in your life you listen to someone, and that someone is Esica Figg!" Anger overrode Tewdric's timidity. "How much of my hard-earned silver have you handed over to him?"

"Too much!" Helled's face darkened with loathing. "But I mean to get all of it back."

Ichtheus was not surprised to hear that Figg's campaign of terror had been in operation for many moons. Even though the moneylender had been absent from Kilterton since the Dunburton skirmish, his talons remained firmly embedded in most of the populace.

"These complaints are getting us nowhere," grumbled Egglebart. "We must get on with the job in hand, for time is of the essence." He selected four burly farmers as leaders and instructed them to report to a clearing in the woods at dawn. "Remember," he added, "to bring along all the weapons you can muster."

Overnight a heavy frost destroyed every vestige of autumn colour. Puddles iced over and frozen grass crunched underfoot. Winter had set in with a vengeance.

A group of villeins waited in a woodland clearing, each man clutching an odd assortment of weapons. Oric ran to join them, rubbing his hands together in a show of mock bravado. "Bit chilly this morning, eh?" He stepped on to a sheet of ice and his feet catapulted from under him. Skating helplessly along upon his backside, he slammed to rest against Egglebart's shins.

The man who glowered down was not the Egglebart that Oric knew. The face, with its one staring eye, was grim. A domed helmet hid his carrot-red hair, and in his left hand he clasped a black shield with a white bovine skull painted upon it. Though Egglebart had not seen battle for some time, his chain mail was rust free.

Oric scrambled to his feet. *This,* he thought with a shiver of dread, *is no game.*

All day long the men of Kilterton trained for battle, and the clash of their weapons reverberated throughout the forest. Whatever the ill-assorted group lacked in skill, they made up for with enthusiasm. Man and boy, they all wanted rid of Esica Figg.

Lanaval and Meerig, leather tanners recently arrived in Kilterton, were not fighters; nevertheless, they wanted to help Sir Edred's cause. Dressing up and pretending to be war wizards seemed the next best thing to using a battle axe. Any soldier worth his salt knew that war wizards cast spells to sap their opponents' strength and blunt their swords. Every man, woman, and child was aware that war wizards filled the enemy with dread. The tanners were fakes, but Esica Figg would be none the wiser.

Disguised by her dead father's battle regalia, Helled drilled alongside the men. She had learned the skill of archery at her father's knee; now she had murder in her heart.

At the end of another long day, everyone repaired to the inn. A quantity of ale was swiftly disposed of, not to mention every morsel of food the landlady could produce.

For a second night Guwain sat apart from everyone. Thoroughly peeved, he quaffed ale. A serving wench sashayed past with a laden tray, and Guwain pinched her bottom. Many more pinches and pots of ale followed. The more Guwain drank, the more belligerent he became. At bedtime, Ichtheus gave him a prod.

Guwain did not move.

"What ails you, boy?" Short on patience, Ichtheus shook the Bayersby heir. Guwain crumpled on to the floor.

"Put him to bed, Oric," Ichtheus snapped. "The young fool has imbibed over-much liquor."

"Much more of his disgraceful behaviour," roared Egglebart, "and I shall take my belt to him." He shrugged dismissively. "On the other hand, the headache the young fool will suffer in the morning may inflict sufficient punishment."

Chapter Thirty Five

Battle Orders

Hersica worried about her future as she shambled from Diggitdow Farm to St Griswald's Church. If Figg failed to commandeer Bayersby Manor, she could find herself in the next world alongside her sons. Instead of backing the moneylender, she decided to rob him and escape.

Hersica recalled the night that Figg, thinking himself unobserved, had hidden his plunder in St Griswald's Churchyard. She remembered every grave site he had desecrated, and she cackled with delight. The moneylender would have a fit when he discovered his stash was gone.

Hopping from grave to grave, Hersica clawed up clods of earth. She found nothing. Fear squeezed her heart, for her own small stash was also secreted in the churchyard. She kicked aside a pile of dead leaves to expose a moss-covered urn, and plunged her hand inside the stone ornament. She almost fainted with relief when her fingers encircled the pouch that contained her money. But still she wanted more. To enjoy the retirement she envisaged, Hersica needed all of Figg's wealth. But where had the crafty maggot hidden it? Resigned to spending more time with the moneylender, Hersica added Helled's jewellery to her meagre stash, and shoved the urn back under its pile of leaves.

-oOo-

Blood-curdling screams sent Ned racing up the stairs to Figg's turret room at the top of Scutterskiff Keep. The moneylender stood over Joe, his fist raised ready to deliver another blow.

"Hold hard," Ned cried. "Stop beating the boy; the poor little fellow is already half dead!"

Figg scooped a handful of clothing from a large chest and shook it in Ned's face. "The boy is supposed to look after my apparel. Not only has the rodent wrecked my best mantle, every one of my undergarments is green with mould." He hefted Joe's small body with the toe of his boot. "Get this scarecrow out of my sight before I finish him off once and for all."

Ned carried Joe's limp form down stairs. *One day, Figg shall pay for his cruelty,* he thought.

Glad to see the back of the two urchins, Figg massaged his throbbing temples. He seemed to attract naught but imbeciles. The boys were nothing but a nuisance, Mother Morghan was neither use nor ornament, and Hersica Horzefell was conspicuous by her absence.

Figg stepped onto the ramparts and glowered down upon the mass of human dross that brawled in the outer bailey. The master-at-arms blamed lack of funds for his failure to recruit good warriors; Figg believed the problem was caused by insufficient discipline. He kicked at a rat, sick to death of parasites both animal and human.

-oOo-

Lady Myferny threw down her embroidery, her eyes full of tears. "Edred! You promised me that you were done with battle.

"In view of recent developments, my promise was somewhat rash." Sir Edred took hold of Lady Myferny's hands. "You surely have no desire for Esica Figg to usurp my position?" Noting how quickly anger replaced his wife's tears, he concluded with a wry smile, "No, I thought not."

Lady Myferny snatched her hands away from her husband's grip. "How did Figg accumulate the wherewithal to wage war against us?" she demanded. "I thought the man was naught but a small-time moneylender."

"Not only has Figg cheated the folk of Bayersby and Kilterton with his moneylending tactics, I believe he is also responsible for all the robberies that have taken place." Sir Edred perched his buttocks on the edge of a table strewn with female paraphernalia. "Ichtheus has informed me that Figg has put together an army and that he intends to challenge me within the next few days.

Lady Myferny slanted her violet eyes at Sir Edred. "Ha! Figg will not live to set foot on Bayersby land – my brave knight will see to that."

More at ease in a man's world, Sir Edred left his wife to her needlework and strode into the compound. He dispatched a scout to spy on Scutterskiff Keep, and set about drilling his serfs and farmers in the making of war.

-oOo-

The hasty departure from Lake Brinwath had prevented

Ichtheus from gathering the herbs he needed, and he hoped that Lady Malla had a plentiful supply that he could dip into. He placed his depleted stock of medicaments, together with his apothecary's instruments, in a borrowed cart and climbed aboard.

Dian chased the cart across the yard. "Wait, Master Ichtheus!" Lady Myferny has given me permission to accompany you, providing I remain at Dunburton."

"Aye," replied Ichtheus. "I would be glad of an extra pair of hands, for there will be injuries aplenty. Hop up beside me, lass, we will ride along together."

Chapter Thirty Six

Into Battle

Under sir Edred's orders, Guwain remained at Bayersby Manor. Thoroughly peeved he mustered the few male servants who were too old to make the journey to Dunburton, and drilled them until they were ready to drop.

Torrential rain replaced the clear frosty weather and, drenched to their skins, Sir Edred and his entourage rode their horses throughout the dreary day. Bayersby foot soldiers with shields, swords and axes, wallowed along behind their leader in a sea of mud.

Etheldrida had spent the night preparing food. Hunched and soaked, she drove her laden cart in her husband's wake.

The Kilterton and Bayersby men arrived at their destination, and more than eighty saturated souls milled around in Dunburton's village square.

Sir Oswold backed his horse and a cartful of medical supplies into the biggest barn the village had to offer. "What terrible weather," he growled, helping Lady Malla down from the cart's bench seat.

Etheldrida squelched into the barn, water squirting

from her boots with every step she took. "Is there room in here for me and my cart?"

Ichtheus and Dian helped to unload and store away supplies. They had almost completed the task when a noisy commotion outside caused them to run to the barn door.

A scout, sent to spy on Scutterskiff Keep, dismounted from his sweat-lathered steed. "I am the bringer of bad news," he yelled. "Figg is almost ready to leave Scutterskiff Keep." The scout snorted disdainfully, "As ready, that is, as Figg's bunch of ne'er-do-well mercenaries will ever be."

"How many soldiers does Figg command?" demanded Sir Edred.

"Not more than fifty, but few of them are true warriors," replied the scout. "But they do have some nasty war dogs and, by the look of them, the poor beasts ain't been fed for days." The scout leered, his teeth gleaming whitely beneath his black moustache. "But as far as I can tell, they ain't got no war wizards."

"Vicious canines are easy to fix," said Egglebart, calling out a pair of young squires. "Catch a few stray chickens, wring their necks and ask Master Ichtheus to dose the carcasses with a strong sleeping draught. Figg's dogs will fight over the food instead of attacking us. All thanks to Master Ichtheus' potion, the hounds will be rendered useless in no time at all."

Sir Edred nodded his approval, and beckoned Egglebart to follow him into the barn. They discussed battle strategy together with Sir Oswold, and ended the day in prayer. With God on their side, they could not fail.

-oOo-

Clad in chain mail and a domed helmet, Oric looked older

than his tender years. Ichtheus smiled to hide his feelings and sent up a silent prayer for the safe return of the youth he had taken into his home and his heart. "God speed and keep you, lad."

Dian was next to offer her good wishes. She put on a brave face and handed a small package to Oric. "'Tis nothing much, but I thought you might like to carry this into battle with you."

Thrilled that she had thought of him, Oric opened the gift. A lock of Dian's hair nestled inside a linen pouch. "Thank you, thank you very much," he mumbled, quite overwhelmed. He pinned the token over his heart, and leaned down to kiss Dian's cheek.

"Please, please be careful," Dian begged. Tears pricked the back of her eyes and, not wanting him to see her cry like a baby, she hastened back to the barn.

With the image of Dian's pretty face etched deeply upon his mind, Oric spurred the horse he had borrowed from Sir Edred, and rode to catch up with Egglebart and his men.

The Bayersby and Kilterton army marched, barely stopping to rest. They arrived at the northern tip of Lake Brinwath as the day drew to a wet and windy close. Tired but enthusiastic, the men set up camp in the woods.

Next morning, rested and dressed in his full battle regalia, Sir Edred leaned out from his saddle and clasped Egglebart's proffered forearm in a warrior's farewell. "God speed, my friend! May victory soon be ours." Without further ado he cantered his horse into the woods, sending great clods of wet earth over his foot soldiers.

In a more sedate fashion, Egglebart, with Oric at his side, led his band of men in a southerly direction. Almost abreast of the keep and under cover of the woods, they climbed a gentle slope until they had a bird's-eye view of the isthmus and the lake.

"Judging by the racket coming from the keep," said Egglebart, "Figg's men have been carousing all night. I doubt their drink-induced courage will carry them past the first clash with our weapons."

To Oric's left Uther, Tewdric, Nathaniel and Niall the blacksmith crouched behind a fallen tree. More Kilterton men straggled amidst trees on the slopes above. Concealed in dense undergrowth, Helled Bascoomb also waited.

The portcullis cranked up and the keep's massive doors swung open. Egglebart flexed his muscles. "Prepare for action!"

War dogs, snapping and snarling, dragged their handlers' full tilt onto the causeway. Two mounted warriors followed the dogs. Finally the drunken rabble of Figg's army spilled out of the keep. They lined up in a ragged line beside the lake to await Cadoc's orders.

Partway down the spiral stairs, an unfamiliar horn blast sent Figg scuttling back to his turret room. He stepped onto the ramparts, and pushed his head between the castellation's to see what was afoot.

Two naked war wizards leaped about on the grassy expanse beside the lake. Painted blue from head to foot, they looked like demons from hell. They screamed and whirled and wobbled their backsides. They pointed human shin bones and spewed vile curses. Atrophied animal parts hung from belts around their waists and one of the men brandished a human skull on top of a pole.

Terrified by the spectacle, Figg's men failed to notice Egglebart's party creep silently out of the woods. Drums rattling, horns blaring, Sir Edred's men wheeled in from the opposite direction.

Too late, Figg's men saw that they were trapped. They turned tail and ran back along the isthmus toward the keep. Sick to his stomach, Figg realised that his plot was rumbled.

Chapter Thirty Seven

Destruction

The drums and horns stopped. So too did the war chants, and the two wizards melted back into the woods. In the ominous silence that followed, the Lord of Bayersby's challenge rang out loud and clear.

"Prepare to die!"

Cadoc searched the baily for his leader, but Figg had vanished. In desperation, the master at arms ordered his dog handlers to release their charges.

"Throw down the chickens," Egglebart bellowed. "They will entertain Master Figg's canines until the sleeping potion takes effect."

Sir Edred and his men were as unforgiving as Figg's bullies had been during their campaign to maim and steal from the folk of Bayersby and Kilterton. The clash of weapons and the dull thud of axe upon shield reverberated across the countryside. Dismembered limbs dropped still twitching to the ground and severed heads rolled in the dirt. Figg's men died where they fell, looking like so much butcher's offal. Rainwater washed their lifeblood into the lake until the shallows turned red.

Desirous of saving their own necks, Rafe and Cadoc sought an opportunity to escape. Separated from his entourage, Sir Edred presented the only obstacle between them and dense forest. Engaged with an adversary, he failed to see the warriors advance with their swords at the ready.

To save Sir Edred, Oric galloped his horse full tilt into Cadoc's charger. The blinkered animal reared in terror, unseating his rider. Cadoc slammed into the ground, the weight of his armour snapping his neck upon impact.

Sir Edred's original adversary turned tail and fled. Sword held high, Rafe moved in for the kill. "Get out of my way, I mean to have my freedom."

Oric swung his axe to deflect the warrior's downward thrust and sustained a deep wound to his own arm. Nevertheless, the impetus of Rafe's sword strike carried on to slice into Sir Edred's thigh. Ignoring the blood that poured from his own wound, Oric followed through with a mighty blow, piercing Rafe's leather helmet with his axe blade.

For a few eerie heartbeats the stricken warrior remained upright. Eyes glazed he stared ahead until he toppled from his horse, dead before he hit the ground.

Sir Edred swayed in his saddle, his leg laid open from thigh to knee. Despite his own painful wound Oric held the big man upright until Ichtheus came to their aid.

Over the apothecary's head, Sir Edred locked eyes with Oric and slowly nodded his thanks.

At close of day the heavy rain ceased and banks of thick cloud parted to reveal a golden sunset. A roll call of exhausted and blood-spattered men confirmed that Niall the smithy and Nathaniel, the gentle shepherd from Rigg Farm, were both dead.

Swallowing a lump in his throat the size of a hen's egg, Ichtheus gently closed Nathaniel's eyes. "Farewell my dear friend, rest in peace." He made the sign of the cross and recited a short prayer.

Tewdric had broken his arm when he was knocked from his horse, but he had managed to spear the drunken fool who had unseated him. Fellow men at arms suffered everything from severe gashes to minor cuts and bruises.

Figg's army fared less well. Most volunteer mercenaries were dead and the few that survived hastily surrendered.

Ichtheus administered to the wounded of both armies. *What an appalling waste of life and limb,* he thought.

Sir Edred's men poured into the keep and began a noisy search for anyone left behind. Ned and Joe, loudly proclaiming their innocence, were dragged from their hiding place under a spiral stairway and hauled away.

Sick with fright, Figg cast around his room for somewhere to hide. A clothes chest disguised as a seat presented the only suitable place. Throwing out items of apparel, he folded himself into the cavity beneath the cushioned seat. A heartbeat later his turret room door crashed open. Clasping his hands together, Figg silently prayed for his own salvation.

A hefty kick to the side of the seat jarred Figg through to his bones. "No one would want to steal that ugly piece of furniture," stated a youthful voice.

Drenched in cold sweat, Figg shut his eyes tight. God help him; he was within a hair's breadth of being discovered.

"Tell you what though," said another voice, "I will have them few clothes strewn about the floor."

"And welcome," replied the first youth. "Whoever they belong to must be as thin as a rodent's tail."

Curled in a foetal position, Figg's legs became numb from the restricted supply of blood, but still he dare not move. A plaited horsehair rope in the bottom of the chest dug into his flesh.

All day long the Kilterton and Bayersby men clattered around the keep and its battlements. Figg almost died of fright each time he heard someone enter the room, but no one touched the worthless seat in which he hid.

Hours later, when all seemed quiet, Figg climbed out and massaged life into his numb limbs. Removing the plaited rope from the bottom of the chest, he crawled on his hands and knees to the eastern side of the keep. Out of sight of the lakeside, he secured one end of the rope to a castellation and threw the other end over the side. The rope snaked down until its tip entered the water beside a small boat.

About to make his escape, the appearance of a diminutive figure froze Figg into terrified immobility.

Helled Bascoomb pulled the string of her bow back to touch her lips, and let fly with an arrow. "Remember me?" she said.

Chapter Thirty Eight

Figg's Nightmare

The arrow nicked Figg's shoulder, and dislodged him from the battlements. Black cloak flapping like the wings of a demented bat, he plummeted into the deep water at the keep's base.

Helled leaned over the parapet and waited for a few heartbeats. When Figg failed to surface she dusted off her hands with smug satisfaction. *The end of a piece of filth, and serve him right.* She returned to the turret room and searched through the moneylender's possessions, but she found nothing of value. Still disguised in her father's battle regalia, she mingled with Sir Edred's men. Tewdric was nowhere to be seen, and Helled wondered if she might be a widow. Not caring one way or the other, she returned to Diggitdow Farm and the welcoming arms of her two daughters.

Panic-stricken, Figg kicked wildly to free himself from the weed that threatened to envelop him. Even though death stared him in the face, he refused to release the precious bundles of black powder from his beneath his tunic. Multi-coloured lights flashed beneath his eyelids and, on the verge of blacking out, his fingers brushed an anchor chain. He grasped the lifeline and hauled himself upward. Breaking the surface beside a boat, he gulped in life-saving breaths of air.

-oOo-

Oric moved amongst the men of both armies. He closed the eyes of the dead, and tended the living. The pain etched upon his face was plain for all to see, and Ichtheus ordered his apprentice to accompany Sir Oswold to Dunburton with a cartload of casualties.

Ichtheus turned his attention to the Lord of Bayersby. He had sewn Sir Edred's wound together with horsehair, but blood oozed through bandages. "You must rest that injured leg, sir. If you fail to slow down your wound could burst open again. Surely some other able-bodied knight could take over your few remaining duties."

"I shall not rest until all the men are taken care of." Not content with looking after his own soldiers, Sir Edred also insisted that Figg's deceased mercenaries receive a Christian blessing. When he could do nothing more, he finally agreed to return to Bayersby Manor.

"Allow me to help you dismount," said Ichtheus. "I will organise a litter for you."

"Stop fussing, man!" Sir Edred had no desire to be carried home. "I rode out of Bayersby Manor and, by God, I shall return in the same dignified manner."

Uther accompanied Tewdric back to Kilterton. Despite his broken arm, the butcher had only one worry. "How do you suppose my Helled will cope now that I am incapacitated?"

"Well enough, I imagine," Uther replied, thinking that some honest, hard work would do Tewdric's ill-tempered wife a power of good.

Dian almost knocked Oric over with her warm welcome when he arrived back at Dunburton. Then, seeing he was wounded, she ran to fetch help.

Lady Malla peeled the blood-stained dressing away from Oric's arm and sucked in her breath when she saw his wound. "Dear boy, you must be in a good deal of pain."

"Aye, 'tis a bit sore." Oric turned away to hide the tears that blurred his vision.

"I gathered a substantial amount of shepherd's purse during the summer months," explained Lady Malla to take Oric's mind off his pain. "Some folk refer to it as toywort, pickpurse or shepherd's scrip." Lady Malla shrugged. "Whatever it is called, the insignificant little plant contains splendid healing properties." She scooped a generous dollop of ointment from a jar and smoothed it on to Oric's arm. "No doubt Master Ichtheus will already have taught you the benefits of this medication."

Oric failed to answer, for his teeth were tightly clenched.

"Would you finish off for me, please Dian, I am needed elsewhere."

Dian wrapped a strip of clean linen around Oric's damaged arm and tied off the ends. "All done," she said, and patted Oric's cheek.

Oric tried to stand, and was shocked when his knees buckled.

"Oops! Better to lie down before you fall down," said Dian, helping Oric to a vacant bale of straw. "I am sure you will feel as good as new after a sound night's sleep."

Ichtheus and Egglebart arrived at Dunburton with the final cartload of the wounded men for Lady Malla to care for.

News of Sir Edred's victory reached Kilterton and family members travelled to Dunburton to escort their loved ones home. Dian returned to Bayersby Manor along with the other able-bodied serfs, and in no time at all the derelict village was deserted.

Last to leave, Ichtheus climbed on to his borrowed cart. "I should like to revisit my old shack. A few days respite before we return to Bayersby Manor might do us good. Can you cope with the journey back to Lake Brinwath, Oric?"

"'Tis not the distance that troubles me, Master Ichtheus. My concern is Esica Figg. What if he has returned to the keep with more men?"

"Ha!" Ichtheus snorted. "I doubt Figg has the stomach to make another challenge, he will be far away by now."

-oOo-

Under cover of darkness Figg paddled his boat away from Scutterskiff Keep. Too exhausted to go any further, he made for a small island in the centre of the lake. For several days he lay low and nursed the wound in his shoulder. He slept rough, ate earth-worms along with wild garlic, and slaked his thirst with water from the lake.

-oOo-

Ichtheus' cart remained where he had abandoned it beside the lakeside shack. "We are lucky it is still here," he remarked as he entered the building. "It seems that Figg's knaves have stolen everything else that we left behind." He chafed his hands together. "It is colder than a grave in here, let us light a fire?"

"Not until I see what is blocking the chimney," said Oric. "Shall I climb up and take a look?"

"Aye, lad, the sooner the better," Ichtheus replied, trying to still his chattering teeth. "But do have a care for your wounded arm."

Oric began the ascent, his injury slowing his progress. A bird had built its nest in the top of the chimney. He poked at it but the obstruction remained firmly wedged. Bracing himself, Oric drove his fist into the twiggy mass. It popped out and he lost his balance. To break his fall, he jammed his feet into the wall at the back of the fireplace. Several rocks rattled down.

Startled, Ichtheus jumped back. "Are you alright, lad?"

"There is a cavity at the back of the fireplace," Oric exclaimed. He plunged his good arm into the hole and yanked out a large sack. Further down the cavity he discovered another sack. And another!

Ichtheus tipped out the contents of the sacks and was soon surrounded by gold nuggets, pouches of coins, jewellery, torques, silver candlesticks and goblets.

Chapter Thirty Nine

A New Beginning

The disastrous battle with Sir Edred had taught Figg a valuable lesson. His next bid for Bayersby Manor would be made with a band of well-seasoned warriors. He had ample wealth to pay for a new, better army – all he had to do was to retrieve his plunder from the shack on the shore of Lake Brinwath.

After dark Figg left the island, and rowed his boat across Lake Brinwath. Inside the shack he lit an oil lamp. Bile threatened to choke him when he saw that his hiding place had been discovered. After all the robbing and maiming, conniving and plundering, he was almost back to where he started. But not all was lost, for the waterproof pouches remained attached to his belt. Figg laughed like a madman as he imagined the havoc he would inflict with the lethal powder.

-oOo-

Mother Morghan's dreams of wealth were dashed upon the

return of Sir Edred and his triumphant army. She locked herself in an outhouse and indulged in a fit of temper that made her head throb.

Under Ichtheus' watchful eye, Oric dressed Sir Edred's wound each day, but the leg remained stiff.

"At least I am alive!" Sir Edred said, slapping Oric on the back. "Had you not dispatched that pair of warlords, I would be naught but worm fodder." To show his gratitude he rewarded Oric with a piece of silver and small plot of land on the edge of High Moor.

Gentry and villagers applauded when Oric returned their stolen items. The effusive accolades were more than Guwain could stomach, and his hatred for the apothecary's assistant grew. He spent much of his time devising ways to destroy Oric's credibility.

Not satisfied with the pouch of silver she had already received, Helled Bascoomb threw a tantrum. His patience spent, Sir Edred sentenced her to three submersions on the ducking-stool.

"Serve the hellcat right!" Uther muttered. "A few dunks in a chilly pond might cool her temper."

Ned and Joe were brought from Scutterskiff Keep to Bayersby Manor. Unwilling to execute boys of such a tender age, Sir Edred sent them to work for Mother Morghan. To keep the boys in line at night, Oric ordered Parzifal to stand guard. The dog took his duties seriously and the two boys were terrified of him.

"Never mind the dog – I will look after you, Joe." Ned patted his chest. "I have Figg's parchment hidden under my tunic. Once we escape from this hell-hole I will find someone trustworthy to read it." Ned gave his friend a cock-eyed grin. "Master Figg never kept anything worthless; I reckon this parchment could lead us to riches."

Hersica learned the outcome of Figg's rout from Mother Morghan and, having nowhere else to go, she decided to remain in St Griswald's crypt until something better turned up.

-oOo-

The day before Yuletide, Oric purchased a pretty comb from a pedlar. He took Dian for a walk and, in a sheltered glade, he proffered his gift.

"It is beautiful, Oric." Dian showed her delight by securing her wayward curls with the new comb. Then, sensing that Oric's mood was sombre, she asked softly, "Is something troubling you?"

Oric sighed deeply. "So much has happened, I hardly know where to start."

"Why not begin at the beginning?" Dian suggested, "I am a good listener."

"Master Deveril, the Dunburton alchemist, entrusted me with a key." Oric paced up and down in agitation. "He told me that it would open a door to great wealth. But he also warned that some terrible disaster might occur if I allow the key fall into wrong hands." Oric stopped in front of Dian and regarded her with troubled eyes. "But the old man died before he was able to finish his tale."

"Oh, my!" Dian gasped. "What kind of disaster do you suppose he had in mind?"

"I have no idea, but I shall feel responsible if anything dreadful does happen."

"Is the key in a safe place?" asked Dian.

"Yes, it is hidden with Master Ichtheus' valuables." Oric took hold of Dian's hands. "Do you remember the broken chest I found at Dunburton Manor? It bears the same double knot that is inscribed, in miniature, upon Master Deveril's key."

Dian nodded, her curls bobbing. "I wondered why you dragged that old thing back to Bayersby Manor!"

"I found a small quantity of black powder inside the chest and, since Master Deveril was an alchemist, I thought the substance might be the raw material for making gold. Master Ichtheus and I tried several experiments all to no avail. But the substance is extremely volatile when introduced to fire." Oric's eyes grew round with concern. "What if the person that broke into Master Deveril's chest found more of the black powder? Maybe that is the danger that Master Deveril tried to warn me against."

"Whatever the perils," said Dian, giving Oric a hug, "we shall seek Deveril's treasure together."

"It is good to know that you are on my side," replied Oric, squeezing Dian in return. The furrows in his brow diminished, and he managed a small smile. "The news is not all bad. Sir Edred has given me a small plot of land and a piece of silver. Now I am a man of means, I shall grow my own herbs and build a hut in which to experiment with new medicaments. But I saved the best news until last. Master Ichtheus has promoted me to full-fledged apothecary."

-oOo-

To celebrate his victory over Esica Figg, Sir Edred hosted a Yuletide feast that folks remembered for many years.

Sated with good food and elderberry wine, Oric crawled into his sleeping place. Across the hearth, Master Ichtheus was already snoring. Oric's heart swelled, for he had grown to love the old man like a father. But he would never forget Master Deveril.

Before he drifted off to sleep Oric made a pledge. With Dian's support, he would continue his quest until he unravelled the mystery of the alchemist's key… however long it took.